15 YEARS YOUNG

Kathryn Louise is one of the most anticipated adult fiction authors to hit the literary scene in 2022.

Kathryn's love of literature started at school and college after studying English Language and Literature. Born in Berkshire in 1980, she continues to live there with her family.

Her inspiration for writing a series of books around adult fiction came from a desire to entice her readers into a fantasy world of love, lust and romance. Each book ends on a cliff-hanger, leaving behind an audience excited for the next instalment.

A list of upcoming books by Kathryn Louise
appears at the back of this book.

15 YEARS YOUNG

Kathryn Louise

Where love meets lust…

First published in Great Britain by Kathryn Louise in 2022.

A CIP catalogue record for this book is available from the British Library.

Printed and bound in Great Britain by Publishing Push.

978-1-80227-571-1 (paperback)
978-1-80227-572-8 (eBook)
978-1-80227-644-2 (hardback)

Dedicated to all my family,
– Kathryn Louise

Prologue

My heart racing, my body flowing with adrenaline and the burning sensation running down my neck was filling me with dread. I would wake most mornings with this feeling. The feeling that something bad was about to happen. But what?

I was fifteen in 1995 and what a difference it was to that of a fifteen-year-old in today's world. Considering the change in materialistic luxuries, such as mobile phones, social media, hair straighteners or acrylic nails, brow tinting and aesthetic eyelashes. You could say it was a good thing not to have had those and the stereotypical images we model ourselves on today but regardless of those, I still compared myself to everyone around me.

I had a great upbringing; my parents were incredible. They still are. I love them to bits. They loved me and my two sisters so much and gave us everything we could possibly want. We lived in a growing town called Bracknell in Berkshire, an overflow of London where our parents and grandparents had moved to for work and more affordable living. They worked hard and instilled the ethic: work hard, play hard and you get what you work for. I have some great memories of us growing up. We travelled to many places and experienced the cultures and food of the world.

Although my sisters were six and nine years my elder, we were all extremely close. They tended to do a lot together being closer in age, whilst I had many an adventure with my friends separately. My two closest friends, Sarah and Zoe, would quite often join me on family holidays, or we would go for horse riding lessons together, organise sleepovers where we wouldn't sleep all night or go to parties and tell our parents we were somewhere else. I'm pretty sure all teenagers told their parents they were somewhere other than where they really were. Every Friday night, we would stand at the local shops asking strangers to buy us cigarettes and alcohol.

So, here I am still asking myself why I had so many worries at a time in my life when things were so simple. All psychologists ask about your childhood as if they are looking for a reason as to why you turned out the way you did and believe me, I have seen a few counsellors and psychiatrists in my time. In 1995, when there were no photoshopped images of celebrities or body images to compare myself to, I still constantly felt self-pressured into looking a certain way, being a certain person that everyone liked and wanted to be adored by all. I would remind myself daily – things could be worse, things could be way worse. But it didn't seem to help one tiny little bit.

I try to think of all the positives in any scenario. Look on the bright side I say but there is only so much positivity you can instil before reality hits you again and again. It doesn't make situations easier, but it helps me cope with life's little challenges. I can't help but think, *is it me? Am I attracting all the drama?* Maybe I like chaos in what could be a calm world. Maybe I was meant to have all these issues so I could learn and grow from the experiences. Nope, I think we all just live in one fucked up little world where we are never happy with what we have. Always wanting more, and more is never enough.

Do I fit in? What do I wear? Do people like me? Am I too fat, too thin, too short? Looking back, I had nothing to worry about. Life was easy. No troubles. No cares in the world. Yet I felt like the world was on my shoulders. Challenge after challenge was thrown at me. I had a brain, in fact as far as it goes, I was highly intelligent. I didn't struggle with schoolwork at all, but I couldn't be bothered. The most important thing was being liked and enjoying each day. My attention span was, at most, five minutes and then I would be distracted with something else. Perhaps this was my problem. In fact, I *know* this is my problem. I could put a label on it and say I had attention deficit hyperactivity disorder, or I am a manic depressive, but how would that help me and how would I cope with it? I know I constantly need stimulating; my mind and body need to be persistently interacted with otherwise I lose interest, or my mind plays games with me. To be quiet or not have something I am working on leads my mind to wander and that has dangerous consequences.

I quite frequently woke up with feelings of anxiety and dread; a feeling that would scare me. I didn't know what was happening to my body and expected the worst to happen. I couldn't explain it at the time and it would frighten me. I often found myself wondering if I was different. Was there something wrong with me? Why did I wake in the night, my heart pounding and with no explanation as to why? Only time helped me understand and control my demons.

The only thing I have ever truly accepted is that I was, and still am, a dark character. Very dark. But this is what makes me, me and totally unique. I just need to channel it, otherwise it occasionally gets me into a lot of trouble. I like everything that is naughty. If you told me not to do it, I would and that applies to life, school, work and even sex. Secret after secret I kept hidden; a book of untold stories and memories that if I was to tell even a stranger, they would look at me in disbelief. From sex to drugs, infidelity, lies and deceit, but tangled within this spider web is a myriad of love, lust, faith and commitment. This is all for me to know and me only, or maybe now it isn't. This is the start of my story, and this is where it all began...

Chapter 1

Family Life

My grandparents were always a huge part of my childhood. As both my parents worked long hours, my nan and grandad were like my second mum and dad. They picked me up from school or I walked to their house when old enough. I would spend school holidays with them and every family event they were there: birthdays, get togethers and Christmas. I was lucky to have them in my life. I knew a lot of my friends who either weren't close to theirs or theirs had passed away.

My grandparents lived in a lovely, terraced house about two miles from us. A cosy and comforting home, full of nick-nacks and ornaments. My nan collected plates that they had hung on the walls in the kitchen, and my grandad had several dark wood cabinets that displayed his model cars, soldiers and album upon album of first day covers. He would religiously go to the post office on the first day of every month and pick up his stamps and first day covers and then spend a week sorting them into his albums. As animal lovers, they had two Border collie dogs, Jenny and Cleo, who went everywhere with them, and two beautiful, highly affectionate Siamese cats called Lila and Pixie. Everything about my nan was funny and completely untraditional. Just like me, she did everything she was told not to. Her response to my grandad every time she was told off was 'sod off' in a jovial manner. This happened a lot.

I was a lot like my nan, a true tomboy. Always in trousers, never a skirt or a dress. I think I saw her in a dress twice: a funeral and a wedding, of which she complained about nonstop. She owned a moped that she would ride to the shops and would play football with me at the park. The youngest of seven siblings, she was the seventh child of a seventh child and to her she believed it was special, a good omen. It dates to the seventeenth century where folklore deemed it as a 'lucky child' and she most certainly was. She came from a very poor family; everything was passed down from her elder brothers and sisters and relied on war stamps for food and supplies.

My grandad, on the other hand, had a very wealthy upbringing. His grandfather was a bookkeeper at Kempton Park Racecourse in the late 1800s. He made a substantial amount of money and built up a portfolio of properties in and around London that was later handed down to his father. My grandad was the first family to have a car in their street around 1930 when he was just eight years old. He went to a private school and was very well spoken and dapper.

They met each other at just twelve years old; two very different backgrounds but lived near to each other. I loved to hear the stories of them playing at Bushy Park together when the air-raid sirens would sound, and they would have to run for cover. They stayed close friends for years, despite my grandad being posted to Malta with the Navy and my nan working as a switchboard operator during the war. They wrote to each other without fail for years. They kept boxes and boxes of their old letters. It wasn't until he returned that they began courting, were married in 1949, had my mum in 1951 and my uncle in 1953. I found their story incredible: true childhood sweethearts from the age of twelve. I guess I wanted something similar, a soulmate, someone I would be with for the rest of my life.

I have so many funny memories from growing up with both of them and it was hilarious. They were like a comedy act. They would argue constantly about the stupidest of things, but it took me away from the seriousness of the real world. My parents were always busy working — don't get me wrong, we never went without — but it meant I was with my nan and grandad a lot. My biggest memory takes me back to after school. I would walk to their house with friends, splitting just before their street. I would ring on their doorbell to the sound of the dogs barking and scratching at the door to greet me. My nan would be in the kitchen making me a hot chocolate and my grandad would be setting up the table in the living room. There would be two packs of cards, a jar full of copper coins, a pencil and some paper he had cut in half for score cards, as well as the sound of BBC Radio 2 in the background that he would whistle or hum along to.

For hours we would sit there and play a game called canasta, using the coins as gambling money. I cheated each day, and I played every trick in the book just to win. I think they knew I was but were just happy to play and spend time with me. I can still recall the fun we had, the music playing in the background, how we lost track of time each evening by being buried in the competitiveness of the card game. Coins strewn across the table, the laughter as we either lost or won a round. By the time my mum would turn up and collect me after finishing work, we would be mid-game and she would have to wait until we had got to the end. Not once did they tell me to do my homework or read. It was all fun and games. Oh, how I miss those days. Not a care in the world, just laughs, fun and good times.

My nan was the most undiplomatic person. She spoke her mind, even if it upset others. My grandparents were both soldiers for the Salvation Army which meant they were involved in fund-raising for the homeless, always helping wherever they could but it also meant they were part of a community. They knew so many people and spoke to everyone. The more troubled someone was, the more time they gave. She saw something in me. They both knew I struggled and the more I was told to do something, the more I did the opposite. I think they liked the unruliness in me, the naughtiness and that I had a mind of my own.

I will never forget their love, enthusiasm, their ability to not care what people thought and their kindness to others. I could only hope to be the type of grandparents that they were to me, to my grandchildren.

Chapter 2

In the Army

I've always been a bit of a tomboy; the smell of gunpowder still sends me back to a time when my dad and I used to go to Bisley Army Barracks and shoot handguns. We would pack a rucksack crammed full of sandwiches, crisps, sausage rolls, cakes, a flask full of hot chocolate or tea and he would take us to the range at the crack of dawn. Although I was the youngest, and the only female amongst the gun club members, it was something I looked forward to every month. A time when just my dad and I bonded. We laughed, we were extremely competitive, and we had great fun. I owned a Glock pistol, which looked plastic and was originally used by the Austrian military, but I liked it because it looked hard core and similar to the ones you see in films. My dad had a Smith and Wesson .357 Magnum revolver — a beautiful silver gun with a black handle — and a Browning 9 mm. The Smith and Wesson had a bit more of a kick to it, and was an awful lot louder. The Browning was a more of a fun gun, quicker and something to practise with.

The cold never seemed to bother me then, nor did the loud gunshots, and the time would fly. All morning we would fire at rotating targets, quick fire rounds and have competitions for the worst, fastest, and most accurate shot. Maybe it was because I was the youngest, but I had a good eye. I had mastered my breathing technique before firing and was a regular winner of many awards. I knew none of my friends had the same interest as me and it wasn't something they did, especially as a fifteen-year-old girl. But when I went shooting, I loved it. I excelled at it, and it felt completely natural. I asked my dad on several occasions if it was possible for me to be a sniper or to continue it as a profession, but he just chuckled to himself. Little did he know that I was being serious.

It wasn't just the shooting that made me a tomboy. I loved cars, my clothing attire was jeans or tracksuit bottoms and a hoodie, trainers and hair tied back into a ponytail or a bun. My mum tried so hard to get me to wear dresses, skirts or pretty outfits and, of course, I rebelled. I would wear the opposite of everything she said she liked. Was I trying to make a statement? Why did I want to be so different? Was it me just being so bloody arrogant and rebellious? I look back now and apologise to her for being such a complete pain.

The memory I remember the most was walking through the town's shopping centre and there was a stand and big banners with the Army symbol displayed at the front and a few young adults dressed in camouflage uniforms handed out leaflets. As I slowly walked past with my parents, a pretty girl smiled, handed me one of the leaflets and said, 'It's not just for boys' in an almost nonchalant way. I said thanks, smiled and kept walking.

My mother turned to me. 'Hey, did you not want to stop and see what it's all about?'

'No,' I said, even though I did and kept walking.

'Are you sure? It looks right up your street. Maybe see what they say and if it's not something you're interested in, we can head home.'

Reluctantly, but only because she had suggested it, I walked back.

'We're recruiting for Army Cadets. We're based at the Coopers Hill site in Bracknell and welcome all thirteen- to eighteen-year-olds, girls or boys. We take part in loads of activities from shooting to assault courses, camping, map and compass, first aid, drill and basically everything that the adult army does just in a controlled environment. We have fully qualified instructors, most of them ex-army. If you would like to join us, come along to Coopers Hill every Tuesday and Thursday evening from 7-10 p.m.' She gave me another smile and waited for a response from me.

'Okay, great. Thanks,' I said and turned to walk away.

'Any questions?' my mum asked, half expecting me to have some.

'No, I'm good. Thanks for your time,' I responded.

Inside, I was thinking this was exactly something I would want to do but I didn't want to seem too eager. *Look interested, be polite and then think about it when I'm home and make my decision*, I thought. My only reservation was what my friends would think. Would they laugh at me? Anyone doing anything out of the norm was teased at school. Cadets would be on that list. If I was going to go, it would have to be kept quiet.

When I got home, I studied the leaflet the girl had given me. *It does look quite exciting*, I thought. I made the decision to ask my parents if I could go but I didn't want to mention it or for any of my friends to know. The fact they did shooting there was a big bonus for me.

Even though I was used to doing things on my own as the youngest sibling, I was as nervous as hell when my dad drove me that Tuesday to the cadet hut just outside of Bracknell town. Going to a new place with new people and doing something completely different wasn't in my comfort zone. He waited with me in the car until I recognised the girl that had handed me the leaflet. I declined my dad's offer of walking in with me and said I would come back in a minute to let him know what time to collect me.

The cadet hut was just like our school terrapins; a flimsy wooden frame raised above the ground. Metal see-through steps with a rail led to an empty room with posters and signs plastered across the walls. At one end, there were two smaller rooms, one had been made into a tea and coffee serving room with a kettle, a sink and a few cupboards. The other room had shelving units full of what I could see were uniforms, including boots, berets, jumpers, trousers and equipment. At the other end, there were male and female toilets. I approached the girl I previously met, who I later learnt was called Lisa, and smiled.

'Oh hi. Glad you could make it. Give me a moment to quickly sign in and I will introduce you to the instructors and walk you through how it all works.' She remembered me and seemed friendly. At least I knew one person there. I felt a bit more relaxed.

'Is it okay to quickly let my dad know what time he needs to collect me? Did you say 10 p.m.?' I asked quickly before running back to let him know.

Just as I re-entered the hut, without looking where I was going, I bumped into a boy coming out. A full on awkward frontal bump that almost knocked the wind out of me. I'm so clumsy and careless.

'Oh, wow. I'm so sorry, totally my fault,' I said as I looked straight at him. And there he was, towering above me over six feet tall. I was only five feet one inch and believe me the one inch counts every time. He had the bluest of blue eyes, dimples as he smiled, perfect straight teeth, freckles across his nose, slim build and dark, dark hair. He seemed familiar. I thought I recognised him although I had never met him before in my life. It was like something had been knocked into me, a potion or an aroma of intrigue as to who he was and what his name was. I stood still, fascinated and just stared into his mesmerising eyes.

'No worries.' That was all he said. He took a long-pleased look at me and carried on in a hurry. He seemed shy. I liked that.

That evening was one of the most stimulating experiences of my life. Lisa introduced me to so many new people. Army instructors were teaching the various groups different lessons, all of which were fascinating. Shooting to rifle dismantling and re-building, first aid, map and compass, basic training, marching, assault courses and survival techniques. These were amongst the things I would be learning in the coming weeks. There was even a mixture of girls and boys, like myself, interested in adventure. I thought I would be the only one. The best part to all of it was that everyone was friendly,

9

helpful and no one seemed judgmental. You were there to learn, to have a good time and you all pulled together as part of a team. The way it should be rather than the way it was at school. Time seemed to fly. Three hours felt like thirty minutes, and it was over in no time at all.

I chatted to my dad the whole way home, telling him about all the things I had done and all the things I had coming up. I showed him all the uniform I had been given and how to wear it. If anything, it would teach me to be smart, to iron my own clothes, for lines to be down the front of my trousers, my boots to be clean and polished. To take pride in the way I looked and to try to be organised and ready for action.

I told my mum about the camps I would be going on in the summer and half term breaks along with all the people I had met. I think they were both pleased I had finally found something that was me, that I finally enjoyed and would keep my body and mind stimulated. If nothing else, maybe it would make me grow up a little bit and learn to look after myself. Maybe this was a taster for me joining the real army.

Army Cadets was my first introduction to the big bad world of sex. Whether that was my age or whether it was something I had suddenly been exposed to, I'm not sure. The age range was up to eighteen years and a lot of the camps were mixed. There was designated living accommodation for males and females where we slept and there were instructors of both sexes, but the rest of the time it was all together.

The amount of experimentation was such an eye opener. I saw and heard things I had never experienced before. Of course, I had kissed a boy before, and there had been the odd fumble and touch but nothing of real meaning. After only the first couple of weeks at Army Cadets, I had been approached by quite a few of the boys there. They flirted, they asked me to go out with them and we kissed but the one I really wanted to approach me was the boy I bumped into that very first evening. After the first time I met him, we kept bumping into each other. He even went to the same school as me. How had I not noticed him before and why was he so shy? Maybe he didn't like me, that was why he was the only one that didn't make a move. His name was Daniel.

Chapter 3

The Big Beginning

I tried to keep Army Cadets a big secret from all my school friends. There were two popular groups at school: one for the girls and the other for the boys, of which I was in the girls' gang. I had known most of the members of the group since I was five and at primary school. Image was everything. You dressed and acted a certain way and if you deviated, you were out. I can honestly say that anyone outside of this group was teased, picked on and bullied. When I look back now, it was cruel. Teenagers were horrible to each other and every day at school was torture. It has been clamped down on in today's schools but back then you were picked on for anything outside of the norm. The teachers said and did nothing to discourage this type of behaviour and I believe this also shaped the person I am today: trying to fit in with society at every opportunity.

I had also hit quite a rebellious stage in my life. Whilst I was always fighting against control my whole childhood and doing the opposite of what I was told to do, I seemed to be drawn to anything that would shock. My parents would let me go out with my friends, but I had to be in by a certain time. If I wanted to go to a party, they wanted to know I was safe. Normal parenting, worrying about the welfare of your children, but I didn't make it easy for them.

I wanted a tattoo. I was told no. So, the first thing I did was go to a tattoo shop and get one. We were fourteen. Zoe and I made a pact that we were going to get a small one, same place — along our knicker line so no one would be able to see it.

One Saturday morning, we got a bus into town, pocket money in our hands, heading for the local tattoo studio. The man in the shop had a Mohican, tattoos on every part of his body, piercings in his nose, eyebrow and ears, and wore leather trousers and an Iron Maiden T-shirt.

The door rang as we opened it, rows of flip charts on the walls contained images of various designs.

'Morning, ladies,' he greeted us as we walked in. We heard the buzzing sound of the tattoo guns in the background and the radio playing.

'Morning,' we both said sheepishly. We knew we weren't old enough, but we were there to see if we could get away with it.

'What are you looking for?' he asked, looking up occasionally as we flicked through the different images.

'Just a small one please. I think I like this one.' I pointed to Tweety Pie along with all the other cartoon characters. Small, funny and completely unusual — just like me.

'Tweety Pie?' Zoe looked at me with a titled head, confused and laughed out loud. 'I love it!'

'Okay, give me five minutes and I will be with you.' He finished his current client. They stood up, thanked him for the artwork, paid and left the shop.

Was it too late for me to change my mind? I was slightly dubious but now I was here, I had to go ahead with it. My parents would kill me if they found out. Oh well, too late. *I'm going for it.* My rebellious behaviour kicked in.

'Take a seat. Where do you want it?'

Zoe and I edged forwards to the seat in front of him. He changed the needle in his gun to a new one and started arranging the coloured ink on the table.

Shaking, I undid my jeans, rolled them back and said, 'Here'. I pointed to a place on the top of my hip where the waist of my knickers normally sat. *No one will ever see that unless I'm naked*, I thought.

'Okay, sit down. Make yourself comfortable. And you?' He turned to Zoe and asked her what she was having.

'I think I want a pair of cherries, but I'll make up my mind when she's finished having hers done.' She watched what he was doing tentatively.

'Ready?' He looked me straight in the eyes.

'Yep.' I took a deep breath in as if I was expecting him to cut me open like a knife attack to the hip.

'You will feel a slight scratch.'

It felt like an uncomfortable scratching sensation. Not unbearable, but it wasn't pleasurable either. He used a tissue to wipe the blood away as he drew the outline of my favourite cartoon character. I looked periodically at Zoe's face to see her expression. She was biting the cuff of her coat and looked apprehensive. It wasn't that bad if I was honest. It hurt, but I quite liked pain in a strange way — it made me feel alive.

Before long, he had finished. The yellow colour was bright, the whole thing was only about five centimetres high. I laughed to myself. It was funny and it was something rebellious that I had done.

'Are you all right? All finished.' He was cleaning his gun and wiping down the area around him. He placed some Vaseline on the area he had just tattooed, smearing it around so it would help stop the bleeding and passed me a tissue to wipe the rest of the residue.

I got up, looking at it in the long mirror opposite his chair. I smiled. Now it was Zoe's turn.

'Little lady, what are you thinking?'

Zoe stood there, quiet as a mouse before turning to look at me admiring mine.

'I think I'm going to give it a miss. I'll come back in next week.' She had her head down but looked at me out of the corner of her eye, waiting for my reaction.

'You what?' I snapped back. 'We were going to get one together, you bitch. You can't not have one done.' I called her a bitch in a friendly way; she knew I was joking but equally she had just dropped me in it. It was a pact; we were going to have one done together.

'I know, I know, but that looked like it hurt. Plus I want a different one and I don't have the money. Come back with me next week and I promise I will get it done.' Zoe pleaded with me. How could I resist. I loved her to bits, so I agreed.

I paid the man, buttoned back up my jeans uncomfortably and we walked out of the shop. We walked back to the high street, arm in arm laughing at what we had just done.

Of course, she didn't go back the following week, or the week after and on Monday morning at school, everyone knew. All my friends asked to see what I had got done. Pulling up my white school shirt and dropping my skirt slightly, I showed them. I liked the fact I was naughty; the first person to get one and everyone laughing, reminding Zoe she needed to get one done too.

Although I was rebellious and naughty, I was one of the quiet girls and I didn't like the way the girls acted against others sometimes. I tended to hide behind the group, spending most of my time with the boys who were so much easier to get along with, less bitchy and had far less dramas and issues. Have you ever seen the film Grease? It was just like that with the T-Birds and Pink Ladies, everyone wanting to be part of the group. I had told my two closest friends, Sarah and Zoe, that I really liked Daniel. Of course, I had to tell them where I had met him and from that point on, the secret was out. Yes, I was teased a little but not as much as I had imagined and worked up in my own little head. The focus was now on Daniel. Both the boys and girls were checking him out and at every opportunity were trying to set us up. If that wasn't embarrassing enough, he now knew I liked him too.

There were two large housing estates in Bracknell: Easthampstead Grange and Home Farm, both of which were in an area called Great Hollands. There was a large field and a park connecting the two. I lived in Easthampstead Grange and Daniel in Home Farm. Sarah, Zoe and I would walk home from school with Daniel and his two best friends, Alfie and Jack. We would walk along the long school drive at Easthampstead Park School, through the field, past the park and then we would all split in different directions towards home. We did this for weeks without either of us making the first move and all our friends knowing and teasing us until one day after school, I walked home, dumped my school bag and coat at the bottom of the stairs because I was too lazy to hang it up and got changed. Sarah wanted to stay at my house until her mum got home from work and Daniel, Alfie and Jack wanted to go back to the park to hang out. All out of our school uniforms, we headed back to the park and sat on the swings talking and laughing. Enjoying time in the fresh air and not a care in the world.

'So, are you both going to ask each other out or not?' Alfie was the first person to raise our like for each other. He stood up, picked up a stick he found on the floor and started drawing a large circle in the wood chippings. I had no idea what he was doing and by the look on everyone's faces, no one else did either. He then divided the circle in half with a line.

'I have an idea,' he said and laughed out loud. Alfie was bold. He always said what he thought. He was very outgoing and quite naughty at school as he didn't care what he said and always had an opinion, but he was a boy that would do anything for you. The type of friend everyone should have by their side.

'Dan, you get up and stand in that semicircle and Rose, you stand in that one.'

My full name is Rosemary, but everyone called me Rose, except my family who called me Rosie as my mum said it sounded pretty. The only time my parents would call me by my full name was when I was in trouble and that was frequent.

'What?' I said, embarrassed that everyone was watching us.

Daniel's face flushed bright red. 'No way. You're such an idiot, Alfie.'

I started to learn that he didn't like confrontation, nor did he like to draw attention to himself. He preferred to stay quiet and intermingle with his peers, watching everything, not missing anything but always standing on the outside looking in.

'Come on, guys. Otherwise, you'll never get together as neither one of you will make the first move.' Alfie started to push Daniel off the swing and towards the circle.

Sarah did the same to me and so we both ended up standing in the middle of the park in a stick-drawn circle of wood chippings.

'Now, both of you close your eyes until I tell you to open them.' Alfie smiled at both of us as we stupidly did as we were told.

Then we both heard a scrambling of feet and finally quiet. As we opened our eyes, both Sarah and Alfie had run off and we were left standing there opposite each other on our own. Although it was extremely awkward, we both laughed out loud until we were left in an uncomfortable silence. Alfie did what he set out to do though; it brought us together and finally we were talking.

'I guess now we're here, maybe I should tell you that I really like you and I've wanted to ask you out since the day I first saw you at the cadet hut, but I was way too shy. All the other boys had made a move and I didn't want to look stupid. I guessed you already had your eyes on someone else and not me.' He leant forward, gently pulled me in to him, wrapped his arms around me and kissed me.

It was a long, passionate kiss. His tongue slipped inside and joined mine. It felt natural like we had kissed so many times before. I felt comfortable and not awkward at all. I could have stayed with him for hours in that park. I didn't want to stop chatting away to him. He had me hooked like he was my complete world, totally unaware of our surroundings or anyone that was around us. He had a hold on me that I couldn't explain. I know what they mean when they say love at first sight. We had the same things in common, we liked the same things.

His hand slid down my back to my side and finally clasped my hand. We sat holding hands on the park bench for over an hour. The temperature began to drop, and we were both shivering.

'It's getting dark. I better walk you home,' he whispered to me.

As we walked the five-minute walk home, I could see him keep looking at me. He smiled like he had just won a prize, a doting look, besotted with me. I had never had someone like me in that way before. It was like I now belonged to him and he to me. A couple that no one could separate.

Chapter 4

My World

From that point on, I was besotted with Daniel and he with me. We went everywhere together, we spent break times together, we spoke on the phone as soon as we got home. Each night he would come to my house, or I would go to his. We were best friends. We liked the same things, we got on so well, I would have done anything for him.

I met his parents, he met mine. In fact, they were both very similar: the same morals, manners, we had a similar upbringing, same toys and the same values. His family welcomed me with open arms and so did mine. The only issue we each had was jealousy; the risk of him getting attention elsewhere or me getting attention from anyone other than him riddled our relationship. Yes, there was trust. There wasn't any reason at this point not to trust each other but the risk of losing one another and what we had tormented us constantly. You could say it was unhealthy. We were infatuated.

It was only a couple of months past our sixteenth birthdays and our Friday and Saturday nights had changed from sleepovers with our friends to spending them with each other, mainly at house parties or the local pubs and nightclubs. Our favourite was The Keep, a dark, dingy nightclub, that stayed open till 1 a.m. and never asked us how old we were and served us alcohol well into the night. It always had a sticky floor and stunk of cigarettes and sweat. You knew you had a great night out when you woke in the morning and your hair smelt of smoke and needed a good wash.

This particular night was different. We had been asked by one of the boys from Army Cadets to go to his house for his birthday. I had been looking forward to it for weeks and I knew this night was the night I wanted to lose my virginity. I had told Daniel and it was all me and my idea. I didn't want to put him under pressure as he was a virgin too, but I wanted us to be the ones to do it together. I knew very few people at school who had done it, so once again, I didn't have anyone to ask for tips. We had to figure it out for ourselves.

We met each other at the local shops. We got some alcohol on the way, and we walked together to the party. I could tell he was nervous and, although I didn't want to show it, so was I. You would have thought I would have wanted somewhere special for our first time, somewhere romantic, candlelit perhaps, gentle music playing in the background but looking back I wouldn't have had it any other way.

We knocked on the door, and Jamie opened it, dance music blaring out loud. I could see someone being sick in the kitchen behind him, people were shouting and dancing in the front room and disco lights bounced off the walls in all colours.

'Hey guys. Come in. Drinks are in the fridge or bottle opener on the side if you have your own. Help yourself to cups. Oh, and mind the sick on the floor!' He was smashed and could barely walk. Jamie was a really sweet boy. I think he always tried to fit in and had a great, dry sense of humour. I felt quite sorry for him as his mum was elderly and it looked like everyone at the party had trashed his house, with glasses smashed on the floor and drink spilt all over the sides. It would take him forever to clean up the mess in the morning and I wasn't even sure if his mum knew this party was happening. I wasn't even sure where she was.

There were drinking games going on, shots were being passed around and before long, Daniel and I had joined the queue of drunkards wrecking his house. By 10 p.m., his neighbours knocked on the door asking if he could turn the music down a little, which he did. But five minutes later and it was back up again.

I whispered to Daniel to see if we could go upstairs and spend a bit of alone time together. We both knew what that meant. Looking back now, was I too pushy? It was all me wanting to do it and he was just going along with everything I wanted. Surely all guys want to do it but perhaps it was normally them being the instigators. I couldn't say for sure.

We walked upstairs hand in hand. I could hear my heart beating out of my chest; nervous and excited all at the same time. This was it. We were finally going to do it and lose our virginity. As we opened the first door, unsure of what to find, we turned on the light and found a double bed with unmade duvet covers, a large wardrobe, a desk with books strewn across it with Jamie's name on the front. It had to be his room. His bedroom was vibrating with the sound of the music from below and we could still hear people laughing and shouting. I sat down on the bed with Daniel nervously standing just inside the doorway.

'You sure about this?' he said as he quietly shut the door behind him.

'Absolutely,' I replied.

I moved back on the bed so he could join me. I had a long wrap over skirt on and a T-shirt top so as I edged backwards, my skirt began to pull apart revealing more and more of my legs. Daniel positioned himself between my legs and as he lay on top of me, we kissed slowly.

'I love you so much,' he whispered as his cold hands disappeared up my top and into my bra. I had quite big breasts for a young girl and my nipples were hard to the touch from his gentle hands cupping and squeezing them. We had touched each other plenty of times but being at home, there was always the worry of someone walking in or being caught.

I reached down to find he already had an erection, so I stroked and rubbed the outline of his cock with my fingertips. The more we touched each other, the deeper and harder our breathing became. Not once did I have any doubts in my mind about what we were doing. We couldn't lock the door, so we didn't have complete privacy, but it felt right doing it then and there.

We didn't get undressed. We didn't need to, our lust was overpowering, and it didn't feel right getting naked in our friend's room. I undid his belt, unzipped his jeans and released his erection from his boxer shorts. He pulled my knickers down to my ankles and smoothly slipped a finger into my already wet pussy as I groaned at the pleasure. We were so ready for each other. It was the next step in our relationship; the party going on around us was unnoticed.

Daniel reached into his back pocket and pulled out his wallet. In the side compartment, he had a couple of condoms he had placed in there earlier to be safe. Using his teeth, he got one out and with his other hand tore off the corner and passed it to me, like a professional. Only having done this once before in our sex education class at school, I held the slippery tip in my fingers and slid it slowly over his shaft. We then returned to kissing and touching, continuing the pace of seduction. As he moved closer to me, us both writhing in time back and forth, I felt the tip of his cock start to enter my pussy. I didn't hold back, I went with it. He applied gentle pressure and, with a slight uncomfortable pain, he was inside me. It felt like he had reached a seal inside me but then pushed past it, breaking it and reaching further inside me.

To mask the pain and not ruin the moment, I concentrated on our hands, him kissing me, touching each other and our whole bodies together while he was gently penetrating in and out of me. His breathing got quicker and quicker. He had his eyes tightly closed, caressing me the whole time until he came. Our first time together. It felt so special, a moment that we would both remember for the rest of our lives. We were both hot, steamy and our eyes met. No uncomfortable silence or awkwardness. He smiled and slowly pulled out.

'You okay?' he said as if he had intentionally hurt me.

'Yes, I'm fine.' My hips felt tight and I had a burning sensation inside me. It was painful but not unbearable.

At that precise moment, the door burst open, and Jamie was at the door.

'Are you guys having sex in my bed? Clear up the mess when you leave!' He then laughed, trying to hold himself up, then slammed the door and disappeared.

I think this broke the ice with us and what had just happened. I pulled up my knickers, adjusted my skirt, bra and top and he did the same with his jeans.

You see in films or read in books that the first time is romantic. Both people are caught in lust and love, a special moment. Whilst it was all of those, it hurt, it was painful, and I didn't reach the state of euphoria that people always talked about. Did we do it wrong? Maybe it was because it was the first time. The second and third time would be way better. This was something I needed to get better at and experience the type of pleasure that was so widely talked about.

'We better go downstairs and join everyone,' I said as we both got up and made our way back to the party. I felt uncomfortable — like I needed a shower or to clean myself — slightly shaken and disorientated but I felt like a woman. I was slightly confused about the whole experience but I guessed I had to be broken for the pleasure to begin. I was a virgin no more. And there was no one I would have rather done it with.

We stayed at the party for another hour or so and then he walked me home. We acted as if nothing had happened. We didn't mention it at all but we both had a smile on our faces and the look that we gave each other was stronger than ever.

By Monday morning at school, as I entered the courtyard area, everyone was in groups whispering and looking at us. Jamie had already told the whole school we had had sex in his bedroom at his house. I was distraught, everyone knew our business. What a surprise, the boys were high fiving Daniel and saying well done and the girls looked at me in disgust apart from Sarah and Zoe. They wanted to know all the details: what was it like, what happened, how did it feel, was he good?

I felt hurt and violated that the whole school was talking about us. Walking to our classrooms, I could feel the stares in my direction, people covering their mouths as they whispered about us. I should have cared less and not worried what people were saying but it made me feel sick. The rumours multiplied, like a string of Chinese whispers, about what had happened that night.

'Hey, I'm really sorry.' Daniel walked up to me apologetically.

'It's not your fault, although you are getting most of the praise and I am getting the dirty looks from everyone.' I raised my eyebrows in disbelief.

'It's none of their business what happened, just laugh it off. Who cares but us, right?' He had a way of calming me down and telling me not to care what people thought. I liked that Daniel always made me feel safe. It was us against the world.

'I guess.' I shrugged it off.

'I better go to class, but I'll wait for you outside the gates after school, okay?' He gave me a kiss on the head, patted my rucksack and left me to walk across the playground.

We only had a few weeks before summer and that was the end of school, so why should I care that I was at the centre of gossip? It was going to be the greatest summer ever. I needed to get my exams out of the way and look forward to the next chapter in our lives – college.

Chapter 5

Valentine's Day

It's funny how when you get to a certain age, you think you are so grown up and can conquer anything. Yet your parents know the truth and constantly remind you that you are still a child. That's exactly how I viewed myself at seventeen. I was Miss Know It All. No one could tell me what to do. My life was in control, and I was prepared for anything. Well, let me tell you this now. I was clearly not prepared. In fact, this was probably the first time in my life where I thought, *oh shit, how do I get out of this one?*

We were two teenagers in love and wanting to do what adults do. We wanted to go for dinner on Valentine's Day, we wanted to stay in a hotel, go to sleep together, wake up together, have the immature sex that we used to have at that age and just simply be. From our first experience, sex had gone from better to amazing, experimenting, trying new techniques. It was incredible.

Too scared to ask my dad as he was quite old fashioned, Daniel was never allowed to stay over and had to leave the house by 11 p.m. so I wasn't tired for college in the morning. Thinking she would say no, I asked my mum, to which she said yes. Oh wow, she said yes.

The Fines Bailywick Hotel was an inexpensive boutique hotel about a mile from where we lived. We booked the night away and a three-course meal at a local restaurant that was in walking distance. We had a lovely meal but couldn't get served alcohol as we weren't old enough, but we did manage to get a bottle of Sheridans and a few beers from the corner shop on the way. We knew eyes were on us. We knew people were watching us, but what were they thinking? That we were a cute couple? That we were way too young? Or maybe something else. Or maybe it was all in my head and people weren't thinking anything; they hadn't thought of us that way at all.

I'd never felt this way before, nothing seemed to matter. I didn't have anything else on my mind other than wanting to spend the night with Daniel, to cuddle up with him, to fall asleep together and wake up in the morning together. Not only that, but we also wanted sex together without having to be quiet, or worry about someone accidentally walking in or being caught. We wanted the feeling of being with someone and it not being frowned upon because we were so young and didn't live together. This was something we had never ever done before, to be totally free with not a care in the world. Little did I know at the time that this would be the first, the last and the only time we would spend the night together and not have a care in the world other than the two of us.

Our meal was full of open conversations, talking about what we wanted to do in a few years, places we wanted to visit and what after college looked like. My plan, as had always been, was to pass my English A Level and then to continue to a degree in English Language and Literature. My chosen university was Royal Holloway in Egham. I had it all mapped out as clear as day. My dream was to teach secondary school children English, to make them want to learn and to make Shakespeare, Maya Angelou and other famous writers interesting.

For all the students that struggled with punctuation or learning the subject, I wanted to be a teacher that wanted to spend time with them. A route to making it easier to understand. Currently, it seemed most teachers dismissed a pupil and made them stand in the corridor the minute they didn't listen or were distracted, without knowing or taking the time to understand that it was because said pupil didn't quite get it and were too embarrassed to raise a hand. Why be a teacher if you don't take the time to really help and have the patience? I saw too many people make it all the way through secondary school without being able to read and write properly.

Daniel, on the other hand, was torn between a career in the trade; carpentry was his preferred route. He had a passion for building and making things and he was extremely talented. He had an attention for detail and was a perfectionist. I had seen his work in our woodwork classes at school and he was very good. Everyone was talking him into business studies though. It was promoted as being a safer profession, better paid and guaranteed. He had chosen the business route but still worked on a Saturday as a landscaper and carpenter so he had both options to fall back on. In that respect, he had his head screwed on. He thought about things first before rushing and making a rash decision. I was the opposite. I wanted everything now and quickly, not thinking about the consequences of my actions. We worked well as a team; where I would want to do something in a hurry, he would slow me down, tell me to think about it and then move forwards.

We walked from the restaurant to the hotel in the pitch black with only the moon and the occasional headlight to guide our way. We giggled, we laughed, and we flirted with each other all the way. It wasn't just a physical attraction for us. We actually got on well as best friends and enjoyed each other's company.

Once at the hotel, it was a little awkward but more for the fact I didn't want to disappoint. I had high expectations for the night and wanted it to be a night to remember. We'd slept together before, but this was on a whole new level. What if this turned him off? What if he suddenly stopped liking me or something embarrassing happened that he would tell all his friends about? The little things that, at the time, really mattered to me. I had done some preparation in advance of the night. I wanted to be good in bed, someone people talked about and someone all the boys wanted to sleep with at school and college. I don't know why I had this in me. I think it was the desire of people lusting after me. Not that I wanted anything to happen, but I just wanted to be desired by others, even at this early age. The last thing I wanted people to say to Daniel was – why are you with her? He was mine and I had to keep his attention and desire.

We had the night of all nights. We had a few drinks; the television was on in the background playing an old re-run of Die Hard and although we were only young, it was as if we had been having sex our whole lives. I was hooked. The way he touched me, running his fingers over my skin and his kisses were the most passionate I'd ever experienced.

We were a fumbling mess of inexperienced sexual beings. Trying to be elegant and sexy in the way we moved our clothes, I still managed to get my knickers hooked up and rolled around my ankles. He couldn't undo my bra strap as it was stuck, and he was naked apart from his socks. I giggled aimlessly; we had the ability to laugh with each other without taking offense. It didn't turn us off or ruin the moment. The fun side of sex made it less pressurised.

I asked questions like, 'What do you like the most? How does this feel? How can I do it better?' and he did the same. The louder we got, the more the other knew it felt good. I had purchased the ancient Indian Kuma Sutra book the week before, containing everything from techniques to positions. As we lay back on the bed, the covers pulled up around us keeping our naked bodies warm, I flicked through the pages. I read extracts and showed Daniel the pictures. It gave us ideas to try to experiment with. There was the odd page we both looked quizzically at but it was from confusion. A big part of the Kuma Sutra was around breathing techniques and connecting as a couple. Something I hadn't considered before. It made complete sense, but it would be something for us to try to master.

For me, sex was the most important thing in any relationship. Without that, couples failed, cheated and broke down. It was the number one thing I needed to get right. I couldn't risk losing him to temptation in the bed of another woman.

We spent hours trying different positions but my favourite by far was when he flipped me onto my front, raising my hips towards him. I gripped the headrest of the bed, two pillows pushed under my pelvis, and he penetrated me whilst kneeling up. I couldn't see his face or his satisfied expressions, but I could tell how fulfilled he was by his sounds and groans. The bed banging against the wall, the noise of other couples in the same hotel as us appreciating the same alone time.

As much as I loved living at home with my parents, I longed for the time when we would be able to spend every night together, alone. I couldn't get enough of sex with Daniel. I thought about it all the time, and my body ached for it all day, every day. There was no feeling I had ever experienced that came close to it. Each time, it got better and better. I was turning into a nymphomaniac. If we went a few days without doing it or I didn't see him, I felt the pressure building up in my body like a volcano about to blow.

Chapter 6

The Big Surprise

One, two, ugh. Three, four, ugh. Five… ugh. I thought the more exercise you did, the easier it got. Each sit up I did, the more I felt dizzy, the more I felt sick, and mornings were always so much worse. The small, secluded gym I was a member of had mirrors on every wall. It was quite quiet but had a lot of equipment that I used. A musty, sweaty smell filled the air. It was my new year's resolution to get fitter and was planning to go on holiday to Greece with the family, so I needed to get beach fit. Something was wrong though. I wasn't feeling myself at all. The dizziness and feeling sick was starting to worry me. Maybe exercise wasn't for me. Perhaps I had a stomach bug or something. I rode it out to see if I could finish the last thirty minutes of my workout and then headed home on the bus. Unusually tired, I went to bed without dinner.

The next morning, getting ready for college was difficult. The dizziness was still there and a strong sense of wanting to be sick. I can only compare the feeling to that of a hangover. Not hungry but my stomach growled in pain, a cloudy, unable to concentrate headache and so dizzy I wasn't sure if I should go back to bed or not. I had never missed a day of school or college before; my mum's attitude was unless you are dying you get up and you go, so I continued with the same approach. I had Business Studies first period followed by English. Never have I had a lesson drag so much in my entire life. I knew the teacher was speaking and I could hear her dulcet tones, but nothing was going in. It was almost as if I was there in body but not in spirit. My mind kept wandering.

'You okay?' Alison asked me. 'You don't seem yourself and your face is all flushed.'

Alison had beautiful blonde curly hair and piercing blue eyes, a very slim frame, was incredibly intelligent and breezed through college lessons. We were in the same year and had a few classes together at the same secondary school but we had a completely different circle of friends. We didn't really get to know each other until this year. It had only been a few months, but already I felt like we had been close for years.

'Go home at lunch if you aren't feeling so well,' she said. 'I'll tell Miss that you were sick at lunch and won't be in for the rest of the day. She'll be fine about it.'

'I don't know what's wrong. Every morning I feel rough and then it seems to get better by the afternoon. I'll be fine in an hour or two,' I murmured.

'Morning sickness then,' Alison replied. We laughed together until a glare from Miss gave us the stare of all stares.

I know we laughed but the nagging in my head kept telling me what if I *was* pregnant? But I couldn't be. I'm not stupid. We took precautions. I couldn't possibly be, or could I? Of course not, I was just overthinking things. I was taking the contraceptive pill so that protected me but I was sick from drinking too much that night and I was on antibiotics.

Me being me, I decided to go straight to the chemist after college on the way home and get a test. I knew I wasn't, but I thought at least if I did one then it would put my mind at rest, and I could focus on getting myself better. More worried about the sales assistant in the shop and wondering what they would think of me buying a test than what I was doing, I pretended I was looking at other products until it was just me and her. Carefully picking up the box, I nervously approached the counter.

She seemed nice and was probably very non-judgmental but nonetheless the voice in my head was saying she's thinking another teenage pregnancy coming up.

'Would you like a bag with that?' She smiled.

'Yes please,' I replied. I quickly paid and almost ran out of the door, my heart racing. The test was wrapped up in as many layers of the carrier bag as possible so no one could see what I was holding. I stuffed it abruptly in my bag and walked home.

I turned the corner, walking up the driveway to our house at the end of the cul-de-sac. No cars parked outside meant no one was home; the family all at work. Perfect, it was just me and the test. How hard could it be? I slammed the from door behind me, dying for a wee but knowing I had to hold it so I could go on the stick. Well, that was what I had seen in films and presumed that's what you had to do.

I slung my coat on the floor, leaving my bag at the bottom of the stairs where I had thrown it down. I ran to the toilet, ripping open the test and quickly scanning through the instructions so I could get it over and done with. So, now came the point where I took the cap off the test, held it between my legs and tried to aim my urine stream on the end of the stick. It's not quite as easy as you would think it would be and at that precise point, I couldn't go. *Come on, you can do this.* I was trying to breathe, relax and just go. *There it is, I'm going.* It took me five whole minutes to finish. I sighed, and replaced the cap back on it and slowly but surely the window started to reveal. I closed my eyes firmly shut knowing it was negative but had to be sure. I placed the test on the back of the toilet cistern, pulled my jeans up and flushed. I shut the lid, sat down and kept my head in my hands, humming impatiently. It said wait ten to fifteen minutes for an accurate result so I counted the seconds in my head. I added on a few just to be sure.

I turned round, flipped the test over and just stared and stared… One blue line for negative and two blue lines for positive. I had two so that meant… wait a second, I had what? That couldn't be right. I looked at the instructions again in the packet. I said it again to myself, 'One blue, two blue, negative, positive. No way. Right, I'm doing that again.'

I bought a pack of two so the first one must have been wrong. I took off the lid, but I couldn't wee again; I had nothing left. I held it between my legs again shaking, trying to concentrate and focus on going again. I managed a tiny bit, just enough to make it work. Again, the window started to reveal but much slower than the first. I pulled up my trousers again, placed the test on the cistern, shut the lid and kept my eyes tightly closed, just waiting. Hoping…

Sure enough, I waited painstakingly for another ten minutes. I already knew what the result was going to be. I just didn't want to believe it. It felt totally surreal that I was doing this test in the first place, let alone the result and what it could mean. As I turned it over, as clear as day there were two blue lines, not faded or blurred lines, bright blue ones, glaring back at me. It couldn't be more positive if it tried. For the first time in my life, I was speechless and motionless. What did I do now? What did this mean?

I gathered the package contents together, stuffed all the pieces of paper and wrappers back into the box, leaving just the two tests out in my hand. As I walked to my bedroom, all kinds of thoughts were running through my head. *I need to speak to Daniel. What will he say?*

I hid the boxes and evidence in the top drawer of my bedside cabinet and just lay on my bed staring at the swirls in the artexed ceiling of my room. *I'm in so much trouble*, I thought repeatedly. Nothing I did now would change the result and no going back. *I'm seventeen.* I looked round my room at the clothes strewn across the floor, the mugs on the windowsill still full of tea and hot chocolate from the past couple of days that I had not bothered to take downstairs to the dishwasher, posters on the wall of all my pop star crushes. *See, I can't even look after myself let alone another small person.* All my friends at school did child development except me. They all babysit for extra money except for me. I hadn't even changed a nappy before. What use would I be as an adult, as a mother – *useless*.

I heard a car outside; the sound of a car door slamming and keys in the front door. Now I was panicking. They were going to know something was wrong.

'Rose, will you move your bag and coat off the floor? I almost tripped over it!' My middle sister Ashley was home from work. She was six years my senior, and we got on well despite me constantly borrowing things from her room, being a total menace and winding her up daily. She was always so placid, calm and collected. The total opposite of me. I heard her make her way up the stairs until she appeared at my bedroom door, my coat and bag in hand. 'Hey, what are you doing?'

'Nothing,' I said, shrugging.

'I got your bag and coat. Why do you always leave it in the doorway? One of these days someone is going to fall over it. And your room is disgusting, doesn't it annoy you?' she said, smiling at me. She couldn't be angry at me if she tried.

'Thanks, and nope, I like it like this. I know where everything is.' I smiled back.

She turned to walk away.

'Ashley,' I said, 'Can I ask you a question?'

'Of course.' She kept walking but I could tell she was still listening. We always spoke between our two bedrooms. I got up and headed to her room this time. I had to speak to someone, and I didn't feel it was something I wanted to shout about. I pushed both tests up my sleeve and then held my arm, so they didn't fall out.

'Ashley, I need to speak to someone, but I don't want Mum to find out.' I perched on the end of her bed waiting for her attention.

'Oh no, what have you done now?' She turned to face me but wasn't fazed at all. We had been in this situation before, but it was normally about me smoking or drinking, a falling out with friends or some other minor subject. I slowly released the tests from my sleeve and held them up to her. I then hung my head, not wanting to look at her or see her reaction.

'Oh, wow.' Was that all she could say? Then she sat next to me. 'Have you told Daniel yet? What has he said?'

'No, you're the first person I've told. I've only just done the test. I had to do two as I thought it was wrong but I'm guessing two can't be wrong. I… er… don't know what to do or what to say. What would you do?' I'm not sure what I was expecting her to say or do. This was my mess.

'Oh Rose, it's not for me to say or to advise you on this one. You really need to speak to Daniel and tell him first. You're so young but at the same time I think Mum and Dad will understand and go through your options. I'm really not the best person but you know I'm always here for you, right?' She put her arm around me and squeezed tightly.

I knew she cared but I wasn't sure what options I was hoping she would come up with. I wished there was a way I could pretend it wasn't real and forget all about it, keep it a secret and not tell anyone. But this wasn't one of those things that I could just brush under the carpet and forget about.

41

'I know. Thank you,' I said. I could feel my eyes welling up. Crying wasn't something I did very often. I didn't know how to, and it never made me feel better. I always felt that crying was for weak people, and I was a strong, independent young lady. 'Please don't say anything to anyone about this yet. I'll give Daniel a call first and then figure out what I need to do but thank you for listening.'

I stood up and walked back to my room, trying to buy myself some more time to think about what I was going to say to Daniel.

The only phones in the house were in my mum and dad's room and downstairs in the hallway. I would quite often sit in my parents' room for hours on end just chatting on the phone, wrapping the cord in and out of my fingers, twiddling it whilst I spoke. The number of times I had been told off for running up an astronomical phone bill speaking to Daniel after college. Apparently seeing someone all day at college and then speaking to them all evening on the phone was too much and too expensive. I ignored them as per usual and carried on doing it every day.

Their room had pine furniture, a television on a bracket on the wall and flowery bed covers. An assortment of china ornaments, which I would often stare at mid conversation, were placed sporadically on the windowsill underneath white patterned net curtains.

I sat on their bed, picked up the receiver that was perched on their dressing table, the long cord unravelled, and stared at the buttons. *Dial his number you idiot.* I talked myself into going through with it. 01344… I was doing it; how would he respond?

'Hello? Who's speaking please?' Daniel's sister answered. He would always get her to answer the phone first, then if it was me, he would run downstairs, snatch it from her hands and tell her to get lost. We would sit talking to each other for hours.

'Hey Sophie. It's Rose. Is Daniel there please?' Normally I would speak for a bit, ask her about her day and then we would get to the end of our quick exchange, and she would pass it over. This time it was different. I couldn't think of anything else to say. Sophie was two years younger than both of us, a real sweetheart, innocent and so caring. I would refer to Daniel and I as the black sheep of both of our families, the naughty ones, and Sophie along with my sisters were the good ones. She didn't have a bad bone in her body. Unlike Daniel with his bright blue eyes, she had dark chocolatey eyes and dark hair, almost Mediterranean-looking with the loveliest hazelnut skin. She took after their dad's side of the family and Daniel after his mum's.

'Yes, sure. I'll go get him.'

It went silent for a bit and then he picked up.

'Hey. You all right?' Daniel always said this, out of breath from running down the stairs.

'Yeah. I… er… Can I talk to you?' Suddenly I was lost for words. I had so many different versions of what I was going to say but, in that instance, I didn't know how to come out with it.

'You are talking to me. What's wrong?' he replied. I could imagine his confused face.

'I mean, can I speak to you in person? I need to tell you something.' It felt awkward to tell him over the phone. I wanted to see his reaction. I was now panicking. What if he wanted nothing more to do with me or hated me? I wasn't sure I could take that sort of rejection from him. He was my world, the last thing I wanted was for us to break up. What a complete mess.

'What? Now? Yeah, I can do. I was just going to jump in the shower. Can you give me half an hour? Why can't you tell me now?'

'I'd rather show you if that's okay. Half an hour is fine. I'll see you then. Come straight over.' I hung up the phone quick before he had a chance to ask many more questions. Half an hour felt like a lifetime.

The doorbell rang. I opened the door to find Daniel standing there in his Nike hoodie, jeans and Adidas Gazelles. His hair was wet and perfectly gelled as it always was. With his freckled young face, dimpled smile and smelling of Lynx spray.

'You okay?' he said as he stepped in and stood in the hallway. He could see my eyes well up again, just as they did before when I spoke to my sister. 'What's wrong?'

Before I could reply, I took out the tests from the back pocket of my jeans and slowly handed them to him.

'I didn't know how to tell you, but you know how I'd felt rough the past few days? Well, I did a test thinking that it was silly and that it would be negative but just in case… and this happened.' I was nervously murmuring my words, not making much sense. I couldn't bring myself to look at him and I didn't want him to look at me either.

His eyes were locked on what he was holding in his hands. I could see the shock on his face. He didn't say a word, just kept his head down.

'Daniel, say something, anything. I don't know what to do. What do we do now?'

He moved towards the stairs and just sat down. Was he angry? Was he mad at me? What was he thinking?

'Rose, I don't know what to say. I'm seventeen. I can't do this. Is this for real or are you winding me up? We can't do this. How is this even possible?' He had tears in his eyes as well, as he spoke. They rolled down his face. He wiped his tears occasionally with the cuff of his jumper. I had never seen him cry before and I didn't know what to do.

Suddenly, this all seemed real. This was happening to us and not just an episode from a film. I could hear my sister in her room the whole time, quietly moving about, but she was clearly giving us the space and time to talk.

'I need some time, Rose. I don't know what you want me to do. We can't do this at our age. We have no money, no house, we're at college… what sort of life could we give to a baby? It's not possible. Are you actually thinking about keeping it? If we were older then maybe. I always imagined having kids in my late twenties, not seventeen. Are you crazy?' He stared into my eyes. He looked scared and for the first time, I didn't have an answer.

'Daniel, I don't know. I don't know what to do or what to say. What happens now?'

He got up and cuddled me without saying a word, like it was the last hug we would ever have, before walking to the front door and opening it. He stood outside for a moment, facing away from me and then turned and said, 'I love you, Rose, but I can't do this.' He then walked away, his head down until he disappeared from sight.

I shut the door, ran up to my room, threw myself on the bed, buried my head in the pillow and began to sob. I was half expecting him to say everything was going to be okay and let's discuss things, but he was just as much in shock as I was. I could imagine the scared college boy walking home in panic for his future, for *our* future and the realisation of what I had just told him. I also knew he would be worried about telling his parents. As if school or college wasn't bad enough with gossip, Bracknell as a whole was terrible. People often knew gossip about you before you realised it was even a rumour. This would be on the front cover of the Bracknell News by morning – guaranteed.

Chapter 7

Decisions, Decisions

That night, I tossed and turned for hours, so many thoughts running through my mind. Some positive, some negative. Confused to say the least and the only person I really wanted to talk to was Daniel. Had I ruined that? Would he never speak to me again and not want anything to do with me, whatever decision I or we made? How would we know it was the right one?

Completely unlike me, I planned to stay at home for the day and take a long hard think about what I needed to do. I called the college and said I was sick — not like me. This wasn't totally a lie because that morning I was physically ill, I couldn't keep anything down. I had only managed a few bites of butter on toast and a glass of water and already that came back up. If this was how it was going to be every morning for me, then how on earth would I keep it a secret until I had figured out what to do? I spent all morning just in my dressing gown feeling sorry for myself. Back in 1997, I didn't have a mobile phone so I didn't hear from Daniel, and he wouldn't have known I hadn't gone to college until the end of first period. This was the time when normally we would have been in the canteen or in the breakout area together.

I made it to lunchtime. There was a ring on the doorbell. Praying it was just the postman or a delivery as my mum and dad didn't know I hadn't gone to college, I walked slowly downstairs and opened the front door to find Daniel standing there. He looked sad and solemn. His blue eyes even brighter than they normally were, or maybe I noticed them more because he looked like he had been crying too.

'Can I come in?' he said. He never normally asked but I guess it all felt strange. I hated us not talking.

'Of course. I wasn't sure if you would want to see me again,' I replied. We went straight up to my bedroom and just sat on the bed in each other's arms for what felt like ages, neither of us knowing what to say.

Finally, he looked at me and said, 'Rose, you know I love you more than anything in the world, but I can't do this, not right now. I don't know how we can. What life could we honestly give to a child? We're children ourselves, that's not fair. We must think about this logically.' He had already made his mind up, whereas I was torn. *How could you possibly make your mind up in one night?* But on the other hand, I would have done anything at all for him.

'I know what you're saying but is there no way…' I stopped and just broke down in tears. 'I'm scared and don't know what to do. My parents will be so disappointed, and I know exactly what people will say. They will judge us either way!'

48

'No one needs to know.' He stroked my hair and looked at me like a lost puppy, reassuring me that everything was going to be okay. I needed him right now.

'I don't know how this works. If we decide not to, then what happens? Is that something the doctor can help us with? Is it painful? I don't even know how many weeks far gone I am and how it could have happened in the first place. I've been on the contraceptive pill for months and not forgotten it once. I'm sure of it.' I couldn't believe I was talking about not keeping it.

'Maybe if we can get a doctor's appointment, they'll be able to advise us on the next steps and what we do from here. Give them a call quick now and see what they say.' He held my hand giving it a little squeeze, again reassuring me he was behind me.

Reluctantly, I got up and made my way to the phone upstairs, sitting back in my mum and dad's room as I had done to call him the day before. I dialled the number for the local surgery and waited patiently for reception to answer.

'Hello, Riverdale Medical Practice, can I help?' They answered almost immediately.

Not ready for them to answer, I spoke in a meek and mild voice. 'Yes, can I have an appointment please?' I stopped there; did I need to say much more?

'Please can I ask the nature of the appointment?' the receptionist prompted.

'I'd like to see the doctor please.' I was confused as to why she was asking this question, surely it was obvious.

She politely laughed. 'Oh, I'm sorry. Could I kindly ask why you need to see the doctor? It's just so I can find the earliest appointment for the right doctor or nurse. You see some of them have specialist skills in certain areas and I want to make sure you're seen by the right person.'

Well, I wasn't expecting to tell her. I thought it was confidential.

'Ah, I'm er, pregnant. Well, I've done a couple of tests and it's saying positive, so I'd like to see a doctor please. Is that okay? Is that what I'm supposed to do?'

She must think I'm stupid. I've never done this before; I don't know what's what and it's not as if I can ask my mum or dad or even my friends. I was totally on my own, learning as I went along.

'Oh, well, in that case, congratulations. I have an appointment free at 3 p.m. today if that's suitable for you with Dr Smith. Would that suit you or if that's too soon, we can look at some next week for you?'

What do I say to that? Congratulations? Is she mad? I had to think quickly and decide on the spot.

'Thanks. Yes, 3 p.m. is perfect.' That was all I could manage to say.

'Okay, lovely, and your name and date of birth please?' she asked.

I gave her all my details and that was that, all booked in for the afternoon. It didn't give me much time at all to think about what was happening. I needed to get showered, dressed, ready and walk to the surgery. It was only fifteen minutes away and Daniel was going to come with me.

We sat in the surgery waiting room, not saying anything to each other just watching the numbers on the wall until it was our time to go in. This was the biggest decision of our lives so far and here we were petrified about what was to come next. I always expected it to be such a happy time to announce a pregnancy, something that people celebrated and here we were, petrified to tell anyone.

We were called into the doctor's room. I knocked first before entering. It was so quiet you could hear a pin drop. We stood in a long white hospital-looking corridor with several consultation rooms, all with numbers on.

'Come in,' a man's voice bellowed.

As I opened the door, there were two blue, plastic chairs adjacent to the doctor's desk. He had a skeleton hung on a frame, a large computer and a keyboard he was tapping away on.

Without even looking at us or raising his head, he asked the obvious. 'What can I help you both with?'

Thinking he was quite rude and not very easy to talk to, I just blurted it out. 'I'm pregnant!'

I waited for his response. The room returned to silence except for his tapping. He swivelled his chair and looked at me. His spectacles resting on the end of his nose, him looking over the rim of them.

'And you want me to do what exactly?' He almost shrugged and looked at us both in turn uninterested. Not a smile or anything.

'Well, I wasn't sure what the options were, so I thought it was best to come and see you.'

Should I get up now and walk out or just sit here and wait for him to say something? I felt quite lost and humiliated. Maybe this wasn't the best idea coming to see him.

'So, first things first. I can't make the decision for you.' He reached across his desk to a tray that had a pile of leaflets in. He rummaged through them and then selected one that had a picture of a pregnant woman on the front. He handed it to Daniel who just held it in his hand, not looking through it or reading it, just holding it firmly. 'Secondly, if you decide an abortion is what you want, how would you feel if it went wrong and you couldn't conceive again later in life? That's something you would have to live with for the rest of your life. If you decide to keep the child, then I would suggest booking an appointment with the nurse who will take you through the process, check-ups and she will be able to work out your due date. Do you have any idea as to when you conceived?'

He sat there looking at both of us as if he had just given us the answer to all our questions and was expecting us to be ecstatic. I got the feeling he was against abortions and there were no options, that was it.

Confused, I just looked at Daniel, expecting him to say something but he didn't.

'We don't know when we conceived, potentially Valentine's Day.' I held my gaze on him.

'Ah ha, so that would make you around eight weeks.' He pushed his spectacles back to the bridge of his nose, using a mouse to click dates on a calendar on the screen in front of him. 'I suggest you both decide what you want to do and make another appointment with reception for either myself or one of the nurses.'

'Come on, Rose. Let's go and figure this out.' Daniel stood up, rolling the leaflet up in his hand. I did the same, picked up my bag and made my way to the door. We didn't know what else to do. We left the room, almost with our tails between our legs. We walked straight past reception, out of the sliding doors into the fresh air and all the way back home without saying a single word to each other. There was nothing to say. Both of us deep in thought, contemplating our whole life before us.

Daniel stayed with me for the entire afternoon. We spoke about all the options we thought we had available, and it was very clear we had two completely different views. He was scared and worried about the thought of such a responsibility at such a young age and one that we were walking into blind. I, on the other hand, believed maybe we could just do this together. It wasn't the end; it was more the beginning of something wonderful and who cared what other people thought. Well, I did worry what people thought, a lot, especially my parents. That was my main concern. We agreed to tell my parents that evening, together, and to see what their response was.

It was the doctor's words that scared me. The thought of not being able to conceive again or if the abortion went wrong. I would never forgive myself for making that decision. Yet in the process, I was potentially restricting Daniel's life by having a responsibility so early on in life. He hadn't lived for himself yet and here we were debating what to do about another living being.

That evening, my parents had gone to their close friends' house for dinner and drinks. They weren't aware of anything different before leaving the house. I had tried to act as normal as possible. So many scenarios in my head. Both Daniel and I rehearsed what we were going to say repeatedly. It was like a well-practised theatre production. We had to tell them, we needed help.

We were both sat in the lounge. As soon as the car reversing lights reflected in the front bay window of the house, we were on edge, pre-empting the conversation ahead of us. The keys turned in the lock. I could hear both their voices but couldn't quite make out what they were saying. I heard steps heading up the stairs above us followed by my mum opening the door. She looked flustered.

'Everything all good?' She quite often said this when she came in. It was a matter of fact rather than an actual question. 'Your dad has gone up to lie down. I think he's had a few too many and the room is spinning.' She chuckled as though he had been quite amusing that night. My dad would have a drink or two, but very rarely would he be drunk and when he was, it was quite comical.

'Mum, could I speak to you for a second please?' I managed to quickly fit in before she snuck away.

'Yes, give me two minutes. I'll take him a glass of water and then I'll be down. You guys okay?' she asked again but this time it was a question. She looked alarmed.

'Yes, fine. Just need to speak to you,' I said again.

'Okay, two minutes. Be right with you.' My mum was always busy but never busy enough that she didn't have time for me or any of us. She worked extremely hard as a personal assistant at a heating controls company, full time, and was extremely organised and efficient – *unlike me*.

We never ever went without. I had the latest clothes, she was always treating me, they both had nice cars, our home was beautifully furnished, and we went on holiday every year without fail. We talked but I never really confided in her or told her about my secrets like some of my friends used to with their mums. I think I was worried I would disappoint her if she knew who I really was.

In less than no time, she was back with us. She sat down in the armchair opposite us and said, 'Okay, what's wrong?' It was almost as if she was waiting for me to tell her something exciting. I froze. Despite me rehearsing, I couldn't find the words to say what I wanted to.

'We're pregnant.' Daniel bluntly spurted the words out. 'I mean, she's pregnant. We've done a couple of tests and they're both positive.' There, it was out in the open. He had told her for me.

'Oh, I thought it was something bad. Well, that's a surprise!' She almost looked excited. What did she mean, I thought it was something bad? It was. How could this be something good? That was not the response I was expecting.

Daniel's face was the same as mine. I think we were both expecting a lecture or to be shouted at like two naughty children. I looked at him. He looked at me. We both looked back at her.

'Have you considered your options?' she asked, 'We can support you. You must continue your education. How far along are you? Do you know your due date?' She was firing questions at me that we didn't know half the answers to yet.

'Well, we weren't sure whether this was the right option. I don't think we're ready to be parents yet.' Daniel was like a scared rabbit in headlights. 'We don't have any money, or a house and I have no idea how to be a dad. Maybe in a few years' time?'

It was as if he was trying to convince everyone in the room of the decision he had already made. Panicking, he began fidgeting with his hands, tapping silently on the arm of the chair. I just sat in silence, not knowing what to say.

'That's what we're here for. We can help you and support you whatever decision you make. You aren't alone but please don't rush into it and be hasty. There's never a good time to plan for a child. The best things in life that happen are unplanned. It's how you deal with them and how you learn to cope with them that matters.' It was almost as if she had been waiting her whole life to say a statement like that to me. 'I'll speak to your dad in the morning and tell him. I don't think it's wise for me to tell him now.'

With that, she walked over, stroked my hair to one side and kissed the top of my head. She put her hand on Daniel's shoulder. 'Please talk to me anytime if you need anything and before making any rash decisions. Let's sit down together tomorrow. You both look like you need a good night's sleep.'

Was she drunk too? She sounded it. I had never seen her so understanding before, yet something minor like me leaving food on the side and she would shout and scream at me.

As soon as she left the room, I sunk into the sofa and just closed my eyes. I was not expecting that at all. In fact, I felt quite relieved. I turned to Daniel. He had his head in his hands and looked deflated. If the truth be told, I didn't want to get rid of the baby. I didn't want an abortion, even if I was only seventeen but I also didn't want to lose him. The thought of him not wanting anything to do with me or us not being together just wasn't an option, so what did I do?

Chapter 8

Becoming an Adult

It was as if I had gone to sleep a child and woke as an adult. The doctor's word stuck in my mind and replayed repeatedly: 'What would you do if you couldn't have children in the future?' For me this wasn't an option but when I sat down and explained this to Daniel, I felt selfish and difficult.

For the next week, he didn't really speak to me. My dad hadn't spoken to me since either. Every time I walked into a room, he left. When I tried starting a conversation, he replied with short one-worded answers and it became awkward.

Finally, when we were both in the kitchen together, I walked up behind him and gave him a hug. Wrapping my arms around his big body, I felt a tear roll down my cheek. 'I'm so sorry, Dad. Please don't be disappointed in me.'

It was as if I had let him down. My big plans for the future, wanting to be a teacher and go to university were quashed and in place was a life I didn't know how it was going to pan out.

He turned around and cuddled me in, pushing my face into his chest and wrapping me up in his huge arms, just like he used to when I was a little girl and had fallen over and hurt myself. 'It's okay. It'll all be fine.'

That was all I needed him to say. He didn't really do cuddles. He wasn't a highly affectionate person but when he did hug you, it made you feel so safe and that everything was going to be okay.

I knew from that point on that the love, affection and attention my parents had given me over the years was all down to creating the person I needed to be for my unborn child. The type of parent I wanted to be. *I've got this. It's going to be difficult, but I'm going to be the best mum in the entire world. Even if I don't have money, I have more than enough love and affection to give.*

That night, Daniel came to see me. I think the strain of not seeing each other for the week had taken its toll on him as well as me but we needed the time and space to think hard about our long journey ahead. He sat on my bed, slouched in the corner with my pillows stacked behind him and just stared at me full of longing. I wondered what he was thinking and how I could make it somehow easier.

'If it's what you really want, and you've made up your mind then I will support you.' He reached out to me to hold my hand and pulled me to the bed with him. 'It's not going to be easy, but we'll have to make the best of this situation. I love you way too much to lose you.' He looked sad but I knew he meant every word he said.

'Daniel, I'm not expecting this to be easy and I'm certainly not expecting you to pay for everything either. I want to work and create a home for us and our baby.' This was the first time I had referred to it as a baby.

We agreed I would finish my first year at college and complete my A Levels. Daniel would finish his Business Studies course and we would both work as much as we could to save for when he or she arrived. Finally, it felt as though we had a plan, a future, a way of becoming our own little family. I could hardly believe it. I was worried that I came so close to losing him and never wanted that to be the case.

As the days drew on, my morning sickness got worse. From the moment I opened my eyes in the morning, I was ill. I would run to the bathroom and be sick until my throat was burning. My head was pounding, and my stomach had nothing left. I couldn't even keep water down. I had tried everything from ginger biscuits to wristbands for motion sickness. I went from nine and a half stone to just over seven stone within weeks and the worry of health to both the baby and I was increasing.

I was rushed to hospital after collapsing, too weak and not enough nutrition for the both of us. I was admitted to a ward at the local hospital where they placed me on a drip for rehydration. Little did I know that I was diagnosed with hyperemesis gravidarum, a condition where morning sickness turns to extreme nausea and vomiting, causing dehydration and weight loss of ten pounds or more. I had tried everything: anti-sickness wristbands, peppermint tea, ginger and many other remedies that were supposed to help but nothing did. The drip really helped. I felt more alert, and the fatigue lifted slightly but the sickness continued.

Doctors told me to eat little and often, sip water and rest, and prescribed me medication so I was only sick around ten times a day. I was assured the tablets wouldn't affect my unborn child and would help me to keep some fluids down. Could you imagine leaving my desk at college to be sick every ten minutes or leaving a checkout at the supermarket where I worked? My face became gaunt, weak and tired. I struggled daily but for the sake of our child, I took each day in turn. College teachers were great and so were work. They understood that if I needed to leave the room or go to the toilet that I didn't have to ask. Hopefully it didn't distract others around me too much.

I had small yellow tablets to dissolve under my tongue every morning. I would set my alarm at 5 a.m. each day, take a bite of a ginger biscuit, place the tablet under my tongue and try to lie there until I drifted back off to sleep. When I then woke two hours later at 7 a.m. for college, I would feel sick to the stomach, but I no longer had the retching. The feeling resembled a bad hangover; all I wanted to do was curl up in a ball in my bed and sleep. The tablets allowed me to at least eat some nutritional food, but the smell of takeaways, grease, or pungent smells would still set me off.

Daniel was still not allowed to stay with me or sleep over, but he was with me as much as he could, making sure I looked after myself and bringing me anything I needed. Every morning, my dad would bring me a warm, weak tea and plain toast and place it next to my bed. My mum would check each morning before she left for work that I was okay. The only food I could stomach was bland, and my appetite waned but I kept forcing every mouthful. It was tough and I struggled. I was scared but I did it all for our baby and that was all that kept me going day on day.

By the dates I had given my doctor, he had calculated my due date to be around the beginning of December and was given a scan date, expecting me to be around three months. The journey ahead seemed so far away.

I was nervous for the scan. The last few weeks before we attended the hospital, I had been having extreme nightmares. Waking up in a pool of sweat, I worried that there would be something wrong with our baby, but I was assured it was completely normal to worry.

Arriving at the hospital, I was told to drink at least two pints of water before the scan but not to go to the toilet. I paced the corridor, full to the brim of water and bloated. I couldn't sit down and settle. Daniel laughed as he watched me walking backwards and forwards. Both of us eager to meet him or her. We wouldn't find out the gender today; that would be the five-month scan. Today was just to check everything was okay and to confirm our due date.

The nurse opened the door to what was a dark room containing a patient couch and a large screen on a trolley. 'Mr and Mrs Murrell please,' she called out.

Murrell was my surname but we both found it amusing that she had called us Mr and Mrs. Apprehensively we walked in, not knowing what to expect.

'Get yourself on the bed. Make yourself comfortable. Is this Dad?' she asked.

'It sure is.' For the first time, I felt excited. I could feel butterflies in my stomach. As Daniel smiled, he looked excited too.

The nurse was busy preparing her instruments. A petite lady who I guessed was in her early forties. She took out a pair of latex gloves and one by one pulled them over her small hands. She picked up a bottle of what looked like glue and a thick probe. I was slightly worried where she was going to put it. My eyes widened and I dropped my arms either side of me.

'Okay, if you would like to roll up your top to underneath your chest for me and edge your trousers down to just above your knicker line, I will squirt some of this cold liquid on your tummy. Don't worry, it doesn't hurt.' She placed a large, square of kitchen roll over the waist of my trousers.

'Come, come,' she added, ushering Daniel to stand up and join us by the screen so he could see and hear.

Using the doppler in her hand, she smeared the liquid all over my small bump, from side to side and top to bottom. As she did so, we saw the screen appear with a moving bubble. A fast-pulsing sound echoed around the room.

'There you go. Welcome to your baby girl *or boy*.' She quickly glanced at the both of us to see the reaction on our faces. 'The sound you can hear is their heartbeat. Don't worry that it's quick. It's a lot quicker than ours at around 110 to 160 beats per minute.'

At that moment, my heart skipped a beat. I couldn't believe I was listening to another human inside of me. A baby Daniel and I had created. He squeezed my hand and looked emotional — in a good way.

'If he or she stays still, I can show you… that's its head, its spine, legs curled up and arms.' She traced the outline on the screen so we could see. 'Judging by the size, your due date would be around 1st December and looks like quite a fidgety little character so I'm sure you'll be getting some kicks in the coming months to feel.' She had a big smile on her face. It must be quite a rewarding job when scans went okay.

I couldn't believe it; all my worries were eased. I was in love already and I made a promise then and there to do anything in my power to protect and keep safe my baby boy or girl. I just couldn't wait to meet him or her. Judging by the way Daniel was fascinated by the screen, he seemed besotted as well.

We left the hospital feeling lucky. Lucky for it to be perfectly forming inside me and the baby was lucky to have two doting parents ready to welcome them into the world. All we had to do now was to make it through the next six months and to save as much as we could so we were prepared for anything we needed.

By June, I had finished college, so the plan was to try to get a job during the day until my due date. At only four months and my first pregnancy, I had the slightest of bumps so I kept quiet at my interviews in the hope they wouldn't dismiss me for only being able to work till the end of the year.

Nervously I sat through the interview for an admin role at British Telecommunications. The building was an old BT exchange. Although I had prepared with my mum and dad on what questions I would be asked and how to respond, I didn't feel ready. I rang the buzzer at the front of the building and was greeted by a tall, slender lady with dark bobbed hair and a rather stern manner. She had a quiet, well-spoken voice and politely asked me to follow her. I walked through the long corridors and up the steel stairs to the second floor, studying everything around me. I passed through a large room crammed full of desks laid with paperwork and filing cabinets round the outside.

The room was noisy, people on desk telephones and smoking into ashtrays placed next to them. The windows were open, but it was still a dark, smoky room and a busy atmosphere. Everyone watched and smiled as I disappeared into an office at the end.

'Please take a seat,' she said as she sat behind the other side of the desk. She placed her elbows on the table, linked her hands together and smiled at me. 'Don't be nervous.' She opened the CV I had prepared and placed in a folder for her to read.

'Thank you for seeing me,' I said as I watched her apprehensively. *Please, please, please give me the opportunity,* I thought. *I really need this; we need this break.*

'So, it says here that you can type and are computer literate. Have you done any office work previously?' She raised her eyes from reading and waited for my response.

'Yes, I have. I spent two weeks at Fujitsu earlier this year for work experience and I used to help my dad at work in the summer holidays. I'm a quick learner and I work hard,' I added before she continued to read further.

'Tell me a little bit about yourself. What do you like to do in your spare time and what hours are you able to work?' She didn't seem quite as stern as I first thought she was when she greeted me at reception.

After forty-five minutes of questioning and a little more of us getting to know each other, she looked at me and said, 'I think you would be a perfect fit for the role and the office. You seem a lovely young lady and we would love to have you on board. When can you start?'

Pleased that I had been offered the job, I said Monday. I just had the weekend to get ready. It was all moving so quickly but we needed it to.

For the next five months, I worked from 9 a.m. till 3 p.m. I would walk from work to the bus station, go home, get ready and have some food. I would then wait for my mum or dad to finish work at 5 p.m. at which point they would then drive me to Sainsburys where I would work from 6 p.m. till 10 p.m. on Mondays, Wednesdays and Fridays as well as all day on Saturdays and every other Sunday.

Tired and with not enough hours in the day, it was work, work more work and then sleep. At least the sickness was becoming less and less the further along I got.

Chapter 9

Getting Big

By month five, I was starting to show but I hid it well with oversized shirts and tops. At work, I would wear skirts or trousers that were elasticated, so I had room and left my shirt untucked. Still looking smart but without wearing figure hugging clothes that I had been used to.

Outside of work, it was getting hard to find clothes in fashion. There were no stylish maternity shops other than Mothercare and all the clothes were for older women, not teenagers. Each day, I worried about Daniel finding me less attractive the bigger I became. Why would he want me with a bulging stomach when all the other girls wore revealing clothes, despite me carrying his child but it didn't seem to faze him. Almost a recluse, I couldn't go out as I didn't fit in. I was too tired after work and with no money to waste.

I would stand for hours in front of the mirror, moving my hands around my stomach in a circular motion. It was hard to the touch like a solid steel cocoon to protect our growing son or daughter. I found it uncomfortable at night. Before, I slept on my front but had to now lie on my side with a cushion under my bump. And then I felt it. It was like the feeling you get when you have trapped wind but stronger. A movement in my stomach and then when I looked down, I could see my stomach move. A kick, was that a kick? It was definitely movement. A feeling like no other I'd ever felt before. I wanted to share this with Daniel then and there. It was painful that he wasn't with me all the time to experience what I was experiencing but I knew it would happen again when he was next with me.

Today was the day we had our second scan. The time when we could find out if we were having a little boy or girl, but we had both spoken about whether we wanted to find out or not. We both agreed to keep it a surprise and to find out on the day. Today, we would meet our child again for the second time, to hear their heartbeat and to make sure they were okay, growing away inside of me. This time was different to the first.

Yet again, I kept having dreams in the week leading up to the scan. I would often wake up in a hot sweat worrying about whether they had limbs missing or had a defect or problems with their organs that couldn't be detected. I continued to have these nightmares throughout my entire pregnancy, but I guess that was the beginning of the worry you experience as a parent. For their safety and well-being.

Daniel and I sat in the scan room, staring at the screen. The nurse pulled my trousers down to my bikini line and inserted a couple of paper towels so she could do a full stomach scan, just as she did before. Cold jelly-like liquid was squirted onto my stomach once again and the doppler that looked like a microphone was moved from side to side and top to bottom so she could get an image of our baby on the screen. There it was again with its rapid heartbeat. An arm, two arms, a leg. Then the other one. Their head, their back. We could see it all in front of us. It was so magical, so beautiful, clearer than it was the first time and bigger, much bigger.

I now had a bump that resembled a football, all at the front and nothing round the sides. This — I had been told — was the sign of a boy. I didn't care if they were a boy or a girl. I was just happy in the moment, I could cry. Daniel had my hand tightly held by the side of the bed and he looked like he was going to cry, teary eyed. This time happy tears. He looked at me and smiled, squeezing my hand and then looking back. It all seemed so surreal. I felt like we were almost there. We had done the hard part, now there was the actual event of birth to get through.

The nurse clicked away, tracking all measurements, printed off a piece of paper with our baby's image on it and handed a copy to us.

'Congratulations to you both,' she said. It was the first time I felt no judgment. She genuinely seemed happy for both of us, irrelevant of our age, our background or the future ahead of us. Something exciting and not a shock.

Month six was the point in which I had a clearly visible bump. I couldn't hide it anymore. I became slower, more tired and less flexible. Even getting my shoes on or reaching things was becoming more difficult by the day. I had to tell work and I could see passers-by take a second look wherever I went. Was I just being self-conscious, worrying about what people were thinking of me or what people were saying behind my back? I felt heavier and although I was tired, I felt healthy. The sickness was getting easier, but it hadn't stopped completely. I had to keep taking the tablets or I was quite ill. What would work say? Would they fire me? Would they be angry that I hadn't told them before? If anything, I had to tell them because of safety.

I plucked up the courage to tell Esther, my manager. I waited until I knew she wasn't busy; she had just sat down to drink a coffee in the kitchen area. 'Esther… I'm sorry, I know you're on a break, but I wondered if I could talk to you quickly about something.'

She took a sip and said, 'Uh huh, of course, anything. Take a seat.' She patted the chair next to her at the table.

'Thank you,' I said, doing as I was told. 'I… I er, have been meaning to tell you something but I wanted to prove my worth here at work and show you just how hard working I am before I said anything.' I fidgeted on the seat nervously. 'The thing is, I'm pregnant.'

She placed her arm around me and said, 'I know. Well, I had my suspicions, but I thought you might be.' She smiled at me. We had got on quite well over the past couple of months and I had really gotten to like working for her. A bit like an older sister.

'Oh really?' I replied, shocked that she knew but didn't say anything. 'Am I in trouble?'

'Of course not. We need to make sure you aren't put in any danger here at work and that you don't pick up anything too heavy. But we want you to work for as long as you can. Have you any idea as to when you will be working until?' She put her head to one side, looking at me.

I hadn't even thought when I would work until. I was half expecting her to fire me or ask me to leave.

'What's your due date?' she asked. 'I'm so happy for you and congratulations, by the way. It's very brave to have a child so young but if anyone can do it, you can.'

'Thank you, and I wouldn't be able to do it without all the love and support I've had, especially working here. It's been lovely. With regards to my leaving date, I'm not sure, can I come back to you?' I wanted to work as long as possible to earn as much money as I could before I had the baby, but I wasn't sure what women normally did.

'Sure you can and next time don't be afraid to speak to me. I'm excited for you.' She lifted her arm from my shoulders, grabbed her empty mug of coffee and pushed her chair into the table, making her way back to her desk.

Another weight had been lifted from my shoulders. I had jumped another hurdle and made it.

Chapter 10

How Hard Can It Be?

From the back, you couldn't tell I was pregnant. I still had nice skinny legs and my waist was still as it was from behind, but from the side, it was as if I had a football under my top. I still wore heels that were so impractical and skinny trousers or leggings and an oversized shirt. I ignored all the rules that my midwife told me not to do. I was constantly moving furniture in my bedroom, I would run for the bus in the morning because I was always late and rather than eat healthy food, I just ate anything that I could keep down. Mainly chocolate and cakes. I'm surprised I hadn't got gestational diabetes. Other than the sickness, I was fine. I had no indigestion, swollen ankles or any other complaints.

The whole way through my pregnancy, both parents were incredible. Daniel's mum and dad were starting to fuss, and I had gotten to know them so much more than I did before. My mum and dad had said that I could turn their spare room into a nursery and decorate it how we wanted to.

It was quite handy as Daniel's dad was a painter and decorator so all we needed to do was choose the colour of the paint and the design and he would do it all for us. We had planned to spend a night at each house when the baby arrived so it gave each set of parents a restful night rather than disturbed sleep from the crying. We didn't realise the practicality of this until later.

We attended breathing classes regularly. Daniel, myself and then our mums alternated each week. It was more comical than anything else and if I'm honest, the hour-long sessions made me more nervous. I'm not sure I wanted to know that squeezing something the size of a watermelon out of a hole the size of an orange could cause tears and stitches. It was too late now. There was only one way out. I promised myself that I didn't want drugs. I had committed to a natural birth and that was what I was going to stick to. Healthier for me and healthier for the baby.

In a nice way, it seemed like a family baby rather than just mine and Daniel's. Our parents and wider family were so eager for its arrival. The first baby in the family, I guess. As much as I knew Daniel supported me and I loved him so much, I wanted my mum at the birth. Nothing more comforting than having another woman beside me who had gone through what I was about to before.

One more thing I had to tell her about was my tattoo. Just to put another nail in the coffin.

'Mum,' I said one morning while she was getting ready for work, the birds cheeping away outside her bedroom window.

'Uh huh,' she answered, not really listening.

'You know I said I wanted you with me at the birth.'

'Yep.' She was taking all the rollers out of her hair, adjusting each strand into the position she wanted before hair spraying her immaculate hairstyle, ready for the day.

'Well, I have one more thing I need to tell you.' I sat on the bed next to her.

'Go on.' She peered at my reflection in the mirror, apprehensive as to what I was about to say.

'I've got a tattoo. It's only a small one but I thought you might want to know before you see it on the day,' I said, quickly trying to make out that it wasn't such a big deal.

'Why am I not surprised?' She raised her eyebrows but smiled. 'What is it?'

'Tweety Pie.' I laughed.

'Tweety Pie? Wow, you couldn't have got a pretty flower, or a butterfly, could you?' She laughed again. 'But I guess that's just you, and I wouldn't have it any other way.' My mum leant to one side and kissed me on my head. 'Thank you for telling me, but I really must get ready for work. You can show me later.'

Well, that went better than I thought it was going to. Maybe she was getting softer as I was getting older. I thought she would have shouted at me and told me how irresponsible I was.

The time had flown and although I missed seeing my friends, having a drink or two and socialising with them at the pub, I was too tired and worn out to feel that I was missing out on all the fun. My nights now consisted of lying on my bed cuddled up with Daniel, watching our baby kick and move around.

As I reached eight months, my stomach was tight. It was getting harder and harder to breathe and it was as if I was running out of room. At five feet one inch tall, I had a slim frame and not much room left to grow any more, but the blessing was that the sickness had started to subside. Every morning and every night, I lathered coconut oil and stretch mark cream around my growing bump. A thick dark line had appeared down the centre of my stomach and my belly button stuck out so much that you could see it through whatever I was wearing. Amazing how a woman's body copes with such changes.

I had decided to go on maternity leave from BT a couple of weeks before I was due and just work evenings and weekends at Sainsburys so I had enough time to prepare, get ready and get as much rest in as I could before the baby was here. I was told countless times that I needed to get my sleep in whilst I still could.

On my last day, I started work the same time I had done every day for the past four and a half months but as I walked into the office, it was filled with helium balloons, wrapped presents and everyone standing round my desk. I struggled with emotion normally, but this was so lovely and so thoughtful of them. It made me not want to leave but it also hit home that I was so close to becoming a mum and the challenge I had ahead of me.

Esther was sweet. She gave me the most endearing hug and said, 'Will you come back and work with us when you're ready? It's been such a pleasure having you here with us all.'

I think it was the nicest, most appreciative comment I've ever had. At school, I was constantly told I could do better, or I had such great potential but never listened. Finally, I was appreciated for working hard.

We had spent the past couple of weeks buying all the essentials we needed: prams, a cot, clothes, nappies. A large pile in the corner of my room was growing, ready for the big day.

Daniel had been practising driving so he could pass and when the day finally arrived for him to take his test, he passed with flying colours. We had a car; he could drive me to the hospital, and we had transportation for wherever we needed to go. I still couldn't take mine or finish my lessons as I was too big to fit behind the steering wheel. Being so short, I couldn't reach the peddles so we agreed I would start again once I'd had the baby.

One week before my due date on 24th November 1997, I woke up at 2 a.m. and couldn't sleep. I had an unusual stomach pain I couldn't seem to shift but I didn't want to wake anyone, so I lay awake staring at the ceiling for hours. I kept thinking about all the things I needed to do and get done before baby arrived.

I got up to go the bathroom. I got back into bed. I threw the covers off because I was hot and uncomfortable. I then got cold so pulled them tight back on top of me. I was like an oversized whale so any movement or getting in and out of bed was a mission to say the least.

The minutes ticked so slowly until finally it was 6:30 a.m. and I heard movement at the top of the stairs. My mum was finally up for work and my pains were getting increasingly worse. *I must have wind*, I thought, *maybe I need to go to the toilet again and it will help.*

As I opened the door, my mum was there in her pretty silk dressing gown and curlers in her hair.

'Mum, I've got wind and I can't seem to shift it. It's getting uncomfortable.' I'm not too sure what I was expecting her to say or do.

'Rosie, do these pains come and go?' It was as if she was asking me a stupid question.

'Yes, they do, but they seem to be getting worse,' I replied.

'I think you may be in labour. Have you tried timing them to see how far apart they are? They could be contractions.' She walked me back to my bed and sat me down, her arm raised so she could use her watch to count.

I was confused. In the films, you see women screaming in pain or breathing heavily. This wasn't the case. I thought it was genuinely wind. Sure enough, as my mum counted in between the tightening of my stomach and it releasing, they were spaced apart.

'I'll give Daniel a ring, get him to come over and then we need to call the hospital and get you admitted to a ward,' she said as she walked to the phone. She almost had a skip in her step, excited about the day ahead.

Meanwhile, I was sat on the edge of the bed in shock. How could I be in labour? I was a week early. Not now. My bag wasn't packed. The nursery wasn't finished, and I still had so much to get done. I wasn't ready at all. I was expecting to be right on time on my due date.

Daniel must have dropped everything in a panic because no sooner had my mum called him, he was ringing the doorbell. My dad opened the door and he rushed up the stairs, his hair wet from the shower and his face flushed from the cold weather outside. He was out of breath and in a panic.

'That was quick,' I said with a slightly pained voice and took a deep breath. I wasn't in pain, but the contractions were getting stronger and closer together and it took my breath away each time they appeared.

My mum appeared at the door again and had called the hospital. 'You need to head up to Heatherwood Hospital. The midwives are expecting you and I've told them that you're seven minutes apart so you should still have some time but at least they'll get you on the ward and they'll check everything is all right.' She smiled and walked towards me to give me a cuddle. My bump was so big that she just wrapped her arms around the top half of me and squeezed. 'You'll be fine and by tomorrow you will have your own little bundle of joy. It's going to be exciting!' She couldn't wait. She patted my stomach as she left the room to get dressed.

I, on the other hand, was petrified. This was the most scared I had been my entire life, imagining everything they had told me in my breathing classes that I was going to experience. This was the most monumentous event of my entire life and only I could do it. I had no idea what to expect, how long it would last or how much it would hurt but all I needed to think of was our baby. Maybe I would change my mind later but at this point in time, I was still sticking to not having pain relief. I believed that if women across the world could do it then so could I and I also didn't want anything to affect my unborn child. *I've got this. I can do it. I will do it.* If there was one thing I was, and still am, it was strong and stubborn.

Daniel was rushing round the room asking me where all my belongings were in a panic. 'Where's your underwear drawer?' he said, opening and shutting drawers and cupboards like a whirlwind. 'I have a baby grow, what else do we need?' He looked up from the bag he was packing in front of me.

Meanwhile, I was trying to get dressed myself. I pulled an A4 piece of paper from my top drawer of my dressing unit and handed it to him. It was the list of items we were given as part of our prenatal sessions at the local doctor's surgery and breathing classes. It was a guide to help us in preparing, which, of course, I wasn't prepared for as usual.

'Ah okay, so we've got... oh, you need sanitary towels and bra pads. Where are those?' He looked a little out of his comfort zone.

'I'll go get those from the bathroom,' my mum said as she walked out of the room. I think this gave her a reason to be a part of the labour, to be helpful and to give us our space to get everything ready.

'How are you so calm? There are things on here we haven't got yet. Music playlist for the birth, food and drink for the day. The nursery isn't even ready yet. You're a week early, you are never early.' Daniel was clearly in a fluster, and he wasn't organised. He hated not being organised.

'Look, it's fine. I'm not calm inside, believe me. I'm really scared but we don't need a music playlist for the birth. We'll be able to get food and drink at the hospital and we have everything we need. It'll be fine; everything will be okay.' I was talking him into thinking everything would be fine, yet I didn't know myself.

He packed everything into his car, came back upstairs to get me, and we set off. It took me a little longer to walk down the stairs as I felt a lot heavier than usual, and I had a sensation of pushing on my whole lower body, but I managed to get in the car and put my seatbelt on. My mum and dad told me to go to the hospital and that they would follow shortly after.

'We'll be there in no time at all,' my mum said. 'Go and get yourself seen by the midwife and we will see you soon.'

Being pregnant had brought my mum and I so much closer together. We had bonded more than we had ever done. Normally I was closer to my dad but she had been through this three times and knew what was and wasn't normal and I needed her now more than ever. Despite our petty arguments, she was always there for me, and I loved her for that. She could be the most caring person in the world. I could only hope to be the mother to my child that she was to me. Right from the beginning, I wanted her to be at the birth along with Daniel. I felt safe knowing I had both of them by my side to get me through it.

Daniel gently laughed intermittently each time I had a contraction on the way to the hospital. It was the faces I pulled each time my body tightened and then released, gripping the door handle to ease my pain. He kept one eye on me and one on the road checking every so often that I was okay.

The journey was only about fifteen minutes. He pulled into a space in the main car park outside the maternity block at

Heatherwood, stopped the car, walked round and then opened my door for me, offering me a hand to get out. The hospital was a very old, tired building but it was on our doorstep and not far away. We were both born here, and Daniel's mum worked in the orthopaedics ward, so it seemed the logical option. It didn't have a theatre or emergency services, but I didn't want to think about anything going wrong. I was young, fit and healthy. What could go wrong?

I envisaged being met at the automatic entrance doors by nurses, hurled into a wheelchair and whisked up to a cubicle with other mums to be screaming in pain. That's what you see in films all the time. Instead, Daniel and I glared at all the signposts, wondering which corridor to head down and followed directions for maternity ward 2. This was where we were told to go. It was eerily quiet as if it was the middle of the night. We reached the double doors for ward 2 and rang the buzzer. A nice, dark-haired lady greeted us and asked my name. She then proceeded to ask if Daniel was the father and walked us to a small room with a plastic chair, a bed and some apparatus.

'Take a seat on the bed. We'll check your temperature, pulse, baby's heart rate and give you a quick sweep to see how far dilated you are. Then we'll get you to a birthing suite when you're ready. I'm going to quickly get some more gloves and I'll be straight back.' Then she left.

Daniel and I both just looked at each other and froze for a few minutes till my next contraction started. It seemed every thirty minutes they were getting tighter and tighter and more painful but not quicker.

The nurse returned and sat on the other chair in the room. She pulled over a large monitor on a stand that had what looked like a big printer, a screen and leads coming out of it. The longest of the leads had a belt attached to it. She asked me nicely if she could wrap this around my already stretched stomach to monitor the contractions. I lay there, watching the flickering light above me and waiting for each one to clench and tighten. Each time they did, the scale on the screen and paper rose. There wasn't much room left in my stomach, but it didn't stop our baby kicking and moving around.

After this happened a few times, she ripped the paper from the machine, folded it in half and clipped it onto the clipboard that had my name and all my details on the front page. She attached a tag to my arm as if I was now the property of the hospital and asked me to sit up if I was okay to do so. She seemed happy with everything so far, so I followed her guidance on what I could expect next.

'Right, your contractions are still around seven minutes apart, so let's get you to a room of your own and keep an eye on you whilst you're still mobile. Have you thought about pain relief?' She tilted her head slightly waiting for my answer.

'I don't want pain relief,' I replied confidently. 'Maybe just some gas and air?'

'Okay. If you change your mind, just let us know. There's already some gas and air by the bed so use this as much as you need to. If you decide you want something stronger later then we can help.' She seemed lovely; I was hoping she was my midwife and didn't swap with someone one.

As I tried manoeuvring my whale-like body onto the bed, Daniel was bent over next to the side of the bed. He had found the large canister of gas and air. He had placed the mask over his mouth, taking big deep breaths in and moving the dials on the front of the display. Breath after breath he took, clearly enjoying himself. I smiled to myself. He was like a child sometimes so if he was happy and entertained then it was one less thing for me to worry about.

'Hey, this stuff is great. You should try it.' He looked up at me and laughed. I couldn't help but laugh back. At least he wasn't panicking and being a nuisance.

Periodically, several nurses came in to check on me and to check my progress and by the time a few hours had passed, the pain had become more intense. The last lady to come in was a short, petite lady called Bernie. She seemed assertive, did everything in a hurry and was very blunt when speaking. I felt like she would tell me off if I didn't do as I was told.

'How's the pain?' she asked.

'It's getting a lot stronger but I'm okay.' I was telling the truth. It wasn't unbearable, but it was a different kind of pain. Not the same as a papercut or a banged knee but a type of tension that was building and building. It felt like a pulling on the whole half of my lower body as if I was being stretched internally.

'I have a TENS machine here that I am going to place on your back. I need you, sir, to help her with this.' She gestured to Daniel with her hands. 'It will help with the pain. When she has a contraction, turn it on and if she needs more relief, you turn it up, okay?'

Daniel nodded.

Bernie hooked up the pads on different parts of my back, turned it on and gave over responsibility to him. I could feel a vibrating sensation across my back, quite nice and gentle.

I groaned quietly to myself as another contraction seemed to engulf my body. Each one lasted for about a minute or so. Daniel looked at the box in his hand and turned the dial slightly up. He was as high as a kite on gas and air and the slightest thing was making him giggle. Again, it felt quite nice and did seem to dull the pain of the contraction a little.

He laughed, enjoying being in control of this device.

Six more minutes passed where we were making general conversation and then whack another contraction started. Daniel turned the dial up slightly again to help. We were working as a team until the next contraction took hold. Not only did I feel the pain of it, but my back went into spasm. What on earth was that? I looked at Daniel as I let out a moan.

'Oh wow, that hurt!' I grabbed hold of the side rails of the bed.

'Oh, sorry about that. I turned the machine up to full. Didn't mean for it to hurt.'

'Yes, of course it hurt, you idiot.' I held my side so I could breathe more easily, no room left inside my body for my lungs or other internal organs as the baby was so big and pushing against my rib cage. Daniel looked like a naughty boy who had been told off.

As the pain subsided for a few moments, we both smirked at each other. He handed the control unit to me and stood up, a bit off balance from the gas and air.

'I need the toilet. Where were they?'

85

'Back along the corridor on the way in, I think. Don't leave me too long,' I said as he left the room leaving the door wide open into the main walkway. I waited a few minutes and got through the next raft of contractions on my own with the TENS machine and the odd gas and air.

Daniel didn't come back. Had he gone back to the car to get something? Or perhaps he had gone to get some food and a drink. He was always eating so it didn't surprise me.

Then suddenly there was a loud sound of alarms. I could see a red button in the corridor flashing and all the nurses running to the reception point where we were greeted. I could hear shouting but couldn't quite make out what they were saying. Daniel appeared round the door moments later looking all red in the face.

'What was that all about? What was the commotion? I could hear something going on,' I asked him.

'Well, I got stuck in the toilet, couldn't find the light switch so pulled the cord that I thought was the light and it was the alarm. The next thing you know all the nurses were banging on the door asking if I was okay or in trouble. Turns out I was in the women's toilet. So embarrassing.' He laughed uncontrollably before leaning over with his hands on his knees.

The next thing you know he would be fainting or passing out just at the moment when the baby arrived, and when I needed him the most.

There was a familiar face at the door. My mum had arrived and asked if it was okay to come in. Thank goodness, sanity had joined the room.

'You okay, sweetie?' she asked, standing right beside me.

'Where do I start? Daniel has had the nurses running around. He's tested the gas and air and he's been helping me with the TENS machine, so I think we're all okay.' I looked at him and smiled.

He smiled back, leaning on the end of the bed where the clipboard was pinned. He was a pain, but I wouldn't have it any other way.

Chapter 11

The Arrival

Eleven hours later and I was in the birthing suite with an army of people: the midwife, a trainee midwife, my mum, Daniel's mum, Daniel and myself. You could say it was like a mini gathering. The pain and discomfort were masking the fact I had my legs wide open and a lot of people wandering around, occasionally looking there. Not something I was expecting at seventeen years old, but I guess the nurses and doctors saw it every day, to them it was totally normal. To me, it wasn't.

The nurses had kindly called Daniel's mum to see if she wanted to come over from the orthopaedics ward to watch her first grandchild being born. She was on her way over, adding to the amount of people already in the room.

With the pain becoming excruciating, six centimetres dilated, tired and impatient, Bernie asked if I wanted to get into the birthing pool. Having a water birth wasn't planned but if she was suggesting it then it seemed like a good idea.

'If you want to remove your clothes, then we'll all help you climb in.' She started to fill the large, circular pool with lukewarm water.

Now I was in a dilemma. She wanted me to get naked in front of my mum and my mother-in-law and other complete strangers. I was sure they had seen it all before, but I did feel a little embarrassed and awkward. The other issue I had was my tattoo of Tweety Pie. Even though I told my mum, Daniel's mum didn't know. How would she react to that? *Oh well*, I thought, *it is what it is now*. The pain was too much so I just went for it. As I started to take my clothes off, I noticed water across the floor that was making it slippery for me to stand. I suddenly thought my waters had broken.

'Bernie, I'm sorry. Have my waters broken? There's water everywhere, but I didn't feel it,' I said.

Suddenly, everyone looked at the floor. It wasn't my water, but we couldn't work out where it was coming from. Then we realised there was a leak in the pool, and it was emptying everywhere. I had to put a gown back on and climb back onto the bed whilst they rectified the problem with the pool. Yet more people entered the room to mop the floor and bring towels in whilst I was in labour. Everyone except Daniel, he was going on about being hungry and that he hadn't eaten all day. I was trying to hold the pain and Daniel was worried about food. He disappeared for ten minutes to find a vending machine. The last thing I wanted was for him to pass out and miss the special moment.

For the next hour, Bernie was great. I was finally told to push whenever I felt the need to push. Daniel was breathing with me to help control when and how I did it, but after the first couple of pushes, I felt emotional. I began to cry. I was tired and felt like I was way out of my depth. The strong, confident young lady from this morning had vanished and a scared, young and emotional teenager was in her place.

'I can't do it anymore. I can't do this...' I broke down. It felt hopeless like it was never going to end. My whole body felt exhausted.

'Rose, look at me,' Daniel said, looking serious and deep into my eyes. 'You can do this, and you are doing this. Couple more pushes and we get to meet our baby girl or boy. We're all here, breath with me. You're nearly there, come on.' He had my hand firmly gripped. 'Squeeze as hard as you can, come on.'

With both my mum and my mother-in-law standing at the end of the bed with the midwives, tense and with an apprehensive look on both of their faces, I gave a hard push with all my strength.

'That's it, we have a head. You're nearly there. I want you to take a deep breath in and with the last contraction give it the biggest push you can with all your strength left, okay?' Bernie barked her order at me and had her eyes fixed on the head.

I pushed and pushed as hard as I could with everything I had. Daniel's poor hand was purple and had nail marks where I was squeezing so tight. My other hand clenched around the bars on the other side of the bed. I think everyone was holding their breath. I felt a burning sensation as it felt like my vagina was tearing apart, but I kept pushing till I felt a tug then a sudden release. My mum and

Daniel's mum were standing together, arm in arm with tears in their eyes, as they watched the miracle of a child being born.

'And we're out. Good girl.' I could see Bernie quickly stand up, baby in arms but with the umbilical cord still attached to me.

Daniel quickly moved to Bernie, gazing at our baby in her arms.

'Oh Rose, it's a boy and he has your ears.' I did have small ears and it sounded like he had them too from what Daniel had said. He had tears in his eyes and came back over to me, kissing me on the head. 'I'm so proud of you!'

The clock on the wall opposite me had just reached 6:32 p.m., more than twelve hours later from when I realised my contractions had started.

Hearing our son cry, I knew he was okay. His lungs were healthy, and I had done it. As the room was in chaos around me, checking him over, I threw my head backwards onto the pillow and breathed a sigh of relief. It was over. The pain weirdly had just disappeared, I couldn't feel anything at all. I wasn't emotional, I was motionless, taking in everything that was happening in the room and just taking a moment to pull myself back together. Every muscle in my body ached. I lay there like I had passed out. I looked down at my stomach and it resembled a balloon when all the air has been let out, a wrinkled, deflated bag of nothing. It was weird not to have my baby moving and kicking inside me after nine months of growing and protecting him but the only thing that mattered to me right now was that he was out, was perfect and I now got to meet him for the first time.

They had cut the umbilical cord and took him over to the scales to weigh him. He was quickly wrapped in the fluffy blanket that we bought with us. It was white as we weren't sure on the gender. He looked so tiny as Bernie lifted him out of the scales and passed him to Daniel to hold. He seemed so happy as he looked down at his son, gently cupping his head and stroking his small ears and fingers. He walked over to join me; his eyes glued to his son.

'Look, Rose. He's perfect. You're so clever.' He smiled at me. I couldn't be happier.

We had already thought of boys' and girls' names and so Jack Baxter was finally here. It was quite hard to tell if a baby looks like their name, but he suited Jack. I didn't think it was possible to love someone more than Daniel but from that moment on, they both became my entire world.

Whilst Bernie helped me get dressed, cleaned and washed, I had a cup of tea and a biscuit waiting for me on the side table next to the bed. Jack was passed from Daniel to my mum to Daniel's mum and as soon as I was able to see visitors, my dad and my sisters were waiting outside and came in to see us all. Tired and worn out, I let Jack be the centre of attention and watched everyone's doting faces as they met him for the first time.

I can honestly say that although the labour was tough, it was a unique and strange type of pain. I now understand why women go through it time and time again to have a child of their own. I managed it with just gas and air in the end but there were plenty of times where I wanted to give up. The love you feel seems surreal.

Chapter 12

Going Home a Mother

I had gone into hospital a child and came home a mother. I had an overwhelming sense and urge to care and protect Jack for the rest of my life.

That night, I was moved to the main ward. Daniel stayed with me until midnight. Jack was either feeding or wrapped up in his Bristol Maid as close as possible to me. I didn't want to close my eyes to sleep in case I didn't wake to tend to him, but I was exhausted. The next shift of on-call midwives arrived and occasionally came to check on us. The ward was quiet. The lights were off except small bed lamps that the lady opposite me had on and my own. Ten beds in total, five on each side with hospital curtains tied back, ready for the next person.

I had to get up to go to the toilet, but my lower body was stiff as if I had run a marathon. I swung my legs off the bed, but it must have taken me well over ten minutes to find the strength to stand up. Even though I wasn't carrying Jack inside me anymore, it still felt like I was carrying heavy weights; my empty belly now hanging like a saggy paunch. I shuffled along the room, pushing Jack in his cot as I went. I made it to the shared, disabled toilet in the corner. Trying to be as quiet as I could, I sat down but couldn't go. I was scared my entire insides would fall out. Not only that but I had got haemorrhoids from the extent of pushing throughout the day. That seemed to be the only pain I now had, and it was excruciating. Having never had them before, I didn't know what to expect.

As I walked back to the bed, I lay there for hours, waiting for the next time Jack would wake. My mind began to wander. How unattractive I now felt and what Daniel would now think about a girlfriend with a damaged body like mine. Not a typical seventeen-year-old at all. My biggest question was, would my vagina ever return to its original size and would sex feel the same? You would have thought there were other things on my mind, but this was a huge worry for me and I hoped I didn't lose Daniel or ruin our new, perfect little family. It was a valid question, wasn't it? You hear all the time about men who have leave their partners after children. Was this why or was it more to do with women losing their confidence after having a child?

'Pssttt... Hey.' The lady opposite me tried to get my attention.

'Hey, you okay?' I replied, both our babies giving the occasional murmur but sleeping soundly.

'Yes, you?' she whispered. 'I can't sleep. How are you feeling? Did you have a boy or a girl?'

'A boy, eight pounds. I can't sleep either,' I said. 'How about you? Boy or girl?'

'A boy. His dad didn't make it in time but my mum was here. His dad is from Jamaica, but he has the whitest skin like me. I'm hoping he looks more like his dad as he gets bigger and has his eyes. Who does your little boy look like? I started my contractions yesterday morning. I'm so glad he's finally here, I was so tired. They had to use forceps in the end, so he has a slightly pointed head, bless him.' She looked only a couple of years older than I was.

'I only started this morning, so around twelve hours. He has my little ears, but I don't know who he looks like yet.' I thought twelve hours was long but compared to her maybe I had it easy.

I was too tired and worn out to keep chatting so we spent a few moments talking but I must have drifted off.

Before I knew it, it was the morning. It looked cold and frosty outside the window as I peered out to the car park before checking on Jack again. He was starting to stir. My watch was saying 7:02 a.m. I was desperate to leave and see Daniel; he was my missing part. As soon as the nurse came in, I asked when I could leave.

'As soon as you have been to the toilet and the doctor has checked both you and baby, you are free to go. Is there someone we can call?' the nurse said.

'Yes please. My boyfriend. His number is on the clipboard.' I pointed to the end of the bed.

By 8 a.m., all the lights in the ward were back on and I could hear the buzzer at reception. Daniel walked in, he was carrying a car seat for Jack and had the biggest, happiest smile on his face.

'How's my girl and my boy? Did you get any sleep?' He gave me the biggest kiss on my head and walked round the side to where Jack was lying. He instantly picked him up, cuddled him in his arms and sat in the armchair. I knew Daniel would be a great dad but seeing them both together just made me look at them in awe. Never in a million years did I think this time a year ago would I be sitting here in this scenario.

The nurse came round to help me change and dress Jack. I was so worried I would break his chubby little arms and legs by putting on his baby grow or his nappy that I let Daniel do it all and just watched. He was so quiet, the odd little cry or moan but he seemed such a content baby. Perhaps it was the shock of arriving in this new world outside of the comforts of my stomach.

As soon as the doctor had given me the all clear, we carefully bundled him into his car seat and clipped the straps safely around him. Daniel carried him and I slung my bag over my shoulder.

'Nice to meet you and good luck,' I said to the lady opposite me as we left the hospital to head home. She smiled and returned the kind words. I couldn't help but feel anxious that as I left the hospital this was the start of my incredible journey ahead as a parent. It took me forever to walk down the long corridor, still stiff from the previous day.

As soon as we reached my parents' house, Daniel's dad, David, had parked his van on the driveway.

'What's your dad doing here?' I turned to him and asked.

'Let's go in and find out,' Daniel answered.

As my mum opened the door, the smell of paint filled the air. She gave me a hug and prompted me to go upstairs. As I reached the landing, David was painting the walls in the spare room with a roller. It was going to be Jack's new room and nursery but hadn't been done because he was early. I had chosen and purchased the curtains and matching border to go round the middle of the walls. They were cream and had baby elephants and teddy bears on them. The walls were a lovely pastel green. It looked so perfect. His own room. All that was left to build was his cupboard, cot and accessories but for the time being, until he was a bit bigger, he would stay in a Moses basket by the side of our bed.

I couldn't believe the love, help and support we had from both families. They could have shunned us and left us to our own devices but instead they helped us buy all the things he needed and from the look on their faces every time they held him, it was love at first sight. Just as if he was their own son.

This was the first time David had met Jack. He put down his roller, wiped any residue paint on his overalls and asked if he could hold him. Daniel carefully lifted him from his car seat and passed him over. A little wince from Jack. He was all snuggled and warm like a cocoon but now nestled in his grandfather's arms, he was alert and looking around as if to check out his surroundings. It wasn't long before he became restless, letting out a whimpering cry. It was time for a feed again. Despite me being naked in the birthing suite in front of complete strangers yesterday, getting my breast out with my family in full view, was not something I felt comfortable in doing just yet, so as he was passed back to me, I went to my bedroom to feed him.

99

For me, breastfeeding was not the most natural and beautiful thing everyone had described to me. It hurt. My nipples were sore and painful, but I knew it was the best and healthiest route for Jack. It was almost frowned upon for you to bottle feed your child, according to the midwives, so I did as I thought I had to being a new mother. The most important thing for me was the time I took to bond with Jack, to spend half an hour several times a day, just me and him, gazing at his beautiful dark blue eyes and him looking back at me with such need and dependence.

That night was the first night Daniel was able to stay overnight. It felt like a sleepover with friends. He had a bag packed with his toothbrush and other belongings. Going to bed together and waking up together, our little boy next to our side; it all seemed like a dream, finally us all together. The following night I would stay at his house, Jack in a tiny travel cot and us cuddled together in his single bed. We barely slept. Every couple of hours, Jack would wake either wanting a feed or just to be near to us. We were shattered. All the sleep in the world beforehand couldn't prepare us for how tired we were now.

It would be the first night I had stayed at his house too. Waking up to his family in the morning and living with them half the week. Everything was new to us. We only had two weeks off from work and college, time to get used to our new world. I wanted to make the most of the time I had with everyone around us. The tiredness was overwhelming; my body was in a state of change. Each day my stomach was retracting back in, but my appetite was non-existent. I had to eat to ensure Jack was getting all the vitamins and minerals he needed to grow so I was force feeding myself everything that was good for him.

I warmed to motherhood like it was something I was always meant to do. I would have done anything for him and didn't want to leave him with anyone including Daniel. For the next few weeks, we ate, slept and breathed nappies, bottles and feeding times. We were both like walking zombies. As we didn't have much money, we used towelling nappies. We had a small bucket in the bathroom, full of disinfected water to place the dirty nappies in when we changed him. There was a certain way you had to fold the towel, place a liner in the middle and then fold round him, secure with a safety pin and then waterproof pants that would go over the top. They were an absolute pain and a lot more effort than disposables, but we got used to it. Nights were difficult. We jumped at Jack's every murmur so he didn't wake the rest of the family but quite frequently we were so tired it would take us a while to wake up, so then did the rest of the house. I would have my foot out of the end of the bed, rocking his cot as I struggled to keep my eyes open, yawning the whole time.

Mid December came and we had to return to work and college. I looked after Jack during the day but had college two evenings per week and worked weekends, while Daniel returned to college and worked two evenings and a weekend. We were like ships passing in the night. On the weekends when we both worked, our parents took it in turn to look after Jack for us — they loved time with their grandson and before long, Jack didn't mind going to people other than me. As long as he had plenty of cuddles and a bottle of milk, he was content. It broke my heart that we weren't always there with him, but we had to be realistic. The only way we could afford to eat, to clothe him and to survive without our families paying for us was to work every hour we could. As far as college was concerned, if we didn't finish our education, we didn't stand a chance of getting a decent job in the future. Frequently, Daniel and I would fall asleep before we could finish our coursework, but with big black bags under our eyes and a non-existent social life, we made it.

Daniel's best friend, Alfie had joined the Army straight after leaving school, but he always made a conscious effort of coming to see us when he was on a break. I had known him since I was five and, in a way, he was like a brother to me. He and Daniel were like partners in crime, if there was trouble to be had, they were both there. He was the type of friend that would do anything for you and always there if you needed him. A rock, a true gentleman too. Five feet ten inches, blonde hair, hazel eyes and the funniest laugh. He was cheeky, naughty and always wore tracksuit bottoms and the latest trainers. He knew my family well and I knew his.

As soon as he heard that Jack had arrived, he was on leave and came to meet him. It was as if he had never left. He took to Jack like he was his own son. He had bought him his first pair of trainers, although it would be a long time before he could wear them. The gift was so special. The doting uncle that would guide Jack through life.

Chapter 13

Happy 18ᵗʰ

Most teenagers are thinking of which club to visit for their eighteenth birthday and what to wear. For me, it was dinner at a restaurant with family, Jack just over two months old and by our side. I had managed to fit back into my skinny jeans and lose all the pre-baby weight I had gained. Daniel's birthday, on the other hand, meant Jack was now approaching four months and was a little easier to take care of. He still didn't sleep through the night but at least I felt more comfortable leaving him for longer periods of time during the day and night.

With some of the money I had earnt from work, I purchased my first mobile phone, meaning I could speak to my parents at any time and make sure Jack was okay or I could speak to Daniel and communicate. Prior to this, getting in touch with anyone meant finding a payphone, making sure you had enough twenty pence pieces to make the call and remembering the number to dial. First world problems, I guess, but this made things so much easier, and I felt even more at ease.

I was nervous going out; what to wear, how to style my hair, doing my makeup and generally leaving the house for a night out was daunting. We got a lift to our local pub, The Crown Wood. I didn't miss the smoky, busy atmosphere but I did miss all our friends and the time to be yourself; a normal teenager rather than having to think about all the things you still had to do when you got home. The responsibility. It was still there but for the next couple of hours I could enjoy myself. So many hugs, so many kisses from people I hadn't seen in so long. The alcohol went straight to my head because I hadn't drunk for well over a year.

Although Daniel was really enjoying himself, I just couldn't settle. My mind couldn't switch off. Constantly thinking about Jack, nervous about his well-being, even though I trusted my parents implicitly. I was just unable to relax and enjoy the evening. I made the decision to leave and head home. Daniel decided to stay and see the night out and meet me back home later. I walked all the way back home as I couldn't afford a taxi and didn't want to disturb my mum and dad. In heels and a short, short dress, it took me over half an hour, my feet aching and frozen to the bone but back in the warm with my baby boy.

At eighteen, I was so insecure and so jealous. I knew Daniel doted on me, and he loved me to the core but all I could do was compare myself to others. Constantly questioning his desire for me. Yes, he loved me but was he attracted to me still? Whilst he was at the pub drinking, I was thinking about who he was chatting to. It was a strain on our relationship. I would think, *how could he possibly be attracted to me if I thought I was disgusting?* Putting on so much weight after being so ill during pregnancy had left me with stretch marks below my belly button. I thought they were ugly; I was embarrassed of them when naked. While other eighteen-year-olds were wearing short tops and bikinis, I had to cover up. He called them my battle scars as a result of carrying our boy, but I took that as him humouring me.

Although our family had been incredible at supporting us and caring for Jack, it wasn't fair on them having sleepless nights, baby items everywhere and to some degree us taking over their house. We started to look at getting our own place. It was a scary thought at our age, being completely self-sufficient. I was wary but sure it was the right thing to do. We had been saving and saving but needed assistance from the local council to help pay rent. My mum had a colleague at work that was looking to rent his house and agreed we could live there at a reduced rate on the basis that the house needed a bit of care and attention, some furniture and a few appliances. It seemed all too good to be true but at the thought of having our own place for our perfect family, we jumped at the chance.

We started to plan for moving out. My parents were a little upset, but we all knew this day was going to happen. We just didn't expect it to be so soon. They had become attached to Jack and used to him being there all the time. The house was a five-minute drive away so I knew I would still be round all the time and they would be round ours. We met Jim, the owner, at the house. The plan was for us to walk round and make a note of all the things we needed and get a feel for the space we would have.

We turned up to the house. It was a terraced property with large windows and a garage to the back in a block of others. As we parked the car, I looked up at the windows to find dirty-looking net curtains and dark window frames as though they had never been washed in all their years. There were books piled high against them, cardboard boxes and some other items all leaning on the glass. In between those was the face of Jim peering out, he stood there for a few moments and then disappeared. *That was strange*, I thought.

As we walked up the small, concrete path to the front door, paint peeling from it, I was slightly disappointed that what I had imagined the house was going to be like was quite different to what it appeared to be, but I hadn't been inside yet.

Jim opened the door. I guessed he was in his late fifties. His hair brown and unbrushed and a few days' worth of stubble. He shook Daniel's hand and leant in to kiss me on the cheek, but I stepped back nervously. It was as if he felt we had met before and he was a close family friend. I felt awkward and uncomfortable but ignored it and tried to focus on the house and making a list of what we needed along with the rent payment arrangements and bank details. I wasn't a big fan of people being in my personal space or affection unless it was Daniel or my parents or friends.

My heart sank. The house was in an absolute mess. As we walked through the front door, the small square kitchen on our right had what looked like a kitchen that dated back to the 1960s: orange and brown cupboards and tiles to match, a flickering neon tubed light. The ceiling was a greasy yellow from cooking fat, the sink was overloaded with used crockery and the taps coated in limescale. The

106

floor had tiles that were damaged and peeling but I kept thinking, *maybe with a bit of a clean and a tidy it won't be so bad.*

It got worse. As we went to the front room, it was piled high with books, ripped furniture, a carpet in desperate need of hoovering and the smell was disgusting. Upstairs, the two bedrooms and bathroom weren't much better. It would take us weeks and weeks to make this house our home, but what alternative did we have? With very little money and options, we had to take it. I couldn't believe he lived in a place like this and more importantly didn't clean or clear it before we had come round to view it.

'Would you mind if we painted?' I asked him.

'Of course, make it your own, do what you please,' he replied instantly. He gave me a side smile that I found weird.

'And where will you be staying?' Daniel questioned him. We had presumed he had another place to live.

'Oh, I am… staying with friends and then I'm thinking of going away for a while so I'll move all my belongings to the garage and store them there till I return.' With that, he turned around and started making his way back down the stairs, so we followed.

'Thanks for showing us round. When do you think the house will be empty for us to start getting it ready?' I said.

'No problems. I'll be out by next Friday, so you can have the keys from Saturday morning.' He handed us his number in case we had any more questions and a few papers relating to the property and opened the door for us to leave.

I was happy to be out in the fresh air again, clear from the stench of the house and its pungent smell. I had my head down as I walked to the car, disappointed in what we had just been to see but trying to think of the positive side. We had already agreed to the rent payments and frequency, the council had signed them off. I guess we should have looked at the house beforehand, but this was the only thing we could afford. We had no alternative.

As we got back in the car, Daniel held my hand. 'It's disgusting but I'm sure with a bit of a paint, some new curtains and some cleaning, it will look lovely in no time. We just might have to leave all the windows and doors open for a few days to get rid of the smell.'

We both laughed but as I looked up to the house again, Jim was standing in the window just staring.

'Let's go home,' I said as we pulled away. I should have trusted my gut instinct. There was something strange about him and the house, but I couldn't put my finger on it.

Chapter 14

Home Sweet Home

S aturday came in a flash; we got the keys to our new house. I was so excited to start making it a home for the three of us. There weren't enough hours in the day as it was without spending every day and every night till gone midnight scrubbing, cleaning, bleaching, clearing and painting. We left all the doors and windows open to air the rooms. We were making progress, and it already looked like a completely different place.

We then noticed something strange. In each of the rooms, there was what looked like a security system, but we couldn't work out where it was wired to. It appeared freshly installed, not dirty and dusty like everything else in the house. The devices were only upstairs as well and not downstairs. Why? *Who would want to break in and steal something from here?* I thought. *And surely you would want to see an intruder entering the property.*

We traced all the cables and power back to the garage but noticed there were three large padlocks holding together steel brackets, securing the door. There was no way we could open that, and he hadn't given us the keys.

'There's no way we're moving into the house until these are removed, and I don't want you going to the toilet here. You can wait till we get back to your parents' house. They must be connected to somewhere where he's watching us. How weird. I don't want a pervert watching us.' Daniel was angry. I'd never seen him act this way before. 'What a creep,' he said clearing all his tools away.

The following day I returned to the house to drop off some curtains and a few more cleaning products that we had bought. I had Jack with me in his pram so I could walk there and back. As I reached the front door, I noticed it was slightly ajar, but I didn't remember not shutting it the night before. I pushed it gently. I was startled as it swung wide open, and Jim was standing there in the hallway.

'Hi,' was all he said and smiled.

'Oh hi. Sorry, did I leave the door open? I—'

He stopped me mid-explanation. 'No, I just thought I would remove the security system that you both wanted taken down.' He looked at me, tilting his head as if he was confused.

How on earth did he know about us wanting the system taken down? I thought. *And more importantly, how did he get in?* He must have been watching *and* listening to us. Confused, I just kept quiet. I got the bags that I came to drop off from underneath the pushchair and placed them just inside the door.

110

'I best be on my way. I need to head back.' I tried to hurry away.

'I can give you a lift, if you like?'

'No, I'm fine thanks. The walk will do us both good and I don't want to disturb Jack. He's sleeping.' I'm sure he was just being nice and polite but something about him made me uneasy. Never get in a car with a stranger, I was told, and he was definitely a stranger, despite us renting his house from him.

'Also, I know you need a new fridge and a cooker. If you come shopping with me in the week, I will buy you one. It should have come with the house really,' he said as he followed me out the door.

I froze. I wasn't sure how to reply to that. We did need one and we were struggling to pay for everything. We had been looking at second-hand ones that were more affordable. What harm could it do to go shopping with him if he was going to buy them? It sounded a little like bribery but what the heck, needs must.

'Are you sure?' I turned around. 'If they were supposed to be part of the house then, if you don't mind, it would be really appreciated. We really need them.' I was trying to be polite, but I also couldn't turn them down. One less thing for Daniel to have to worry about sourcing.

'Of course. Meet here Monday morning at 10 a.m. We can head into town then.' He shut the door and I left to walk home.

For some reason, he made me nervous. How did he know about the cameras and us not wanting them up and why did he just let himself in, especially if I was there on my own? There was just something about him that made me uneasy. I was probably overthinking it, but it was just a feeling. I always wanted people to like me and as a result,

I agreed with everyone, even if I disagreed. I couldn't say no, and I would never speak my mind. This time was the same. Even though I should have mentioned something to Daniel or my mum, I kept quiet and didn't mention a word. If he was that much of a threat to me, he wouldn't be buying the appliances for the house.

Monday morning came and I made my way to the house; Jack all wrapped up in his pram with his car seat clicked in on top. As soon as the house was in sight, I could see Jim was already there and waiting in his car for me. He left it running but opened the door to open the boot and give me a hand strapping Jack into the backseat, then kindly opened the passenger door for me to get in. I fastened my seatbelt and waited for him to get in and start driving. It had the same horrible, dirty and musty smell as the house. It was so strong, making me feel slightly sick. He looked as though he hadn't had a shower for days. He had unironed clothes and more stubble from before. It could be his body odour that was creating the stench along with the scent of coffee pouring from his mouth as he spoke, but I didn't want to get too close to smell him. I hate awkward silences, but I couldn't think of anything to say, and he just drove, eyes focused on the road.

'Did you have a good weekend?' I broke the quiet, fidgeting around awkwardly.

'Erm, yes, good thanks. Didn't really do too much. You?' He looked over from the corner of his eye but instead of looking at me, he looked at my breasts. I had a T-shirt on, so it wasn't exactly revealing but he stared and looked distracted as if he was thinking something in his head. I shuffled a little in my seat to hopefully move his glare. His eyes moved from there, down my body. I felt uncomfortable in his company.

'Yes, good thanks.' I looked in the back of the car to check Jack was okay. He was watching everything outside the window passing him, content as usual and babbling. I turned back to face the front of the car and found him looking directly at me, smiling. Thankfully, we had just reached the large public car park outside the electrical superstore and as I reached down to undo my seatbelt, his hand touched mine by accident as he grabbed the handbrake and firmly pulled it up. We still said nothing to one another. I jumped up and quickly opened the door and got Jack out of his chair. I felt like I was using Jim for the appliances, that I should have just said 'no it's okay we will get them', but we really did need the help, so I just ignored the situation and put it down to me overreacting.

As we walked to the shop, he seemed to walk behind me. Each time I slowed down or stopped, he did too. We approached the automatic sliding doors and wandered around the store, looking at each of the fridges and cookers on display.

'What do you think?' he asked. 'Any that you like?'

To be honest, I wasn't too fussed. *A fridge is a fridge*, I thought. *If it keeps everything cold, then I'm happy.* I wasn't too fussed about colour and we had quite a large gap in the kitchen for room, so weren't restricted.

'Why don't you bend down and open the freezer door at the bottom?' He pointed to the unit in front of us. 'Make sure you're happy opening and shutting it and enough space in all the compartments.'

I thought this was quite a stupid idea. Of course I would be able to open and close the door, so I bent over to open and pull the containers out. Completely innocent, I looked behind me to where he was standing and found him just staring at my bottom. Shocked at what he was doing and how he had his eyes locked on me as if in a trance, I jolted back upright and slammed the door.

'That one will do fine. Thanks.'

I quickly moved onto the cookers, trying to have a look before he could join me, but he was there, right behind me, following everywhere I went.

'So, that's the fridge sorted. What cooker would you like? I'm sure a girl like you is great at cooking and is a big feeder.' He stopped and smiled in a cheeky way.

What on earth was that supposed to mean? 'A girl like me.' I just ignored his comment and instead turned to the cookers, looked at the first one with a reasonable price tag and decided. I think he was testing me. The more he letched after me and the more he made me feel uncomfortable, the worse he got. It was as though he was liking it. I tried to hurry the assistant along with the ordering and paying of the appliances, said thank you to him for getting them and wanted to get out of the shop and back to the car as quickly as I could. My heart was racing; I needed fresh air and to get away from him.

Getting back in the car was a big mistake. I should have taken Jack's pram out of the boot and walked home but I didn't. He seemed a bit on edge as if he was frustrated and he seemed to go from a slightly creepy but polite man to incredibly impatient.

'I have to pick something up so I will take you back to the house and drop you there. You can walk from there,' he said abruptly.

'Yes sure, okay.' I panicked thinking I was making something of a situation that wasn't happening and appeared rude and ungrateful for the items he had just bought us for the house.

'When we get there, you can say thank you for what I've just bought you, if you know what I mean.' He still kept looking ahead at the road but whilst his right hand steadied the steering wheel, he dropped his left hand down and placed it on his groin. He used his fingers to stroke himself as if it was completely normal.

I was in total shock. 'Excuse me?' I said as my heart began racing again. Thank him for what he has just bought me, I repeated in my head.

'Don't plead innocence. Such a beautiful girl, you're clearly not a virgin.' He laughed a dirty, evil laugh and pointed to Jack in the back as if he was the evidence of me not being a virgin.

I felt sick. I wanted to get out, but Jack was my main priority. I needed to get him out of the car and get as far away from Jim as I could. He saw me look at Jack and then back at the handle on the door. He quickly brought his left hand back to the wheel and then pressed on the door lock button, triggering all the central locking in the car. I started to panic; I was afraid.

'Why are you locking the car?' I said as I tried unlocking it, but I couldn't. I didn't want to scare Jack, but I was worried. 'Please, I don't want to seem ungrateful, but you're really scaring me.' I was completely vulnerable.

Instead of pulling up outside the front of the house, he drove round to the back and parked in the block of garages. Secluded and out of view of any of the houses.

'I'd rather not have the appliances than do this. Please open the car and let me out.'

Jack began crying as if he knew what was happening. I gave the door handle a tug again to see if it opened. It did. It clicked and released. As I leant forward to undo my seatbelt and get out, he reached towards me grabbing my shoulder and tried to pull me back in. He only managed to get hold of my coat, which I slipped free from, leaving it behind on the chair. I quickly opened the back door, grabbed Jack's car seat out and then proceeded to the boot to get his pram.

Jim was visibly angry. He began shouting at me. 'I'm only joking, you know that, don't you? You're being very dramatic.' He didn't get out. He stayed behind the wheel but watched my every move.

I clicked Jack back into the pram and started walking very fast home. That was no joke, I was shaken. It wasn't until I was out of sight and well on my way that I realised I left my coat behind but there was no way I was going back. I reached home in next to no time, my hands shaking from the cold as well as what had just happened. I couldn't get the keys in the door. Trying to steady my hand, I took a deep breath.

Focused on getting Jack and his pram up the front doorstep and into the house, I slammed the door behind me, standing there leaning with my back up against it, taking another big deep breath in, calming myself down. I was angry but I was also confused. I did

116

have a bad feeling about him, but I wasn't expecting that. I should have never gone without Daniel; he would call me stupid for putting myself in that situation and potentially putting Jack at risk. At least I wouldn't have to see him again and I would change the front door lock, so he didn't have a key to the house. I had to keep it quiet, so I said nothing.

It took us another two weeks of painting, decorating, repairing and getting the house ready to move in. We were gifted a sofa; we had my bedroom furniture and everything else we needed we would save up and get in the future. Just as we were doing the finishing touches to the kitchen, there was a knock at the front door. My heart went into overdrive. Was it him? Was it Jim? I hadn't seen him since the incident in the car.

As Daniel answered it, a delivery driver had the fridge and cooker I had chosen. 'A delivery for you, sir. Can I bring them in?' He handed us some paperwork and as Daniel nodded in response, the guy walked back to the van and started unloading.

'Oh perfect. Maybe I had the man all wrong and he is nice after all. That was good of him to get those for us.' Daniel knew he had offered to buy them for us, but he didn't know I had gone with him to choose them.

'Yes, maybe,' I replied and then proceeded to carry on with hoovering the carpet ready for the rest of the furniture to go in the front room. I hoped I never had to see him again.

Despite that day, the house was now looking lovely. It smelt of fresh gloss paint. Everything was clean. New curtains, new carpets, even the kitchen looked like new. It might not have been perfect but for us it was our little home and our first place for just the three of us. It was going to be great. Although I missed my parents dearly, it was home sweet home at last. I didn't want anything or anyone to ruin this for us. All that was left now was to move in, but was it the last of Jim?

Chapter 15

In the Shadows

It was moving day and I had butterflies. I'd never been on my own before. Daniel and I had never lived together on our own. Both our parents were so supportive and helpful, we would miss them so much. They were only a five-minute drive away, but it was yet another new chapter for us. Four journeys back and forth with a car full up of all our belongings ready to go in their new home. Jack was quite unsettled; I think he knew it was all change.

On the last trip to the house, it seemed to be colder inside the house than it was outside. I was worried the heating had given up and our first night in the place would be freezing. As I entered the front room with only a sofa, a small rectangular rug and a coffee table to furnish it, I noticed the back door was open, and the curtains were flapping in the breeze. That was strange as neither one of us had gone through the back door or into the garden and I was the only one with a key. I shut the door, locked it with the key from my keyring and pulled the curtains closed. I thought nothing more of it.

Tired from all the carrying of boxes and unpacking everything, we decided to take a short walk to the parade of shops in the next street up from us and get fish and chips for dinner. Jack had just had his food so we could get him to sleep by the time we were back. It felt quite strange. No one to tell that I was just popping out and when I would be back. Remembering to lock everything up before I left, turn off anything electrical or lights and take my keys with me. Our own little responsibilities.

As we walked down the front path, I glanced back at the house and had a warm feeling, a sense of achievement for turning what was once a grubby, filthy house into a warm, cosy home. Even the front door looked brand new. Stripped back and re-painted.

The evening was getting dark and with just the streetlights to guide us, we picked up our food from the local fish and chip shop and a couple of essential items like milk, bread, tea bags, and sugar and headed back home. As we walked along the side of the road, I was certain I saw Jim in his car drive past us. What on earth was he doing coming out of our road? Had he knocked on the door? He knew we were moving in today. Perhaps he was just passing but it made me feel uneasy. As he drove past, he looked straight at me. Our eyes both hit each other as they followed him down the road making sure he didn't turn around and head back. He said he was staying with friends while we rented his house, but he never said where that was. It could have been the next road up from us.

Trying to get it out of my mind and Daniel still none the wiser, we got in through our new front door and started to put away all the items we had just got, grabbed a couple of forks from the drawer and then headed into the front room to sit and eat our dinner. But it hit me like a steam train. The front room was freezing again. The back door was wide open and the curtains once again flapping in the wind. I wasn't going mad. I shut and lock the door, I made certain of it. But then I noticed my coat. The same coat I left in Jim's car that day was just hanging on the corner of the door as if it had been there the whole time. He wasn't just passing. He was here at the house. He was teasing me again, knowing I would see my coat and know he had been here, inside the house. I took my coat off the door and threw it on the back of the sofa, shut and locked the door, shaking.

'You okay, Rose? You look like you've seen a ghost.' Daniel crammed another chip in his mouth as he walked into the room and sat down. 'Wow, it's freezing in here. Did you leave the door open again? You've got to be more careful than that, anyone could walk in.' He turned on the television and started flicking through the channels.

Again, I kept quiet. The longer I didn't say anything, the more he would question why I hadn't told him, but I felt horrible. What if he came back in the night? I would have to change the back door lock now as well.

Trying to forget about the door and my coat, I had lost my appetite. I managed a couple of chips and a bit of fish, but I just couldn't eat. Sitting back on the flowery sofa, covered with blankets and throws to match the room décor, I had Jack on my lap. His beautiful blue eyes just like Daniel's, his chubby dimpled cheeks and cute smiles every time I spoke to him made any troubles disappear. I could spend hours just watching and talking to him. How did we make something so perfect and adorable? At six months old, now he had a sprinkling of silk-like brown hair, a little button nose and was always happy if he was being cuddled or close to us. He still wasn't sleeping through the night. He would wake every few hours, if only to check we were still there. Even though the midwives told us not to take him into bed with us, he frequently cuddled up, sandwiched in between the two of us, all snuggled up together.

Daniel finished eating, screwed his empty food wrapper into a ball and placed his fork on the table. He looked at me and smiled. 'First night in our new home. Fancy christening it? We can make as much noise as we like without waking anyone up.' He had a naughty look in his eye that I liked. It turned me on. He didn't need to ask me twice.

'Hell yes. I'll change and put Jack to bed. Meet me up there in five.' I never turned down the offer of sex. I had a theory that if Daniel wasn't satisfied at home then he would look elsewhere. I got up, Jack gripping hold of me, perched on my hip as always. Daniel leant forward to kiss him on the cheek and to say goodnight.

Jack always took forever to fall asleep. He had his last bottle of the night, changed and wrapped in his blanket in his new cot for the night and I was gently stroking his head until he drifted off. It wasn't easy. I would sit next to him the whole time until his eyes closed but he would just look at me smiling. It just made me want to pick him back up again. As soon as his eyes closed, I knew he was asleep.

122

I could see a flickering light in the bathroom. The door was slightly ajar and steam filtered through the gap. As I slowly pushed open the door, Daniel was in the bath, a couple of tealights lit by the tap, bubbles surrounding him and the luscious scent of raspberry bubble bath.

'Are you going to join me before it gets too cold?' Daniel raised his hand full of bubbles and blew them at me. I didn't need persuading as I unbuttoned my jeans, peeling them from my legs down to the floor. My socks were next, then I crossed my arms to lift my jumper over my head, leaving me with just my underwear on. It wasn't sexy underwear. I couldn't afford expensive lingerie, but I wore it well. A black thong, covering my neatly trimmed pussy and a black lacey bra holding in my 36DD breasts.

Even though I had had a baby, I thought my breasts were still pert and voluptuous. I had nice nipples and they sat well. As I unclasped my bra, I cupped and squeezed my breasts as I looked at him straight in the eyes. I used a seductive half smile as I took my hand and slid it into my knickers. My middle finger slipped between my lips, already wet from the thought of Daniel's cock. I took my finger and sucked it from knuckle to tip so he could see how much I could get down my throat. Finally, I removed my panties slowly and in a pile with everything else. I lifted my legs one by one into the opposite end of the bath to where he was sitting. I always used baby oil to rub all over my skin after having a shower, so I was silky smooth to the touch.

Daniel picked up my foot, right in between his body and lifted it so it was directly in front of his face. I had petite feet, only a size four shoe so my toes were dainty and nicely painted. He took a few of

123

my toes and licked and sucked them in a way I didn't think would be sexual, but it felt so naughty that it made me twinge. I wanted him so much. It was as if he had hit a pressure point within my body and had released an irresistible sexual pheromone. I didn't want him to stop.

As he released my foot from his mouth and his grasp, it slid down to where his cock was. At first, I stroked his length and teased it with my touch. I then used both of my feet together to create a clamp around his already hard shaft. In a rocking motion, I began wanking him up and down. His face filled with pleasure, he leant his head back against the tiled wall, closed his eyes and with both hands held my feet tightly around his cock. Faster and faster, he moved them. The water was splashing over the sides and onto the floor but neither of us cared. I found it so satisfying by the look on his face that he was close to cumming so I kept the pace. He let out a few deep groans with pleasure; his lips tightly closed and his face full of tension as he came. My feet were red from his strong grip as he gently released them. My knees were covered in cum which he cupped and threw into the toilet beside us.

'Fuck, that was amazing,' he said as he reached for the shower gel to wash the tip of his cock. 'I love you.'

The sexual desire for him had passed, while I was still completely turned on and desperate to fulfil my needs. He sat straight up in the bath and started to make normal everyday conversation with me. Ignoring my needs completely. I guess I thought sometimes my job was to give him what he wanted; my desires came secondary. The ultimate point of pleasure for me was the ability to make another human have desire for me, to want me in a pure state of lust and to achieve sexual ecstasy when I touched them. That is what turned me on the most. That a man had a look of pleasure with me being in control, I could stop at any point and his state would decrease. If I gave Daniel everything he wanted, if there wasn't anything I wouldn't try or experience, why would he lust after another woman? Or so I thought...

The following day we spent together, finding a home for everything we currently had in boxes. Making the house cosier and getting settled. We were both exhausted and decided to take an early night but just as it was starting to get dark and I took the dried washing up to our room, I turned on the lamp beside the bed and went to draw the curtains. As I took hold of them, I noticed movement outside the front of the house, just under the shadows of the streetlights along the path. A dark shadow stood there, still. As I took a better look, I realised it was him. Jim was just standing there, a long, dark coat and gloves staring up at me. He didn't seem fazed that I had spotted him. I took a step back and gasped. *What do I do?* Daniel came walking into the room.

'What's wrong?' He walked over to stand by me to see what I was looking at.

'It's him. He's there, just standing there.' I tried to point at his dark silhouette.

'Who is?' he said, confused.

'Jim, he's—' I stopped. He wasn't there. He had gone, but where had he gone? 'He was standing right there, watching us.'

'Don't be silly. Why would he be standing there watching us? You're tired. Loads of people walk along that road.' Daniel drew the curtains for me and headed to Jack's room to check on him. I wasn't being silly. He was there, I know he was. I knew that face anywhere.

In bed that night, I tossed and turned. All I could think about was Jim in a weird, scared kind of way. Was he watching and stalking us? What did he want and more importantly, where was he staying? I had changed the lock to the back door so I knew he couldn't get in anymore but the thought of him being outside all the time made me petrified to leave the house on my own.

The following day, Daniel returned to college during the day, so it was my first day without him. I had plenty to do to keep myself occupied and Jack took up a lot of my time. My plan was to cook something nice for dinner when Daniel came home. I was back to work and college again next week too so the time we had together was limited.

I jumped in the shower, taking Jack with me. He would lie in his bouncer chair by my side the whole time. As soon as the water ran through warm, I wet my hair and began to apply the lather of shampoo. I heard a loud crash downstairs which startled me, making Jack quiet. Taking my head from under the shower so I could listen more easily, I paused and was silent. I couldn't hear anything, but I was confident I heard a crash. I listened again and heard something downstairs. I quickly finished washing my hair and got out of the shower, a towel wrapped around my middle and my hair dripping down my back. I lifted Jack from his chair and ran downstairs to find the back door window shattered on the floor. What on earth happened?

There was glass across the carpet and the freezing cold air from outside was blowing in. I searched round the front room to see if there were any signs as to what had happened but all I could see were some papers on the coffee table. As I glanced at the top of them, it had Jim's name and address at the top and warranty details for the kitchen appliances on them. There was also a mug of coffee. I could see it had just been made as the steam was pouring over its side. I didn't drink coffee, someone had made that and sat there drinking it. I grabbed my phone and called Daniel.

'Daniel, are you in a lesson? The back door window is smashed and there's glass everywhere,' I said frantically.

'What? You've smashed the window? Is Jack okay?' He wasn't getting my point.

'No, someone smashed the window and sat here drinking a cup of coffee.' I think he thought I was losing my mind.

'What are you talking about? Give me twenty minutes and I'll head home.' He hung up before I could say anything else.

Shaking, I shut the door carefully, re-locked it before more glass fell out, ran upstairs to get dressed and hunted for the dustpan and brush. This was really starting to scare me. The promise of a family home was starting to feel like a terror house, constantly unable to settle. I wasn't sure what Jim was trying to do, but it was definitely him that had done this.

When Daniel arrived home from college, he seemed pre-occupied. He didn't have a lot of patience at the best of times for me and I found myself doubting what had happened. Had I left the door open, and it smashed from the wind? No, of course not. I wouldn't have made a coffee and then just left it there. If it was Daniel's, it would have gone cold a long time ago.

127

'Why would someone want to break in, Rose, and sit there having a coffee? That's just weird,' he said as he walked around the room and analysed the broken window.

'Well, I don't know, but it isn't the first time. He's been outside the home. I think he's watching us.' I didn't want Daniel to think I was deliberately causing a drama, but the house owner was really starting to scare me.

'Calm down. I'm sure there's an explanation for all of this, and we're blowing it well out of proportion. I'll give him a call. I need to get back to college as we have a module assessment this afternoon, I can't miss it as it's the last one and I won't pass the course.' He gave me a big kiss on the cheek, as he always did when he left me, and did the same to Jack. 'If you're worried again, just call me and I'll be straight back but try not to think about it.' He always had a way of making me feel reassured.

'Uh huh, okay. Love you,' I replied as he grabbed his keys from the side and walked out of the front door.

I started to clear away the cup and the large pieces of glass from the front room carpet, but no sooner had Daniel left then there was a figure by the back door that I could see from out of the corner of my eye. Thinking Daniel had returned and that he had forgotten something, I spoke out loud without looking up.

'Did you forget something?' I smiled to myself as he normally forgot things.

'No, I don't think so,' a familiar voice replied.

That wasn't Daniel. I stopped instantly. I turned to my side to where Jack was sat in his bouncer, checking he was okay and stood

128

up, looking at the man before me. I knew who the voice belonged to before I pinned my eyes on him. It was Jim. What the hell was he doing here, again? He was a middle aged, unshaven and dirty-looking man. His brown, uncut hair was a mess, his clothing all creased and baggy against his unfit body. He resembled a homeless person.

'Oh, you scared me for a minute. Someone broke into the house, so I was just clearing the mess up.' You could hear the nervousness in my voice. What did he want from me? Why was he here and why couldn't he have turned up ten minutes earlier when Daniel was here?

'Why did I scare you? Don't you get visitors from time to time?' he said just standing there motionlessly.

'Yes, but they tend to knock on the front door, not just appear in the doorway.' I was quite blunt, but I think the man was one step removed from reality. Why would that not scare me?

'I think you like people watching you.' He stood there smiling, waiting for my reaction. 'I think you like the attention.'

'Excuse me? Why would I like someone watching me? It's you outside the house at night, isn't it? It wasn't me imagining it. I don't understand, what do you want from me?' I could feel my heart pounding in my chest. Jack sat in his bouncer, completely oblivious to what was happening around him.

'You see, the thing is…' He took a step forward towards me as I began to step away. 'You're in my house, which was fine but now it isn't.'

'I'm not quite with you. You want us to move out?'

He wasn't making any sense. I was confused. His creepy smile had turned to seriousness and his eyes looked like they had turned into dark portholes to his evil soul.

'You said you were staying with friends?' I asked.

'Well, I was staying with friends but there's been a bit of an incident so that's no longer an option now. The only option I have is to move in here with you both.' He took another step forwards, backing me against the wall. He was so close I could smell his breath and his stifling body odour that smelt like he hadn't washed in days. By this time, I was really panicking, watching Jack to make sure he was safe but at the same time trying not to make eye contact with Jim. I wanted to run, I wanted to escape but I had to stay strong and get rid of him. I needed to think fast. I had never been in this situation before. *Think quickly*, I kept thinking.

He raised his right arm and reached out to my head, stroking my hair and the side of my almond shaped face, eventually stopping and touching my chin.

'I'm sure Daniel won't mind sharing the house with me. It would be a shame for you both to leave just as you have finished cleaning and decorating the place. It looks so homely,' he whispered as he stared at my eyes first and then my lips, almost as if he was going to try to kiss me. 'Besides, where would you all go? You can't afford anywhere else. You have to stay here with me.' He could see my eyes start to well up. It was as if he was turned on, the more afraid I was.

Jack could sense the tension as a tear started to roll down my cheek.

'Please don't touch me,' I said as I tried to move my head away from him. I slid down the wall, and almost breathed in to escape from the barricade he had created by standing so close to me with his arms propping him against the wall behind me.

Panicking, I didn't know what to do next. *Do I just turn or try to call someone?* I was limited with options because I had Jack to think about. Just as I thought about grabbing him from his bouncer and running and leaving the house, the front door slammed open, and we both turned to it instantly. Before Jim had a chance to do anything, Daniel appeared. I ran to Jack immediately, unlocking his belt that strapped him in. I pulled him free from his bouncer and then went to Daniel, throwing my arms around him. He could see I was upset and had been crying but he didn't need to say anything.

'What the fuck is going on?' he angrily said, staring at Jim, expecting him to give an instant answer.

'Let's not get too excited here.' He looked intimidated and not quite so brash as he had been to me before Daniel came home. 'I think we all have our wires crossed here. Let's discuss it like adults.' He went to sit down on the chair of the sofa arm, but Daniel stopped him. He looked like he wanted to punch him but was refraining from doing so.

'I was just telling Rose that, due to unforeseen circumstances, I need to move back in. I don't see it as unreasonable as it is my house after all and I could be your lodger. I could stay in the spare room. You don't really need all three bedrooms and the council are paying your rent, so it makes perfect sense.' He raised his shoulders and shrugged as if it was a completely normal suggestion.

'You what?' Daniel said in shock.

'I have to move back in and I—' Jim started to repeat himself.

'Yes, I heard what you said the first time. There's no hope in hell that you're moving back in with the three of us. No way. Not at all. No chance.' Daniel's voice was getting louder and louder and threatening with each word. 'After everything we've done to this house, to think of the state that it was in when we got the keys from you and the hours we've spent on repairing, cleaning and fixing this place, for you to then demand you want to move back in again. It's not happening.' Daniel started to step forwards, getting closer to Jim, their eyes locked on each other like a staring competition. A standoff between two male animals in the wild.

I followed Daniel forwards, Jack balanced on my hip and clutched by my side. I placed my hand on his back. 'Hey, it's not worth it. He's just a sad, lonely old man that takes satisfaction from scaring a young couple and a baby. I don't feel safe here anyway, not with him hanging around.' I shot him a look that could kill. 'We'll find somewhere else. I'm sure our parents would have us all back.'

I squeezed his shoulder to try to calm him down, getting him to step backwards and unlock his gaze.

Daniel leant forwards into Jim, turning his head so his mouth was close to his ear and whispered in a low but serious tone. 'You can have your house back but if I find you anywhere near us again or I find out that it was you smashing the window, or watching us late at night, I will come and find you and I will kill you.'

Daniel then leant even further forwards and whispered something that I couldn't hear. Jim looked down; he seemed a taken back. He knew Daniel meant business. Without looking up or back at any of us, he turned around and walked back out of the house.

With complete relief, I made my way to the sofa. I deliberately collapsed, like a crumbling building, into the cushions. With Jack perched on my lap, I began to sob uncontrollably. Jack gave me the biggest, slobbery kiss on the cheek, staring into my watery eyes. He knew I was upset but was always such an affectionate baby and knew how to make it better. He lay on my chest with his chunky arms wrapped tight around me like a baby kangaroo.

'Fucking idiot,' Daniel murmured as he paced backwards and forwards in front of me. 'I wanted to hit him. I'm so pissed off. Who the hell does he think he is? How long was he here for?' He turned to me, red faced and angry.

'About fifteen minutes or so before you got here. I'm not sure, it all happened so fast I...' I wasn't sure exactly how long, but it felt like ages.

'I'm so sorry for not paying you much attention before when you said he was watching outside. I didn't realise he was such a lunatic. He knew that I wasn't in. I think he watched me leave the house earlier as I noticed the car in the car park earlier but as he wasn't in it, I didn't think much about it. Looking back, it was strange for his car to be here.' Daniel sat on the sofa next to me, putting his arm around both Jack and I and hugged us.

'Look, it's okay. Let him have his house back. I don't feel safe here anyway and he's not staying here at the same time. We'll find something else. The main thing is that we're all safe and okay.' I thought this would be the best option.

'I'll stay home this afternoon so he doesn't come back. We can work out what we do and start to pack up all our things and get the furniture into storage if we need to.' Daniel stared at the ceiling. It appeared he was having a long hard think about what to do next and to calm himself down. He had such an angry temper when things really got him wound up. I had never seen him that aggressive before, but I quite liked it. He made me feel safe when he was around, like nothing or anyone could hurt us. A six-foot, masculine man that was protecting his family was attractive and sexually arousing, despite everything that had just happened and the circumstances. Never did I think that I would be on the receiving end of such a temper but that's for another chapter. I couldn't believe it though, after all the hard work we had put in. But it was a house after all, and not our own at that.

That afternoon I spoke to my mum and explained everything that had happened. Without even asking, she ordered us to come back home and live with them. She said we should give ourselves time to save enough money and then move back out. Perhaps get a mortgage and a place of our very own. Okay, it was great to have our own space and be together, just the three of us. It gave us a taste of independence but not at the cost of our safety.

It took us a few days and with the support of both our parents, we moved all our belongings back into my parents' house with the plan to save again. It would also give me a chance to pass my driving test and get a car for extra freedom. As long as we were away from that creep, I was happy.

Chapter 16

Working 9 till 5

We spent six months saving every penny we could. At just
nineteen years old, Jack had just turned eighteen months.
Daniel and I had by now finished college after two years. Successfully,
Daniel had achieved a Business Studies diploma and I had gained A
Levels in English, Psychology and Business, as well as a certificate in
typing. Although we had spent months and months doing coursework
and exams whilst trying to cope with sleepless nights and a small
child, the real bonus for us was being able to get a real job with our
qualifications during the week with weekends off and better pay than
a minimum wage salary. Finally, we were able to contribute seriously
to our house fund and spend some quality time together, just the two
of us before time passed us by too much.

There was no doubt at all that we wouldn't have been able
to get to where we were now without the help of our parents
and family. The support we had around us was phenomenal.

Helping us, encouraging us and more importantly being a part of Jack's upbringing. So many times along the way, we wanted to quit, to take the easy route and claim benefits, which for some people is the only route. They don't have the support network or things haven't worked out with their partner. For us, it was sheer hard work and determination and a clear goal that we wanted to achieve. It was in both of our natures to work hard and play hard, at least that was one thing where we saw eye to eye.

This episode in our life may have been a slight setback in terms of money and life plans but looking at it now, we were one step ahead of the life game. Money, which would have otherwise been spent on nightclubs and lifestyle choices, went into building a family and settling down together. Travel was always there for us later in life when we had enough time and money to pursue it. Raising a baby and being young enough to cope with the sleepless nights and chaotic schedules was something we breezed through to some degree, whereas older parents would to some degree struggle. We had little to no money, but we made up for it with love and laughter. That's all we needed at the time.

Daniel had managed to secure a job at a large communications firm not far away from home in the data processing team. I was so proud of him. The salary was three times what we had been used to earning and it was Monday to Friday 9 a.m. till 5 p.m. Such a luxury. We celebrated with a dinner out; something we never did as we couldn't afford it.

I made the hardest decision to go to work full time and for Jack to go to either a childminder or nursery during the day. As much as

I didn't want to leave him with anyone other than family and people he was familiar with, I had to do it to give all of us the chance of a reasonable life beyond the limits of our bank balance. One of my closest friends had had a baby girl and offered to look after Jack for me at a reduced rate. It was a case of a friend helping another friend out. I couldn't afford the extortionate rates of a private nursery and she needed money whilst she wasn't working so we mutually agreed how it was going to work.

I was offered a role as a sales administrator for an IT company about a mile out of town. It was perfect. We could drop Jack off with my friend Chloe every morning, then drive to work and collect him on my way home. I would pack a lunch box and a small rucksack full of all his favourite toys, cars and playthings for each day and reluctantly leave him whilst I worked. The first few days were torture. I just wanted to turn the car around and go back to be with him but eventually I would get used to leaving him. I knew he was in safe, loving and more than capable hands.

Aside from the fact I was a mother, I now truly felt like a grown up. Work wasn't anything like I imagined it would be, nor was it anything like school or college had prepared me for. It was better, with more freedom and scope to be myself, who I truly was. No one constantly breathing down my neck, telling me to listen or pay attention. I wanted to be there. I woke up every morning excited to go to work. Well, at least for a short period of time because it was new to me. I worked hard, I excelled in all areas, I was a quick learner, and I was interested to learn for once. I still talked the whole day, but I managed to get all my work done at the same time, making sure I finished first out of everyone. I was extremely competitive, always wanting to be quicker and faster than anyone else and soon I realised that I stood out.

At school, I wasn't very good at sport so I would sit at the back and talk or hide behind the bushes smoking during cross country. Here I was doing something I liked so it came naturally. Finally, something that excited me, just like Army Cadets, using my brain towards its full potential. I seemed to be flying at 100 miles an hour whereas all my co-workers were happy to drift along day by day around me, achieving the bare minimum.

My role meant I had to process all the orders and paperwork the sales teams had sold. I had fallen into this job because of a recommendation from a recruitment agency but before long, I realised I was doing a salesperson's paperwork and they were making the real money. They earnt way more than me, plus commissions, bonuses and company cars. I had to start somewhere but I knew straight away that this wasn't where I was going to stay. I wanted to be a salesperson and earn the money they did. Why couldn't I? I had the brains to do it and I also had the ability to talk to complete strangers and build up a relationship. I would be perfect in sales; I had a knack of talking people into getting me what I wanted, I was pretty sure I could talk people into purchasing a product I was selling. From that point on, I was focused on becoming a salesperson, not just anyone, a top performer, one I could make my son proud of becoming. I wanted a fast car, money and not have the worries I had now. This would all go away if I could get there. My sights were set, and no one could discourage me or talk me out of it. My want to become an English teacher was too far in the distance now.

The characters in the office were what made my time away from Jack more bearable. A new set of friends that I hadn't grown up with or been to school with and completely outside of my comfort zone. I had to build relationships again, but they still wouldn't know the real me. To some degree I built up a work persona, someone confident and that everyone liked. I dressed a different way, not necessarily in designer clothes but in fashionable work attire with a spin on still looking attractive and showing off my curvy, top-heavy figure. I wasn't out to attract men, but I wanted people in the office to still notice me, to ask who I was and to start to build my career.

Claire was the quiet, shy and reserved type. She would have her hair tied back into a neat ponytail, large secretarial looking glasses perched on her freckled, un-made up face. Each day she wore a smart blouse, fitted trousers and flat, black patent ballet shoes. She rarely participated in the office discussions, but she would watch and take in everything around her. Claire arrived at 8:55 every morning, unpacking all the contents of her handbag in the same order and placing it onto her neatly arranged and organised desk and leaving at 5:05 on the dot at the end of the day. She was predictable and did everything like clockwork. If you ever needed anything or had any questions, she was the go-to person. A fountain of knowledge and had been there for over five years.

Teresa, on the other hand, was the loud one in the office, the life and soul of every party, a real character that never failed to make you laugh. Even if you weren't sat next to her, you could hear her loud cackle of a laugh from wherever you were. She had a no care attitude, meaning she didn't care about anything at all or anyone. Teresa would frequently come over and sit on the edge of my desk. I would be asked time and time again to accompany her on a cigarette break, even though I didn't smoke. By the time I had been there a few weeks, I would quite often share half of hers with her. It was more for her to share the office gossip and find out anything that was going on. There was always a drama, especially when she was involved.

Teresa was a bad influence, but I liked it. A day without her in the office was a quiet one. It was as if something was missing, and work resumed without her disturbing the flow of work processes. Those days dragged. Teresa, unlike Claire, always wore short pencil skirts, high heels and a revealing top of some description. A different hairstyle each and every day, bright red lipstick and lovely makeup. Everyone in the office loved her despite her carefree and loud attitude. I wished I was a little more like her.

The third most stand out character was George; he was from Greece and was stunning. A stereotypical sales guy, outgoing and very forward. He was charismatic, chatty and a real ladies' man. His Greek looks meant he had the darkest of hair, gelled and styled to perfection, olive skin and the most luscious dark chocolate eyes. Half the time you didn't hear what he was saying because you were drawn into his handsome looks and charm. I would have bought anything he was selling, there was no questioning why he was one of the top salespeople in the business. He had a red sports Alfa Romeo car that he loved to show off to everyone he met. His chat up lines were cheesy but we laughed anyway. The conversations between Teresa and him were hilarious; they just bounced off each other. It was comical. Between the three of them, my time there whizzed by.

George saw Claire as a challenge, one of very few that saw through his good looks and misdemeanours. He would try daily, and unsuccessfully, to seduce her, but Teresa would just mock him and encourage him even more. The rest of the office kept themselves to themselves. My boss, Ann, however, was a force to be reckoned with. She was a flirt in an unattractive manner, and she spoke down to everyone who worked for her. I saw it as her trying to assert her power and we clashed. On days when she was in the office, I became reserved and concentrated on keeping my head down and finishing my work. When she was out of the office, I interacted more with everyone, and the hours flew.

Daniel never really spoke about work or the people he worked with. I thought it was strange but as he was always quite a shy and timid individual then I guessed this was maybe why. He, like Claire, seemed to watch everything around him but not participate as much as I did. I would frequently ask him how his day was or if anything had happened, to which I got little response. He would reply with one or two-word answers.

'Yeah, good. Yours?' was his usual response.

That's when it all went wrong. My whole world fell apart and my normal loving, trusting nature seemed to change to a cold, black heart and adopt the opinion that I couldn't trust anyone. It came totally out of the blue, completely unexpected. I was too caught up in work that I didn't see it coming.

Daniel had been his normal fidgety self in bed, but he started earlier in the morning. He was up, dressed and was giving Jack his breakfast by 7 a.m. I had never been a morning person and although I got up for Jack every day, I was regularly rushing around, forgetting things I needed to get ready and running out of the front door because I was late. Daniel seemed distracted and distant, but I guessed it was because he was tired.

'Morning,' I said and kissed him on the cheek as he was feeding Jack in the kitchen.

'Morning. Thought I would get Jack ready for you,' he replied. Jack was his normal happy and smiling self. 'I'm in training all day at work so don't call me. Just text and I'll give you a shout when I'm out.' Daniel was making up Jack's drink in his beaker that he took.

'Yes, sure,' I replied, not really thinking too much into it.

I carried on my day as normal. It had been a busy day in the office. The last day of the month meant we were trying to get as many orders and papers processed as we could to smash the numbers we had done from the previous month. I hadn't even had a lunch break. The first moment I had to check any emails or missed calls was 2:30 p.m. Teresa had tried dragging me out of the back fire exit to have a cigarette break so I reached for my phone from my bag and tucked it into my pocket as I left my desk. We were mid conversation before I could fully take on board what I had just been sent. I had received a text message from Daniel, but I didn't really understand what it meant.

'We need to talk later.' No kiss afterwards, no greeting, just those words. What did that mean? I had a bad feeling and was already starting to think of the worst scenarios possible. Was he ending it?

142

Had he had enough? Why say it now? Why didn't he wait until I had finished work and then speak to me?

Teresa asked me what the matter was, but I shrugged it off and told her nothing. I knew she would tell everyone, and I could be making a mountain out of a molehill, so I tried to ignore his message and continue as if I hadn't got it. Try as I might, I couldn't concentrate. I felt sick and had a really bad feeling. What on earth could it possibly be that he needed to speak to me about? Only time would tell.

By the time I had collected Jack from Chloe, had a quick chat about what he had eaten, what little activities they had done during the day and driven home, Daniel's car was already on the driveway. My parents weren't home from work yet, so it gave us time to talk about his text message, but I froze. I sat in the car staring at the steering wheel and running the scenarios over in my head. What was he going to say to me and I to him? How would I react and what was I going to do?

He opened the door; his face looked solemn as if something had happened. I racked my mind to think of anything I had done or said but I couldn't think of a single thing.

'Good day?' he asked

'Well, it was until I got your text.' I was trying to carry Jack along with all his bags and belongings. I handed Jack over to Daniel and walked through the front door, taking my coat and shoes off and closing the door behind me.

'I made you a cuppa,' he said leading the way into the living room. It was as if he was building me up to tell me something he didn't

143

want to. I could read him like a book. I knew when he was nervous, uncomfortable, happy or sad. I had seen it all before.

'I need to tell you something, but I don't want you to hate me, and I didn't know how to tell you.' It was one of those, 'it's not you, it's me' conversations, I knew it. He was almost shaking and couldn't look me in the eye.

'Go on,' was all I could muster.

'I said I was in training today at work. Well, I wasn't. I had a doctor's appointment. I'm sorry, Rose…' He looked as though he was going to cry. I was now worried. It sounded serious like he was ill and was scared to admit the truth. I wasn't prepared for this.

'What… what is it?' I sat down beside him and put my arm around him.

'Don't. I don't deserve it.' He looked at me as his voice trembled and tears rolled down his face. 'I had to go to the doctors because I thought I had caught something. It was a one-night stand. I don't really remember it. It didn't mean anything, but I'm so upset that I could lose you and Jack and what we have that I don't know what to do. I didn't want to tell you but then I thought it wasn't fair that you might catch something too.' He was stuttering and so upset that I couldn't really take in the words. I felt so sorry for him that I didn't know how I was supposed to act.

'You mean you think you've caught an STD?' That was all I could think of. How could this have even happened? I thought we were close.

'Yes… I… I'm so sorry.' He looked at me, my best friend, my boyfriend, my son's father. It felt like a knife had been stabbed into my heart and I wanted to leave it there. I took my hand from on top of his and moved sideways away from him. My head rested in my hands, giving me time to comprehend what he was saying. I felt betrayed.

'When did this happen? I don't understand.' I needed answers but I felt numb.

'A few weeks ago, when I went out with the lads. We went back to a girl's house for a party, and I don't remember much after that. When I got in, you and Jack were fast asleep. You looked so beautiful, I felt so bad. I thought I could forget about it and not have to tell you but then I got an infection and didn't want to risk you getting it or hearing it from someone else.' He sobbed like he really meant it and it was heartfelt.

I sat back in the chair, staring at Jack who was playing happily with his toys on the floor. Daniel was my best friend; I didn't see this coming at all. I had spent all afternoon thinking I had done something wrong, or he was going to leave me when in fact he had cheated and then kept it from me. Where did I go from here?

'Rose, say something.' This time reaching for my hand. 'I'm sorry, I never meant to hurt you. I had drunk way too much. It didn't mean anything. I would do anything for you to forgive me.' He sat there waiting for me to reply.

I wiped my tears away. 'Who was she?' I asked.

'I don't know. I've never seen her before, and I probably wouldn't recognise her again.' He seemed desperate, I didn't know whether to believe him or not. 'I would never do anything intentionally to hurt you. It's been driving me insane since it happened but I didn't want to lose you.'

'Does anyone else know?' I didn't want to be the laughing stock of the town and word travelled fast around here.

'No, I haven't spoken to anyone,' he said. To be truthful, I didn't know whether to laugh, cry, be angry or get upset. I felt let down and sick at the thought of him being with another woman that wasn't me. It was completely out of character for him. How could I trust him now? From now on, I would be wondering what he was doing when he went on a night out and I wasn't with him. How did relationships move on from here?

'I need to think.' I got up, leaving Jack with Daniel and went upstairs to my room. I shut the door and just lay on my bed staring at the ceiling. I felt sick from the pit of my stomach and began to quietly cry. I didn't want him to hear or for him to know that I was upset. He had hurt me, and I didn't know how I felt about it. Never had I felt the need to cheat on him. Yes, I wanted people to lust after me and find me attractive but thinking it and doing it were two completely different things. It was a strain on our relationship having Jack so young and it must have been difficult for him living at my parents' house, almost trapped in a world that was more in my favour than his, but it didn't excuse his actions. There was no doubt in my mind that I wanted to end things, but I wasn't sure how to get over this.

The door handle creaked as Daniel opened the door and walked in with Jack in his arms. 'I'm sorry I've done this to you, and I know you're upset but I'll never ever do this to you again. How can I make it right? I don't deserve you.' He moved my legs out of the way and perched on the end of the bed. He came closer to me as Jack crawled to give me a hug.

'I can't believe you did this to me, to our family. I'm struggling to be near you right now, but I know that I also can't bear to be without you. I don't know what I'm supposed to do or how I'm supposed to feel.' As I sat up, Jack cuddled up next to me. Daniel reached forward and cradled me as I sobbed.

'You know I love you more than anything. I don't know how I let it happen. I have regretted it ever since. I was drunk, I was caught off guard and it didn't mean anything. All that matters is you and Jack. I wish we had our own place, with our own quality time together.' He stroked my hair gently. 'I'm not making excuses. I understand if you hate me at the moment, but I would do anything to take it back.'

I had prepared myself for the worst. I had in my mind that he didn't love me or wanted to finish things, when in fact he did love me and had made one silly little mistake. It was me that he wanted, she didn't matter at all. I tried to convince myself that that was the case. I had to think of it that way. Whilst I couldn't forget what he had told me, I had to learn to forgive him if I didn't want to break up our family. For the sake of Jack if nothing else and there would have to be boundaries agreed by us both. I had to act like nothing had happened in front of my parents or they would suspect something. I was getting good at keeping secrets and hiding away things that mattered to me, so others didn't know how I really felt.

It was a little frosty to begin with. It was difficult pretending everything was okay to Daniel but deep down inside, I was upset and hurt. Taking a trip to the sexual health clinic to get tested was embarrassing to say the least, but again I took it in my stride, acted as though it didn't matter and got on with it. As far as I was concerned, it didn't happen. I didn't want anyone to know the truth and it was our dirty little secret. He had a lot of making up to do and I used it to my advantage. In a way, it made us stronger, and we agreed to start again. Be stronger and better than we were before and work on getting a place of our very own.

His infidelity made me think about faithfulness and whether it existed. Were men really that weak that they gave into desire if a woman was open to having sex? Were women the instigators and men just couldn't say no? I was generalising here. Of course, there were a lot of men that tried it on with women time and time again and eventually the women gave in but if you were in a loving, special relationship like ours and all it took was a drunken night, two adults and a mistake, surely you couldn't guarantee it wouldn't happen again in the future. Whilst some women may not have been able to get past being cheated on, I felt there was no alternative if I wanted to be with the one man who I could honestly say I loved.

In all the situations I had been in, men saw me as an attractive young lady. They were persistent in trying their luck. Take the case of Jim and there had been several others when on a night out but if you were on your guard and said no, they knew where they stood. In some cases, you had to be blunt, but they got the message. I was soon learning that you could manipulate people to get what you wanted. I was also learning that there were some people you just couldn't trust no matter how much you wanted to.

Chapter 17

Number 71

For the next few months, we saved every penny we could along with collecting wage slips, salary evidence and bank statements. We started the process of trying to find a mortgage and a house suitable for us to buy. We tried all the high street banks but with no luck. They saw it as a risk at such a young age and a dependent under eighteen years of age. Our last hope was to try a financial advisor who was a specialist in finding mortgages for those risk adverse applicants such as us.

He was a friend of the family and had come highly recommended. He came to the house in a smart suit and briefcase and walked us through multiple options, examining our commitments, outgoings and combined salaries. He had managed to find us a mortgage albeit with a higher interest rate than normal, but they were willing to lend us £100,000 plus our savings of £5,000. It wasn't much and we weren't hopeful, but it was something. The next steps were for us to speak to the estate agents and find a property we were interested in purchasing and if they had something in our price range.

The very next Saturday, I bundled all the paperwork I had relating to the mortgage offer and placed Jack in his car seat, strapping him in, ready to visit each of the estate agents in turn. This was hopefully the break Daniel and I needed to get over the incident a few months ago. A restart in our relationship.

'Let's go find us a house, baby.' I kissed Jack on his rosy cheeks. He gave me the most beautiful smile and we set off. Daniel was working for some extra money for a landscaper that he had known since school and gave him all the hours he needed. I parked in the large multi-storey car park that was nearby all the shops and had to wake Jack up. The car journey always rocked him to sleep. I transferred him to his pushchair, getting a sleepy smile in return. He was such a content and happy baby, nothing fazed him at all.

I tried the first estate agents in the parade of shops and walked us both into the small office. Its windows boasted lots of house and apartment images on display. All four office staff looked up. They were busy talking on the phone to prospective buyers or sellers, then shortly after, dropped their heads and continued working as if I wasn't in the room. I knew they were busy, so I patiently waited in the reception area, taking a seat on one of the chairs they had placed there for visitors. One by one, they all finished their conversations but carried on working. I twiddled with my fingers, excited to start talking about properties that would be suitable for our budget. As time passed, I increasingly felt like I was being ignored but still sat there waiting. A good twenty minutes passed before my patience ran out. I either needed to get their attention or I was walking back out. I was not wasting any more time sitting here whilst they ignored me.

'Excuse me,' I said, embarrassed to draw attention to myself. No one dared look at me.

'Excuse me please.' I cleared my throat to raise their awareness. The gentleman on the first desk, closest to me, was the first to respond. He looked around at the others, seeing if he was the only one responding, he looked at me and replied. I think he felt obliged to answer me as he was the nearest.

'Sorry, can I help you madam?' He seemed nervous yet polite and came across as not really interested in anything I was about to say.

'Yes. I have a mortgage offer and I'm looking for properties that fit within my budget.' I rummaged in my bag for all the documentation I had brought with me. I wasn't too sure what I was able to get or what the process was, so I was looking for his guidance. His interest peaked as though he realised I wasn't a time waster. As I finally found the papers and handed them to him, his expression seemed to sink.

'Ah,' he said looking up at me. 'We have a roomy one-bedroom flat available but I'm afraid we don't have much else.'

My heart sank. 'Oh, I understand. We were ideally looking for a house with a garden if possible.' I was starting to think maybe we wouldn't be able to get a place of our own after all.

'Not on your budget.' He smiled in a matter-of-fact way, quite rude and dismissive. I didn't have the patience, nor could I be bothered in standing up for myself. If anything, I felt stupid and

151

ignorant. The woman at the desk behind him put a hand up to her mouth and sniggered to herself without even looking up at me.

'Okay, thanks for your time.' I took my handful of papers back off the gentleman and turned to put them in my bag and leave. I could feel their eyes burning a hole in my back. They were all looking at each other behind my back and laughing between them. I felt like a bullied child in a school playground. My fault for even being hopeful and thinking we could afford somewhere for us. It would be *another* year or more to get something half decent.

Just before I reached for the long metal handle attached to the large glass door, the gentleman walked after me and called out. 'Wait a minute, we do have just one more property but I…' He paused as I quickly turned around to see if he was being serious or if this was a joke at my expense.

He hurried back to his desk and flicked through a pile of property documents stacked on the edge of his desk in a metal tray and pulled out a double page overview of a house with a picture on the front of it. He shook it in front of me, prompting me to look at the terraced house he had just found.

'It needs a bit of work but it's 98,000 and well within your budget.' His eyes seemed to be searching for my reaction.

'Really?' I was waiting for him to say he was joking or there was something else I should know but he didn't. At this point, the others in the room had all stopped what they were doing and were listening to our conversation. There must be a catch, but at this moment I wanted to take all that I could get. After the amount of time and effort spent on the last house, I would have bought a garage to live in, just to call it our own and make it ours.

'Would it be possible to view the house please?' I asked hopefully.

'Yes, of course. Is Monday any good? That's the earliest I can do, I'm afraid.' He scanned through a calendar that he had opened on the screen in front of him and stopped on next week's dates.

'I work but I could do Monday lunchtime. Say 12:30 if that's convenient?' I had everything crossed and glimpsed down to Jack, who was playing with the buckle of his pushchair strap, entertaining himself as usual. The estate agent took my name and number, and I took his. Shaking his wet and clammy hands, I walked out, pushing Jack along as we left. Without looking at the house, I already had a good feeling and wanted it, but I needed to convince Daniel that this was the one. My face was beaming. *This could finally be it. Our house that no one can take away from us.* I folded the leaflet in half and inserted it into my bag along with all the other papers, bursting with excitement inside.

'Guess what, Jacky? We're going to look at our new house on Monday. How exciting!' I spoke to him like I would a grown adult, half expecting him to retaliate with a full conversation but instead he babbled with the occasional mum, mum, always dad, dad and a few other small words he had learnt. He pointed at the shop ahead of us. He had spotted some cakes and cookies in the window and signalled to me that he was hungry by making yum yum type sounds. Jack loved his food, especially cakes so as a treat I thought we could get a cake or two to celebrate.

'Okay, let's go eat and look at our house together.'

153

We walked to the shop, selected a muffin each, a hot chocolate and sat at one of the little round tables together. His big, eager blue-green eyes that were once piercing blue were changing to match my emerald green eyes and they were locked on his muffin. The older he became the more he resembled a younger version of my dad. He had more of my genes than of Daniel's, but you could tell he was his son.

I took the brochure back out, placing it on the table in front of me after handing Jack small parts of the muffin for him to eat. I started to read the description but there was only one picture so I began imagining what it would look like inside and how I could customise the interior with what little budget we had left. I had already created a mental image of where the furniture was going to go and was studying the dimensions of each room. Before long, the coffee shop became busy and I was concerned how much the car park would cost the longer I took, so we headed home.

I told my parents all about the house and then again to Daniel when he returned home from work. I had so much enthusiasm, but it wasn't met with the same level of excitement from him. More pessimism than anything else. I tended to look at things with a half full kind of attitude. He, on the other hand, with a half empty outlook. I understood that he was tired and had been busy at work all day. He just wanted to sit back and play with Jack until he went to bed and then relax in front of the television. I couldn't blame him. I would approach the subject again when I knew he was in a better frame of mind and not so tired.

My parents, unlike him, were a little more positive. Perhaps they were thinking about the possibility of getting their house back and us finally moving out. They both offered to come with me and look at the house and give their opinion. They were the ones with experience and would be able to advise me on what needed to be done and whether it was worth investing in. Of course, I took them up on their offer.

That Monday morning at work, I couldn't contain myself. I achieved the bare minimum and counted the hours until I could leave and go to see the house for myself. I had shown George and Teresa the one picture of the house. They were really excited for me and offered to come take a look too for support, but I told them maybe after I had seen it first with my parents and then I would take them back once Daniel had had the final say and approval.

12:15 on the dot I switched my computer screen onto standby and almost ran to the car in the car park, driving so fast and well above the speed limit to get to the address. As I found the street and drove down the steep hill to reach the number I was given, number 71 Ringwood, I arrived at a small row of parking spaces next to a block of garages. I pulled into an empty space but didn't bother to straighten the car either side of my parents. They were already there and waiting for me, very rarely were they late for anything. I was fashionably late to pretty much everything.

All three of us got out of our cars at the same time and stood on the corner of a cul-de-sac of terraced houses, surrounding a large green area of grass in the middle. Just as we were about to walk round the corner and look at the house from the outside, the estate agent turned up. The same gentleman from Saturday that I had spoken to. Still looking slightly uninterested.

'Good afternoon,' he shouted as he began walking over towards us. He first shook my hand as he approached and proceeded to shake my mum's, then my dad's in turn. 'You must be Mum and Dad. Let me walk you round the house, but a couple of things I want to mention beforehand.' He stopped just outside, pushed the keys into the door lock but then turned to us, his file in his hand like a surveyor. Number 71 was the second house from the corner.

'The house requires a bit of work and modernisation, so you need to have an open mind when looking around. The cost of renovating the property has been reflected in the sell price.' He looked down the entire time he was explaining to us and searching in his pocket for where I presumed his phone was. I looked at my parents in turn with a look of surprise. He mentioned that it needed a bit of work, but he didn't mention any costs for renovation or modernisation. I wondered what he was referring to. My face had sunk but I had to remain positive. Like he said, keep an open mind.

The front of the house had quite a plain and standard look to it, two double glazed windows at the top, a larger window to the bottom right where I could see a sink and a tap so that must be the kitchen and to the right of the large window was a wooden protruding box, clad in timber lengths where the grass had grown out of control against it. As I looked closer, the bottom of the clad box was rotten and coming away. The once white plastic front door now appeared a dirty brown and probably hadn't been washed for many years. All these things were fixable though and didn't faze me in the slightest.

As the estate agent slowly opened the front door, I asked my first question. 'When did the previous owners move out?'

156

He paused when opening the door to let us in and stood still in the hallway as he started to reply. 'We got the house in quite a poor condition. The story is that the previous owner was an elderly man who lived on his own. The neighbours hadn't seen him in a while, and they couldn't get a response from knocking on the door. Concerned about his welfare, they called the police. The poor man had diabetes and as a result had lost his limbs, making him wheelchair bound. You'll notice some of the modifications to the house making it wheelchair accessible.' He walked through the hallway, past the stairs on his right and into the kitchen which was the first room.

I noticed all the floors were bare, from the stairs to the kitchen and the hallway, just plain floorboards. All the carpets had been removed and the smell that filled the air was stagnant and damp. *Leaving the windows and doors open for a while will fix that smell*, I thought.

'So, what happened to the man who lived here before?' I continued the last conversation. My dad was studying every room from floor to ceiling making a mental note of all the things that needed repairing.

'Ah, he unfortunately passed away.' The estate agent continued through the kitchen to the open dining room and living room.

'In the house?' I asked, not really wanting to know the answer.

'Yes, unfortunately. In the bathroom but it's been cleaned and fumigated so it's all okay now.' Although he seemed to think it was quite normal, the fact that a man died in this house unsettled me somewhat. I glanced over to my mum. She made a face at me that I knew meant, don't worry about what he said, just look round the house and think about it later. Call it women's tuition but we had a

157

way of communicating through facial expressions in some situations; words weren't needed. This also applied when I was younger and she was angry at something I had done in public. Her death stare meant wait till I get you home and then I will tell you off.

You could barely call it a kitchen. There were only two, old cupboards where the doors were hanging from their hinges. They looked like they dated back to the 1960s when the house was built. The sink was grubby and looked a dirty grey rather than a shiny silver basin and tap. The sideboard consisted of a laminate wooden board that was rotten, stained and peeling perched up by a metal pole at each end. I wanted to move through to the rest of the downstairs but each step I took, my shoes stuck to the sticky, dirty floor. I just wanted to clean and clear everything in the house around me, but it wasn't mine yet to do anything with.

As I entered the dining room, it was empty with wallpaper peeling from the walls and a large set of patio doors. I was stunned by what I saw next.

My dad walked over to me and whispered, 'Remember what he said. Keep an open mind.' He placed his hand on my shoulder and gently squeezed as if to ease my worrying mind.

Outside of the patio doors, I was expecting to see a pretty little garden that Jack would be able to play in when he was old enough, but instead, all I could see were seven-foot-high brambles. I could only make out small parts of a decaying fence at the back where it ended. This wasn't what I was expecting at all, although I wasn't sure what I was expecting anymore. If anything, I felt sorry for the previous owner. How could someone let his house get this out of control? No one to look after or care for him, how sad. All my excitement for what was going to be our new family home had been quashed. I felt deflated and as though the estate agent was mocking me. I wasn't sure if I was ready or even wanted to go upstairs to see the rest of the house.

'I think I've seen enough,' I said to the estate agent who stood back in the hallway, propping himself up against the wall with his arm.

'Hey, your dad said keep an open mind,' my mum said with a smile.

'I haven't seen anything here that we can't fix,' my dad added. 'Let's have a quick look upstairs and then head back to work.' He took my arm and led me up the stairs.

There were two large bedrooms at the front of the building, either side of the stairs, a smaller but still quite substantially sized room straight ahead and then a bathroom in the back left corner.

It was not what I had envisaged but again I tried to remain positive. Thinking about it, if I looked back to what we did to Jim's house, it was impressive. It looked like a completely different property altogether.

In the bathroom, there was an antique-looking dark green bath with dirty, limescale-ridden taps, a basic sink and toilet to match. The flooring had also been removed in every room to match downstairs. The floorboards in the bathroom had dark stains all over them and the smell was intoxicating. The small, patterned window was slightly ajar, but it didn't seem to make a difference to the smell in the room. Why was the floor stained? Was this

159

from where the body had been found? My mind was wandering and imagining all sorts of images, like a crime scene from a film. The reality didn't warrant thinking about. What if the house was haunted? I was unsure how much I wanted this property. Maybe it was better to wait for the next place to become available, even if we had to wait a little longer. I also wasn't sure if we had the money to invest in repairing it on such a large scale.

We made our way back down the stairs and thanked the estate agent for his time, saying we would come back to him shortly with a decision. He nodded his head as if he had heard it so many times before and locked up as we left.

I was expecting my parents to say save your money and have a look again in a year's time but instead my dad turned to me as he opened his car door to climb in.

'Don't be disheartened. You're nineteen years old. Most people move out when they're a little older and then start a family. The house may need a fair bit of work but look at the potential. It's in a nice location, the rooms are a large size and with a bit of a clean, a bit of paint and your own stamp on it, you'll end up with your own lovely home. It's whether you want to put the time and effort into it. Don't make up your mind now. Have a long, hard think about it and then make your decision.' He gave me a comforting smile, a look of support, got in his car and drove off to work.

My mum did the same. 'Let's think about it tonight. Get back to work before you're late and then make your decision, sweetie.' As she drove away, I got in my car but sat for a moment behind the wheel just thinking about what I had seen.

As soon as I got back to my desk, my phone pinged, and Daniel had text me.

'How was the house, baby? X.'

I wanted to call him, to talk it through, to tell him what it was really like, but it was frowned upon making personal calls in the office. Everyone listened in and I didn't want them knowing my business, especially as I had been so excited to leave and had come back feeling down about the house and what a state it was in.

'Interesting. I will tell you all about it later, honey X' I text back. I left it as a short response. I knew if I told him the full story he would say no straight away.

All afternoon I deliberated about the house. Maybe my parents were right about the house. It would be a huge project, but it was the only thing we could afford, and my heart had been set on it until I had discovered the background and seen what a state it was in.

I spoke to Daniel about it at length, and he didn't seem so sure. Yes, the house was an investment, but it wasn't the right time to pick up on such a project. That night I lay awake thinking about the pros and cons. To make the right decision, Daniel suggested we go back and look at the house but this time we go with his parents. His dad was a decorator so it made sense for him to look and gauge exactly how much work would be involved and approximately how long it would take. Daniel seemed more comfortable with this option than taking my word for it and me wanting the house just because I wanted it. I could be a bit of a diva at times. If I wanted something so much, I would keep on and on and create so many justifications as to why I should have it and the person on the other end normally gave

161

in. Therefore, I knew I would be good at sales because I could talk anyone into anything. It was whether their patience gave in or not.

Wasting no time at all, I called the estate agent first thing in the morning and made another appointment for the following day at lunchtime. This time I had my positive hat on and started to prepare myself to note all my justifications about why we should go for it. I met Daniel in the same place in the car park as I had previously met my parents. We waited for his dad to arrive in his large grey Ford Transit van. Both his mum and dad were in the van together. I was a little apprehensive as to what they would both think or say but I let them make their own decision. Daniel walked round the car to meet me and Daniel's mum and dad got out of the van. We all walked to the house together, just as before.

The estate agent walked round the corner at the same time. 'Afternoon.' He nodded politely to each of us. No shaking hands this time except for the point at which he passed Daniel towering above him, to open the door for us. Daniel always had a strong handshake; I think he was showing his authority and a force not to be reckoned with.

As soon as the estate agent opened the door, he backed to one side, using his extended arm to usher us into the property. I let Daniel go first as I had already seen the carnage inside the house. I wanted to watch his reactions. It was less than a minute before I heard Daniel.

'Wow, what is that smell? It's awful,' he said.

I peered round the corner as he was in the kitchen. His hand was up against his face and cupping his nostrils so he couldn't smell. I laughed at the expression on his face: his nose crinkled up and the look of pure disgust in his eyes as they scanned every wall and every nook and cranny of every room. Before he had a chance to finish looking at everything in the kitchen, his attention moved to the view of the garden, or lack of view through the patio doors. As he was experienced in landscaping, he knew exactly how much work was involved in clearing and re-doing that space.

'Absolutely not,' he said as he turned around to walk out of the house. His dad, who had been following him, stood in his way and held out his hand to stop him from leaving.

'Hang on, just wait a minute.' I wasn't sure what he was thinking. He had a look of seriousness on his face but was it good or bad? 'It is quite a mess, and it'll take a bit of time to get it into a habitable state but structurally, it's sound. It doesn't appear to be damp, and the size of the rooms are quite substantial. With a bit of hard work, this could be a nice house for the three of you.' His words mirrored that of my parents. They could clearly see something that we couldn't. Was it our generation that we had been used to such creature comforts? I was never afraid of hard work, but it was the money we didn't have that worried me. We would have to do this entire project on a shoestring.

Daniel's whole demeanour seemed to change as he listened to his dad. It seemed as though he was now taking it seriously rather than just coming along to look. It was like his eyes had just been opened to what was possible rather than its current state. The pair of them paced backwards and forwards, talking between them about what could be fixed and how they would repair certain things. I could see their brains processing the scale of the work. I hadn't even told them about the previous owner passing away yet. I thought I would keep that in my back pocket until they had made more of a decision.

Next on the list was upstairs. I left the three of them to wander round whilst I waited downstairs. It gave me a chance to take a second look and build some ideas of my own. I could hear what I presumed were Daniel's thoughts of the bathroom and chuckled quietly to myself.

'Wow, that's hideous' and 'That's disgusting, how could someone live in this' were amongst my favourite comments I could hear him say. To get a break from the pungent smell of the house, I stood outside and was joined shortly after by Daniel's mum.

'So, what do you think?' I asked her, not sure if I wanted her answer but I was ever hopeful.

'Rose, my darling girl, we lived at home with our parents for many, many years and it took us a long time to be able to afford something like this. It may be a project, but I think it would be a good investment.' Well, I wasn't expecting her to say that.

Daniel, followed by his dad, joined us in a line outside of the house looking up. We stood there for a good ten minutes, not one word was spoken, just staring back up at the front of the house, deep in thought.

'Thanks for your time, mate,' Daniel said to the estate agent as he locked the front door and went to walk back to his car. 'We'll be in touch, but we are interested.' Daniel shone a look over to me. I think for the first time, he didn't need convincing. He had taken on board what his dad had said and saw something in the house that we could work on. I beamed from the inside out.

'It's going to be a busy six months for us all,' Daniel's dad said and laughed. He gave Daniel a couple of brazen pats on the back. 'You know enough people in the trade to help you out here, and you know we'll always help you. We can start with the kitchen and bathroom first, Jack's room second, make it liveable and then work on other rooms as you go. I think you should go for it, as long as you think you can afford the monthly payments?' He looked at us both in turn and shot us a smile of encouragement.

We all walked back to the car park and made our separate ways back to work.

That afternoon, I was so busy at work that I didn't have any time to think about the house, nor did Daniel. He picked up Jack whilst I finished entering the last couple of orders on the system and met him at home. During dinner, we ran through everything to do with the house: the figures, our budget, ideas on what to do first and more importantly, how long we thought it would roughly take. To complete all the necessary paperwork, legal documents, exchanges and contracts would take another few months so it gave us the opportunity to save yet more money to pump into the renovations. We made a great team so we knew if we were going to do it together then it would be a success.

I gave the estate agent a call the following morning and gave him the good news that we wanted to proceed. I think he nearly fell off his chair and was expecting us like all the other viewers to turn it down.

'Okay, great. I'll instruct the solicitors on behalf of the sellers. This is now with the deceased's family, and they'll be in touch.' The

165

estate agent explained the process. 'Congratulations and good luck with the property.' He hung up the phone before I could say thanks.

I couldn't quite believe it; I was excited and apprehensive all at the same time. Little did I know that this was the last time in my life where I would have money in my bank account. From this point on, we scrimped, saved and couldn't afford a single thing but it was going to be one hell of an exciting journey.

Chapter 18

The Keys to the Door

I took us a good three to four months to finally get the keys to the house. An endless amount of paperwork, contracts to sign, documents to review, searches, chasing solicitors for updates and both Daniel and I doing hour after hour of overtime, trying to scrape together every penny we could. Our limited funds meant we searched charity shops and welcomed any second-hand or unwanted items from family and friends for furniture and essentials. Even though we had moved out previously, this time we needed a kitchen, a bathroom and all the appliances to go with it. Daniel was becoming a professional at negotiating buy prices and discounts from retail stores and trade centres, to make our money stretch even further.

During the next ten weeks, we cleaned, we cleared, we ripped and replaced and were at the house each night till gone midnight. At one point, I thought Jack must have thought we had abandoned him as he saw more of my mum and Daniel's mum than he did of us.

I had blisters on all my fingers, and we were both shattered. Daniel had pulled in all his friends that had a skill or a trade to help with the repair of the roof tiles, to replace the wood on the front box and many other areas in exchange for a cooked meal, beers or his services as a landscaper. The house was beginning to look like a completely different place.

As the days whizzed by, its appearance resembled more of a home than a house as it was all coming together at last. Daniel had learnt how to lay a new wood floor throughout the downstairs, he had fitted and installed the kitchen worktops, cupboards and appliances and, with the help of my dad, new radiators and a central heating system instead of blow heaters. No longer did the house smell old and musty, instead fresh paint filled the air, making it feel new and clean.

We had set a date to move in: the first Sunday in October 1999, after a weekend of moving everything out of storage and into the home. Boxes full of photos, clothes, crockery and utensils for the kitchen and everything we could physically package up and take to the house we could. Rather than try cooking a meal for dinner as well as trying to move in, my parents offered to cook us one last Sunday roast so once we had finished dropping everything off, we could go home and sleep for the first time in our new beds, in our new rooms and new house. It felt like the last supper. I was super excited to be moving out, as I am sure Daniel was, but in a way, my parents had been my rock through everything and now I was cutting my lifeline to become independent and start to be the best parents for our darling Jack.

With a full stomach, we helped load the dishwasher with the dishes, cleared the table and said our goodbyes. How exciting, the first night in our new home. The drive was only five minutes as our house was less than half a mile from my parents. Before we approached the turning for the road, a fire engine zoomed ahead of us, lights flashing and sirens on full alert.

I turned to Daniel who was driving. 'Imagine if we had done all of that work and then the house was on fire.' I laughed as though it was a stupid thing to suggest.

'Don't say that,' he said. 'I think I would cry. All that hard work ruined.'

He turned into the road following the fire engine as if we were an escort vehicle. *Surely not*, I thought, *the same road? That's a coincidence.* We only managed to get halfway down the road as the fire engine continued. We were stopped by four men in safety jackets and helmets, waving their hands above their head and telling us to wind down our window.

'Sorry, mister, you can't come down here. There's been a burst water pipe.' He went to back away from the car so we could turn around.

'But we live here. Is it bad?' Daniel kept the car still, shouting back to the man.

'Yeah, bad, mate. All the houses are under water, halfway up the first floor and it's pouring in.' He backed away for a second time, telling us to park our car at the top of the street and walk down.

I looked at Daniel. I couldn't quite believe it. Our house was under water? Surely this couldn't be happening. All our furniture, my car. *Oh my gosh, my car,* I suddenly thought. In a panic, Daniel parked his car on the side of the road at the top of the hill, pulling Jack from his car seat in the back and grabbing my handbag. We made our way quickly down the road to where our house was. We couldn't even get close, the row of car park spaces where I had parked my car was under water. I could only see the top half of my silver Renault Clio. Emergency services were doing their best to pump the water out of the area and into drains further up the street, but the force of the burst pipe was too much, and it was having very little effect. Our neighbours were in a panic. The water was up to their waists, and they were wading through the water to try to rescue all their belongings. Our next door neighbours were on their honeymoon. All I kept thinking was their wedding presents would be on the floor in their front room all damaged and wet.

'Holy shit, our house,' was all Daniel could say. He looked on in sheer astonishment, placing his hand over his mouth and stroking his chin as if to muster what to do next. I couldn't believe it; our beautiful house would be trashed inside. I grabbed my phone from my bag, calling my dad. I didn't know if it would help but he had a pond pump, maybe that would help us to get the water out of the house once the surge was under control. In a panic, I always called him.

'Dad, our house, our house, it's been flooded!' It was all I could say.

'I'm on my way. Be there in five.' He slammed down the phone. I then dialled again but this time calling Daniel's dad. Two hands were better than one, right? Even if it was buckets, we needed all the help we could get.

'David, our house has been flooded.' He could hear the panic in my voice.

'Flooded? Okay, give us ten minutes. I'll get my boots on and be over.' He did the same and slammed the phone down.

The neighbour opposite us, John, started to make his way over to us. He had fishing trousers on so was keeping most of the water off his clothes and was in emergency rescue mode.

'Daniel, Rose, it looks like the water is in all the houses. It's seeped in both the front and the back doors and is now about halfway up the walls. A mixture of sewerage and rainwater caused it to burst and it's going to take a while to clear. Stay that side of the wall and as soon as the fire brigade have managed to bring the water levels down a little, we can get into the houses and start to pump. All the children are upstairs at number 60 and are watching Disney, completely oblivious to everything that it is going on, so if you want Jack to go up there, my wife can watch him whilst we get to work.' John was lovely; a big, friendly and bubbly gentleman. He was clearly one step ahead of all of us.

'Do they think it will take long to clear?' Daniel asked him. The dark night sky was now filled with blue and red flashing lights from the fire engines.

'We aren't sure. They think thirty minutes or so. The pipe is right under the underpass, past the street. They've managed to stop the burst up there, so it's just getting rid of all the water here as we're at the lowest point where it's all gathering.' John seemed to have asked all the right questions from the emergency services teams and was updating everyone else.

171

Both my dad and Daniel's dad came running round the corner in a panic. They must have been stopped by the emergency services as well, parking their cars at the top of the street and running down to help us. Out of breath and looking flustered, they both had their hands on their hips, ready and waiting to spring into action.

'I can't believe it,' my dad said as he hugged Jack and me. 'Have you managed to get inside yet? I hope there isn't too much damage and the doors and windows have shielded a lot of the water.'

'Nope, we can't get in yet. The water is too high now. Our neighbour told us that they are trying to clear it enough so we can walk to the house and get access but, at the moment, it's still too high. The longer we leave it sitting in all that dirty water, the more damage there's going to be to the house.'

Daniel was watching the emergency services rushing back and forth helplessly waiting to get to our house. 'We're insured, aren't we?'

The only saving grace was that I had organised all the house and contents insurance as soon as we got the keys in case someone caused damage to the house whilst undergoing all the renovations. Little did I know that this was going to happen. It still meant us starting all over again and having to redo what damage had been done. Thank goodness we weren't inside as we may have been trapped upstairs.

'I just can't believe it,' my dad said watching all the commotion. 'Literally the day you were supposed to move in. You both have all the luck, don't you?'

We all looked on in disbelief. The emergency services team waded over to us. By now, the water was down to just above knee height and was being pumped away quite quickly.

A short stocky man dressed in waterproof overalls started to explain what was happening. 'We've managed to stop the surge of water to the area and isolated the broken pipe. They're still working on repairing it but at least we can now work on getting the water in the area back down the drains. It should be safe now to enter your properties although you will have noticed the water on the outside against the front and back doors is being held back so as soon as you open them, more water will gush in. Just be prepared for this. Unfortunately, by the time we were called in, the properties already seemed to have suffered water damage and the smell isn't pleasant. I would suggest you take pictures wherever you can and submit them to your insurance companies as soon as possible.' He seemed to be apologising like it was his pipe that had burst. It wasn't his fault, but it was frustrating, nonetheless.

'John, would Rachel mind taking Jack with all the other children in the square for us?' I called over to my neighbour and took him up on his offer for his wife to watch Jack for us. 'I'll only be a short while, but I just want to see what's what in the house and clear a few things if I can before Jack touches anything. Thanks for offering,' I said as I tried walking over to him to give him Jack, but it was like trying to walk when in a swimming pool. The dirty, smelly water swirled around my jeans and my now soaked through trainers and socks.

Jack gave me a little wave as John took him across from the underwater green from our house. The four of us made our way slowly over to the house, unsure as to what we would find. The water was halfway up the front door and pushing to get through. As Daniel pushed his keys into the lock, he wriggled them around forcefully. He couldn't help the pressure as the door flung open and the outside water poured in, joining the water already filling the hallway and kitchen.

Daniel's dad had a large empty bucket and my dad had a pond pump, but by the time we came in, it was too late. The water had already stained the walls in the house and had made dirty brown lines along all the freshly decorated walls. The laminate flooring that we had laid weeks before was soaked through. You could already see parts that were rippled and damaged. There were thick, grimy lines across all the kitchen cupboard doors and against the washing machine. All the cardboard boxes that we had carried in earlier were either floating around or the heavier ones were soggy and falling apart.

'Oh no, all our photographs and albums. They're in that box, it's ruined!' I cried out.

'Quick, let's get that one upstairs so it can start to dry out. Open the box and get the contents out if you can, Rose.' Daniel gently pushed me in the direction of the box. I was devastated, all the hard work and effort that everyone had put in were ruined. What little belongings we had were wrecked. Yet another setback to try to get it all re-done.

The sofa was brown and stained. Instead of the house smelling of fresh paint and air fresheners or candles, it now smelt like it did the day when we first viewed it. I took all the albums and photos upstairs quickly, hoping they hadn't got too wet or ruined. I ran back downstairs to see what else we could rescue. Daniel was standing with his hands on his hips just looking at all the mess. I could see he was thinking what to do next. Even if we pumped water out of the house, there was nowhere to pump it to as the water outside was just as high. I started getting all the largest pots and pans out of the cupboard so I could pick up some of the water and throw it down the sink but even the sinks were gurgling and bubbling away. The toilet water had risen to the brim.

Before long, the water outside was down to around three to four inches in depth, barely over our front step. The pond pump and the larger buckets were all ready to start clearing inside into outside. As I opened the door and peered out into the street, the sky was dark, only lit by the streetlights. What water was left looked like a shimmering pond. The emergency services were starting to pack their hose pipes away and clear up, ready to leave — their jobs were done. Everyone's doors in the small square we lived in were open and I could see all our neighbours rushing around, trying to salvage whatever they could, just like we were. It now meant we were going to have to redecorate, replace the entire downstairs floor and potentially replace the sofa and some of the contents in the boxes.

Always trying to see the positives in everything, my dad turned to me. 'Hey, the good thing is you got insurance. They'll cover you and they're normally quite quick.' He could see I was clearly upset. 'Come here, you.' He pulled me into him and gave me a big hug, wrapping his huge arms around me. 'We can fix it,' he added as he squeezed me. I guess, as long as no one was hurt, the main thing was that the house and its contents could be fixed. They were just belongings.

It took us well over an hour to clear most of the water and get down to the squelchy wooden floor. I had taken lots of pictures of the before and after state of the house. Thanking both our dads for helping us clear anything and at the drop of a hat, I walked over to rescue our son from John and Rachel's house. By this time, it was almost midnight.

Their house seemed less frantic than ours. Some of the water was still in their front room but the giggle of all the children upstairs and some of our other neighbours in their kitchen chatting and drinking tea, made it all seem a lot less dramatic than we were making it out to be. They didn't seem to care that their furniture was ruined or that their walls needed redoing, nor that there was a dirty, stench of a smell in the air.

'Oh, hey Rose. Fancy a cuppa?' Rachel said. She had Jack resting on her hip, carrying him around like a baby kangaroo. He was still bright eyed and wide awake, smiling and giggling at anyone that showed him the slightest bit of attention and boy did he love all the fuss and attention.

'No, I'm all good, but thanks so much for the offer. I'm shattered. I think I'm going to get Jack settled and then head off to bed myself.' Rather than worry myself anymore, I decided to get showered and change into dry, clean clothes, go to bed and worry about the state of the house in the morning. The first night in our new home was supposed to be special. Our first time that we could really be together and enjoy our space.

Instead of a romantic night, I managed to get Jack to sleep in his cot almost straight away and then Daniel and I cuddled up together. Normally if I brushed his side with my bare breasts or wrapped my legs around his muscular thighs, it would start us touching each other and eventually lead to sex. Not this night. I think we were both exhausted and reserved ourselves to just a nice, comfortable, cuddled up sleep. At least we were both safe…

Waking up the following morning was like waking up to the aftermath of a storm. Planks of laminated wood flooring were bubbled and lying all over the place. The smell was awful, and everything needed a good wipe down to clean it. I immediately opened every window and door in the house, not only to let it dry out but to let some fresh air in. It was cold but I didn't care. Rather than start to clear the house and rip up all the flooring, I made myself and Daniel a cup of tea and coffee and we sat at the dining room table, our feet resting on the dirty chairs, just looking at all the mess around us.

'Where do we start?' I said blowing my tea to cool it down.

'Dunno.' Daniel took a sip of his coffee then returned to looking around the room. We both looked at each other and sighed. Another nightmare in what we thought was finally going to be our big break.

We now appeared to be back to square one. Clear and clean the house, wait for the insurance company to confirm what they were going to cover and for the foreseeable future we had to almost live upstairs until all the work had been re-done.

Chapter 19

Letting My Hair Down

The last six months seemed to be the longest six months of my life. Not only did it drag, but it also seemed to be filled with problems and issues. All we did was work to pay for bills that were sky high and rocketing. The house insurance covered some of the work to be done on the house after the flood, but it didn't cover everything, so we had to save all over again. We were tired, broken and disheartened. As a couple, we were feeling the stresses and strains of adulthood.

I had always battled with my inner self, but I felt it more so recently. I needed a constant supply of things happening around me and events to focus on otherwise, if my mind became idle, it would start to go off track and I was dangerous. It was normal for me to fear the worst scenario in any situation. If I had an illness, it would be thinking that it was life threatening, making myself sad that I only had a limited time left on this planet. Despite me having these thoughts and battling with my mind regularly, I very rarely showed it. To anyone who knew me, I was bubbly, outgoing and extremely confident. No one would have had the slightest inkling how I really felt and all my insecurities. I always thought I wasn't pretty enough, not smart enough or not good enough and a general feeling that everyone would be better off if I wasn't here half the time.

My only escape from feeling like this and all the pressures and strains from life was alcohol. When I was drunk or drinking, it was the only time I could relax, and block out the reality of such responsibility. It gave me an excuse to fuck up, to have an excuse for my behaviour and an alibi that if I didn't like how I had behaved then I could just say I couldn't remember what I did. This only worked for so long because the more drunk I became, the more I couldn't remember; it wasn't something I was making up. The mental block I experienced when drunk was scary, but it didn't put me off. The more I drank, the more it was an escapism. I couldn't just have one or two drinks; I would drink and drink till I was comatose.

A night out drinking and getting drunk would normally end in me passing out or causing a huge drama. Either way, I wouldn't remember it in the morning and the blackouts were the worst part. I could never remember where I was, what had happened or who I was with. Relying on everyone around me to recap the events that unfolded during the night. I knew I had a big issue with drinking but just how much of an issue, I couldn't tell. I just carried on regardless. It was irresponsible really, a cry for help maybe. Everyone around me found it funny apart from Daniel. He was the one who was subjected to the aftermath of my ridiculous actions. He had the patience of a saint. Time and time again I messed up. No matter how smashed I was, he was there for me. He picked me up and fixed all my broken pieces.

A week into moving into the new house, now with half the floor ripped up, cupboard doors off and drying in the garden along with a damaged sofa, my mum offered to have Jack whilst we went out for a few drinks with friends. I said I would drive, that way we could leave when we wanted, and I could then pick up Jack early in the morning. We deserved a night out from our busy schedules, what with the house, work and looking after Jack.

Our plan was to meet everyone at the only nightclub and bar in Bracknell there was: Frisco Jerry's. If I parked in the car park outside, I could have one or two drinks and then drive home. Frisco Jerry's was a great place, an open bar that spanned the entire length of the room, three snooker tables and a dance floor at the very end. Right next door was Ardennes, an old underground building that had been turned into a nightclub. Circular by design with a staircase that followed the curve round the edge and a round bar right in the middle. The music was so loud, you left with your ears ringing and drinks were on offer, normally buy one get one free. It was always so busy and so many people we knew went. Every Friday and Saturday you were guaranteed to bump into one of your friends. Also a downside as there was nearly always a fight. Too much testosterone, alcohol and boys trying to win over a girl's attention.

By the time we had dropped off Jack and got to the club, it was 7:30 p.m. Our friends had commandeered the middle snooker table and had drinks ready and waiting for us. A bottle of alcopops for me and a beer for Daniel. As per usual, I was wearing something revealing. I had a sequined short skirt on that barely covered my bottom and a crocheted top on; my breasts overflowing, my push up bra making it irresistible for any of the boys not to catch a glimpse at every opportunity they could. My choice of clothing hid all my insecurities about my body, my image or how I viewed myself.

'Loving the shoes,' Becky said to me as she wandered over, handed me my drink and hugged me like she hadn't seen me in years. Being so short, I would always find the highest high heels I could. If I didn't, I looked so short standing next to Daniel, who was without fail, always the tallest. Daniel being more reserved than me and a lot quieter just sipped at his beer, happy to be out and with all our friends. I, on the other hand, had finished the bottle in less than ten minutes and was off ordering another. They were going down way too well. *I'll leave the car here*, I thought, *and collect it in the morning*. It was my turn to play pool, but I needed another drink, so we ordered a round for the table. Striped ball after striped ball went down. I was winning. Of course I was winning. Miss Competitive was in the room and the more I drank, the more confident and louder I got.

'Honey, calm down, don't you think you've had enough or are you not driving now?' Daniel said to me in front of all our friends. Well, that was the first mistake right there. Tell me not to do something and I would do it, or make me look stupid in front of everyone and I was your worst enemy.

'No, I don't think I've had enough,' I replied. 'In fact, I think I need another. Excuse me!' I clicked my fingers at one of the bar staff and held up my current empty bottle. 'Another bottle please. Scrap that. Another two please.' I was slurring my words but my response to Daniel and my actions made everyone laugh. It only encouraged me all the more.

'Here we go,' Daniel muttered under his breath, but it didn't stop me. I continued.

By the end of the night, I had made an absolute spectacle of myself, but I had danced, laughed, had a huge amount of fun and just like Teresa no cares were given, least of all from me. Daniel had made numerous attempts to calm me down and stop me drinking but it hadn't worked. Like a naughty schoolgirl, I ignored him even more. My actions resembled that of the aftermath of a tornado; I caused chaos and destruction wherever I went and with anyone in my path. I upset people, my mouth was out of control, and it caused arguments, not just with us but with other couples too. As the club was closing, I grabbed my coat from the cloakroom, went to the toilets and stood at the entrance waiting for everyone to join me.

'All right, darlin'?'

I looked around, wondering if that was aimed at me or someone else.

'You off home?'

Sure enough, it was directed at me. A dark, short haired boy was walking towards me. I had no idea who he was and I had never seen him before in my life. Due to the state I was in, I couldn't really make out his facial features in detail.

'Nice pins,' he said by the time he reached me.

I said nothing, I could barely string a sentence together let alone chat to him.

'What's your number or do you fancy coming home with me tonight?' In true 1990s fashion, he was wearing black jeans, white socks, Reebok classics and a Benetton T-shirt.

'No thanks,' I said waiting for the others to join me.

'Come on, you can't be shy. I've been watching you dance all night in that short skirt.' He went to slap my bottom, but I turned sideways so he missed. That had made him mad, so he grabbed my wrist and went to start shouting at me when Daniel appeared from nowhere.

'Get your hands off her.' He shoved the guy to the side by the wall and they stood about an inch apart staring at each other.

'Daniel, don't worry about it. Let's go.' I was way too drunk to deal with a drunken brawl.

Before long, all our friends, one by one, stood behind Daniel like a team of backup and the same happened for the other boy until there was a crowd of twenty something people waiting to have a brawl. The two bouncers from the entrance of the club raced over and split everyone up. They knew us well so tried to diffuse the situation and asked us all to politely leave.

'Fuck's sake, Daniel. I had that. I said no.' I pottered along in my heels to the car. Everyone else in a trail following us.

'Oh, you did, did you? Well, it didn't look like that from where I was.' He tried to keep up with the speed at which I was teetering along.

'Yep, more than capable.' My independence getting the better of me once again. I hated people doing anything for me.

'And you are not driving. We can get the bus home.' He tried to grab the keys from my hand, but I snatched them away from him.

'I most definitely am. If you don't want to get in, don't. But I've only had a couple and we'll be home in five minutes.' In my head, I had sobered up. The fresh air hit my face as soon as I left the club, and I didn't feel drunk at all. At that precise moment, I felt like I could do anything, do it well and with precision.

Reluctantly, Daniel got in the car. I think it was the lesser of two evils. He knew I was going to drive regardless, and it was better that he was in the car with me. The car stuttered as I started the engine, the misty windscreen started to clear, and I made my way carefully out of the car park. It was all going so well. I then freaked. I saw another car's headlights in the rear-view mirror. Thinking it was the police, my foot hit the accelerator, my arms and hands not really responding to the speed of my feet and instead of turning left on the roundabout, the car hit the kerb in front of me. It leapt over the top and straight through the middle of the mound. I panicked, the adrenaline pumping. I glanced at Daniel, he looked mad, really mad. With one hand holding the handle above the passenger door window and the other clutching his seatbelt, he started shouting at me.

'Stop the car, Rose, stop the car!'

I thought he was going to grab the handbrake and pull it up. I immediately pulled into the wrong turning and stopped by the kerb. My tyre felt popped.

'You are out of control. What are you doing? What on earth has got into you? Get out of the car now and let's get a cab home.' He tried to reason with me but the stubborn young lady that I was, I refused to get out of the car.

185

'I'm fine. Look, we'll be home in five. Shut the door and let's go.' I tried convincing him I was fine, but he looked like he was ready to blow. He unclicked his seatbelt and got out of the car. I had a feeling he was going to attempt to get me out but as soon as he slammed the door shut, my foot hit the accelerator once again and the car hurtled off with me still behind the steering wheel. I didn't even look back to see where he was, but I had every intention of driving to the bus and taxi rank and waiting for him there. I could then convince him to get into the car for the second time. I knew I shouldn't have driven off the minute I left him, but I carried on regardless.

There was a long carriageway. I just had to drive along that road, a steep, sharp bend and then the station was on the other side. I would be there before Daniel would. I picked up speed, although I wasn't quite sure how fast I was going because I had double vision. I could see four dials where there should have been two and the road markings were all blurred. As I approached the sharp bend at the end, suddenly something or someone appeared from out of nowhere and darted across the road. It startled me. I tried yanking the wheel quickly before I hit the object, but it was too late. There was a deafening whack against the car. I lost control, the tyres clipped the kerb, the steering wheel span from underneath me and the car jolted forwards skidding across the two lanes and another almighty bang…

The next thing I remember was waking, curled up in a foetus type position, freezing cold on a concrete floor. Where was I? There was a stabbing sensation above my eyes and I had a banging headache. I reached up to touch the part of my head that hurt and realised I was bleeding. My nose in agony, it felt like I had broken it. I was in a small dark room with bars, furnished with nothing else other than a thin mattress bed. Was I in a police cell? It definitely wasn't a hospital; I knew that much as I looked around me.

'Oh, she's awake.' A policewoman walked past the bars and stopped just outside.

'I'm sorry, where am I?' I raised my head off the ground and tried to get up from the floor and onto the bed.

'You're at Bracknell police station. You were brought in a couple of hours ago after crashing your car into a lamp post, but we thought we would let you sleep it off as you weren't making much sense. You were clearly a danger to yourself and everyone else on the road. You're lucky you didn't kill someone out there tonight. You have one phone call, but you aren't going home till the morning, I'm afraid.' She searched for the keys to the cell in her pocket and proceeded to open the door, walking me to the phone hanging on the wall in the corridor.

Wow, I had fucked up. How did I explain this to Daniel? He would be fuming with me. I picked up the receiver and started to dial our home number. 0… 1… 3… 4… 4… There was a short pause followed by a ringing tone. I dreaded him picking up.

'Hello,' said a sleepy but deep voice.

'Daniel, I've fucked up. I think I crashed the car and am being held at Bracknell police station. They're holding me overnight.' I rushed the words out of my mouth as quickly as I could so he didn't have much time to tell me off.

'You're what? Are you okay? I've been wondering where the hell you were. I thought you had gone to your mum and dad's. I waited and waited but you didn't come back.'

I went to reply but the phone made three loud beeps and then the line went silent.

'That's it, I'm afraid. Back to your cell you go. You'll be released at 7:30 a.m. and if you're a good girl and stay quiet, we might let you go at 7 a.m. instead.' She was sarcastic, but followed me back to my cell, locking the door behind me.

This was scary in a whole new way. What had I got myself into? What was more concerning was that I couldn't remember a single thing. From leaving the club to how I got here, the whole thing was a blur. I needed help from Daniel to pull the pieces of the puzzle together, but my fear was that he wouldn't talk to me. My thoughts turned to Jack. I needed to pick him up in the morning. If I had crashed my car, where was it now, how bad was it? What would I say to my parents? I knew I was a grown up, well, supposed to be, and I had moved out, but it wasn't very big of me to go and do this.

I sat in the cell, facing the corner, hugging my knees, pulling them tight in against my chest. I was freezing, still wearing the clothes from last night. I shivered and had goosebumps all over my body. It served me right really, but I couldn't sleep, thinking about what I could have possibly done. Although I liked the feeling of drinking and becoming drunk, I didn't like the feeling of blackouts. It was like a complete mental block, erased from my memory, unable to recall any events that happened within a certain timeframe. What if I had hurt someone? How would Jack cope without a mother or Daniel without a partner? I could have lost him, or I could still lose him. Then what?

For most people, their body consumes the amount of alcohol that their body can cope with until they get to the point where they can't stand, they feel ill, or they can't speak. My body, instead, decides to shut down and pass out or have a complete memory blank. I don't seem to suffer from hangovers either so the desire to put me off having a heavy night is almost non-existent. The only trouble is that it wasn't responsible as a parent or as a girlfriend so I tried to take that into consideration but the minute a drink hit my lips it was like I just couldn't resist. I couldn't say no, it was an addiction, a drug to me and no matter what anyone said or did, it simply made me worse.

The hours in the cell dragged by. I found myself tormented by the inability to remember anything. I had flashes of certain images but nothing that I could piece together. I made a pact with myself to calm down, to act responsibly and take control of the matter. As soon as I was out, I was going to promise to Daniel that I would limit myself to drinks the next time I went out. Maybe there wasn't a next time that we would be going out, but I had to show him that I could do it.

I stood up. I sat down. I paced the room; it was only about two metres by two metres so I could do roughly seven or eight steps before turning around again. I noticed the eyesight in my right was greater than in my left if I kept shutting one at a time and stared at a mark on the wall for far too long with all sorts of thoughts filtering through my mind. I had an attention span of five minutes at the best of times so being in a small room with me, myself and I and nothing for entertainment was making me worse. The alcohol was wearing off, and my head was banging. I had clearly hit my head last night and my neck was stiff from the impact of whatever I had hit. I was in a sorry state, but it could have been a lot worse. I could have hit and killed someone. What was I thinking?

Finally, the lady police officer approached my cell once again and asked me to follow her to the desk opposite the entrance of the police station. 'If you walk with me, we can give you some of your belongings back and get you to sign a disclaimer,' she said in an abrupt fashion.

'Okay.' I just did as I was told. I was clearly in the wrong here and didn't want to make matters worse. I hung my head in pure shame. Another police officer was behind the tall desk and was writing something down on a piece of paper. He turned it round so I could read it.

'If you could sign at the bottom, please, to confirm that you are taking back your belongings that we temporarily held. We have one mobile phone, a small black clutch bag, a purse and a set of keys. Is there anything else you feel is missing?' He looked up for me to answer.

'Erm, no, I think that's it.' I took the pen and signed my name. I noticed some blood on my hand — presumably from my head or nose or both.

'We took your fingerprints last night and you waived your right for a legal representative, pleading guilty to the offence of dangerous driving whilst under the influence of alcohol. Is that correct?' Again, he looked at me to confirm.

'I, erm, I don't really remember but I guess so, yes.' I was so confused. What happened last night? What did I do?

'Finally, you met with the on-duty nurse, she cleaned your face for you, but we felt the need to detain you overnight so that you could sober up and were not a danger to anyone else before letting you go. You will be notified in due course of your court date. Do you understand everything I have said to you?' His face was emotionless. He must have to say the same thing to people daily and must be sick of dealing with idiots like me.

'Yes, I do.' I touched my head where it was throbbing and nodded at him solemnly.

'Okay, your car is in car park space six. You are free to leave.' He took the paper and pen back from me and turned around to carry on his duties, leaving me to go home. Only I didn't want to go home. I didn't want to see Daniel as shameful as I was, but I was desperate to see my baby boy. At least he would give me a big, loving cuddle. I didn't deserve it at all.

I put my purse in my bag and threw it over my shoulder. Keys in hand, I walked to the car park to find my car, hoping to remember something from last night. As I walked to space six, my face dropped. The silver Renault Clio that I drove out at the beginning of last night was not the same car that was parked in front of me. Instead, there was a small silver car with the whole front bonnet completely caved in, the radiator was exposed, both the front wheels were damaged and facing outwards, and the windscreen smashed. It would be a miracle if I was able to drive that home. I tried opening the door, but it was a struggle. The edge was stuck on the side panel that had been bent inwards. I sat in the driving seat with a heavy heart, put my keys in the ignition and placed my bag onto the passenger seat. The steering was extremely hard, but I managed to pull away. I couldn't really see out of the windscreen with a clear view, so I had to hang my head out of the wound down window to check the traffic at each junction.

Tears rolled down my face the whole way home. I was disgusted with myself.

As I arrived home, pulling into the street, there were no free car parking spaces, so I had to drive into the block of garages and park in front of ours. Stiffly, I got out of the car, my neck and back ached, I had the headache of all headaches and a gash right across the ridge of my nose. It was still only 8:02 a.m. so I tried my best to be quiet, but the birds were still chirping in the trees as I shamefully walked back to the path leading to our front door. Quietly turning the keys in the lock, I was stunned to find Daniel filling up the kettle at the kitchen sink as he turned, his eyes meeting mine.

'Oh my God, look at your face, you complete idiot. What were you thinking?' His tone was enough to say it all. It was worse than when my parents used to tell me off. I knew I was in the wrong, I knew I had fucked up in a big way.

'I know, I know.' I hung my head in shame.

'What the hell happened? One minute you were there and the next minute you drove off and I couldn't stop you. I was so worried wondering where you had gone or what had happened when you didn't come home. I'm so tired. I haven't slept worrying about you.' He seemed more concerned about my welfare than giving me a hard time.

'I don't know... I... My head hurts and my nose... None of it makes sense. I can't remember. I don't even remember leaving the

club. What the hell happened?' I walked into the downstairs toilet to look in the small, wall hung mirror at why my head hurt so much and found that I had a deep cut on the side of my forehead, a cut on the bridge of my nose and my lip was swollen from what looked like my teeth going through it. I had a quick flashback to last night and images of me skidding round the sharp bend, trying to avoid something or someone and crashing into a lamp post; the radiator smouldering as if it had been pierced by the bumper. That would explain the bonnet of the car and the injuries I had sustained but after that I still couldn't remember much. I walked back out holding my head. I sat on the bottom step of the stair and began to cry. Daniel joined me on the step and held me tight.

'Rose, as much as I'm mad with you, I'm worried. Are you okay? I don't understand what gets into you. You could have killed yourself, then what would Jack and I do?' His face just as emotional as mine. Why, after everything I had done, did he still want to help me, to save me from myself? I didn't deserve him at all.

'I'm going to lose my license. You know that, don't you? I can't believe I was so stupid. Back to walking everywhere and getting the bus.' I was angry with myself.

'We'll manage, as long as you're okay, but you need to sort your drinking out. I can't cope with you behaving like that when we go out. It's embarrassing.' He placed his hands on both sides of my head and pulled it down to look at my wound. 'I think that should have had stitches. You must have taken quite a hit. What state is the car in?' he asked.

194

'It's not good. I think it'll be written off.' At this point, I just wanted to get showered and changed and to pick up Jack. I would think about the car later. My mum would worry when she saw my face. Maybe it was better that Daniel picked up Jack and made up an excuse as to why I hadn't. Daniel agreed to pick up Jack and I went upstairs in the bathroom to make myself half respectable again.

I stood in the hot, steamy shower; the water running through my hair and onto my face. I winced each time it touched my cuts and bruises but the more it hurt, the more I wanted it to hurt to teach me a lesson. I liked the pain. I liked the feeling that my body encountered, it made me feel alive. I felt like my body had to experience pain to repair itself. Punishment for my actions.

Although I cried from time to time, I never really broke down, but on this occasion, my body was screaming. I was shaking in pain. Not the pain from the accident but the pain from how I was feeling inside. Things always got on top of me. It was my way of blocking out the real world. Things always seemed a good idea at the time but afterwards I had to wake up at some point and take responsibility for the actions I had taken. This not only affected me, but it also affected everyone around me: Jack, Daniel, my parents. The inconvenience of not being able to drive again or have a car and rely on others to get me where I needed to be, work, Jack to his babysitter and so on. I was such a disappointment.

I closed my eyes, letting the water run over my naked body, placing my hands on the tiled wall either side of me and letting everything out. The water began to run cold giving me a sharp awakening. Bringing me back to reality and telling me to get myself together.

195

Daniel and Jack would be back soon, and I needed to be respectable. I needed to be the mother and girlfriend they both needed. Getting myself washed, dried and changed, I made my way downstairs just as they both walked in the door. Daniel talking away to Jack and him laughing. They had a cute way of talking away to each other that made me dote on them in such a loving way. By boys, my entire world, they deserved so much more than the person I sometimes was.

Chapter 20

Sand, Sea and Sex

Although I wouldn't have changed it for the world, our life was chaotic. Daniel and I had worked so hard to give Jack the start in life with everything he needed. As a couple, we hadn't had a chance to enjoy our time together, as normal couples would. The car crash incident hadn't helped. The court date hanging over our heads was causing a strain on our relationship, and we needed some downtime. He suggested we take a short, cheap break away in the sunshine and leave Jack with our parents for the week. I was reluctant. It sounded great, and I understood why he wanted us to get away but the thought of not being with Jack for a week was tough.

'He'll be fine. It's only a week and Jack will love being with his nan and grandad.' Daniel pleaded with me to consider.

'I feel bad. Can't we take him with us?' I tried to negotiate with him, but I think he had his heart set on us getting away, just the two of us.

'Rose, come on. We deserve this. Just me, you and some sunshine.' His eyes beamed at me; he had a way of convincing me to give in.

'I suppose, but where were you thinking?' Expecting him to say somewhere close.

'Spain, Greece, Portugal. Where do you fancy?' He seemed excited.

Daniel drove us into town to visit the travel agents and once again were limited to a budget on where we could go. All the places we wanted to go were way too expensive and out of our price range. In the end, our options took us to a budget hotel in Zakynthos, Greece. I was sceptical but my mum and dad were so excited of the thought of having Jack for the week that they had booked it as holiday from work and had planned to do lots of things with him. It made me feel less anxious knowing he would be distracted from us being away and would thoroughly love it.

Nervously, we booked it. I shopped for some summer clothes to wear, we borrowed some suitcases and counted down the days to flying. The closer it got, the more excited Daniel got. It was like he had never been on holiday before. The night before we were due to leave, I couldn't sleep at all. Thinking about what I would do if Jack needed me and I was so far away from home. I had to push all those thoughts to the back of my mind and enjoy it, to hold Daniel and I together. I would make it a holiday to remember, one never to forget and for him to know again the reason why he loved me so much at the beginning.

I had worked out and trimmed down to look incredible in swimwear, for Daniel to have the most stunning girlfriend that every man wanted and that he had. I carefully organised all of Jack's clothes, toys and everything he needed whilst we were away. We dropped him off at my parents and I felt like it was the last time I was going to see him. I couldn't stop kissing and cuddling him, not wanting to leave Jack behind so eventually I stood up.

'If I don't go now, I never will. I love you, baby.' I squeezed him tightly, locking that memory in my heart forever and passed him over to my mum.

My dad helped us get our cases in the car and drove us to the airport. London Heathrow was only around forty minutes away and whilst Daniel chatted the whole way to my dad, I stared out the window, watching the other cars on the road. I focused on seeing my baby again in seven days' time when we returned.

Heathrow was crammed with holidaymakers. It was the first time I had been away on holiday, not only on my own but without my parents. Two firsts in one go. I had to just sit back and relax and enjoy the time away now. Dropping off our bags, we made our way to the bar. We had a couple of drinks each before the screens told us to make our way to our gate to board the plane. I felt like I was missing something, like a part of me had been left behind where normally I would be carrying Jack on my side and showing him the big planes out of the window. I could imagine his little face full of excitement and pointing to show me.

'Switch off,' I heard Daniel say to me. He grabbed my hand and led the way. Easier said than done but I had to make sure I didn't spoil his week away as well as mine. I squeezed his hand back and apologised for being distant.

The plane journey was better than expected. I wasn't too bad with flying, but I wasn't the best. Having a smoother journey meant I could finally sit back, watch the blanket of cotton-looking clouds below us and look forward to landing. It was time to concentrate on Daniel and me. Putting the spark back into our relationship that sometimes we had neglected because life had just made us so busy that we had forgotten about us time.

After he had had his one-night fling with that girl, it had knocked my confidence for six, but it was never mentioned again. I didn't want him to think of what he had done with someone else other than me. What I had to do now was to make sure he didn't even want to look at another woman besides me and that meant being the perfect girlfriend, a seductress, giving in to his every desire. I swigged back another sip of the vodka and coke I had in front of me, kicked off my shoes and pushed my seat to recline as far as it would go. With my right hand, I pushed the arm rest so that it was in the upright position and tried to get Daniel's attention.

He was drifting off to sleep with his headphones wrapped around his neck loosely. I ran my hand first down his arm and then across to his thigh. Without moving, he opened one eye and looked at me. At first, he looked like he was startled but then he looked at me as if he was wondering what I was doing. I moved it further over to reach his cock. He opened both eyes and shot me a panicked look. I just smiled and continued to rub it up and down whilst making sure no one else on the same row as us could see.

'Rose, what the fuck are you doing?' he whispered like an adult telling a naughty child off.

'What do you think I'm doing?' I tried to wink unsuccessfully, smiling and giggling quietly. 'What do you want me to do?' I was trying to be seductive. I moved my body towards his and pulled my blanket over him, covering my arm as I played more aggressively.

'Seriously, you can't do that on here.' He found it funny but wasn't playing along with my game.

'Why not?' I asked rhetorically.

'I'm not doing this here. People will see.' He genuinely looked concerned that someone would see.

'Okay, so come in the toilet with me. I'll pretend I'm ill, and you can help me. No one will know what's going on.' It was my turn to talk him into something I wanted.

'Have you been drinking?' He reached down to find my arm and to stop me, but I could feel his erection through his jeans. He must have been turned on so why stop me? His hand held mine, but he moved it back to my lap and held it there.

'As much as I want you to do that, you must stop. As soon as we are at the hotel, you can do whatever you want but not on here.' The serious look on his face made me listen, but I was as horny as hell and the more he told me not to, the more I wanted to. I could tell he wanted it too but, on this occasion, I did as I was told and rode out the rest of the journey watching the tiny screen in front of me until we landed. Stopping my urges to play with him seductively.

As soon as we were grounded, we undid our seatbelts, grabbed our bags from the overhead storage, waited in line with all the other passengers to leave the plane until we could leave and walked down the metal stairs onto the airport terminal tarmac. The minute we stepped outside, the humidity hit us. The heat was penetrating, and the sun was so refreshing. Daniel was right, it was good to take a break from reality, to escape the chaotic world around work, children and responsibilities. Still thinking about Jack but also thinking this week would be good for us to reconnect.

'Ah, sunshine,' he said looking at me and smiling. He seemed happy, content, just like he used to when we first met. The stresses and strains of life back home seemed to peel away from him like a second skin. 'Love you,' he said reaching for my hand again. Sometimes I felt that he held my hand like a lifeline.

'Love you too, honey.' I smiled back.

One by one, we were piled onto a hot minibus, back-to-back with the other aircraft passengers, resembling sardines in a can. Everyone sweating and blowing into the air to cool themselves down. The UK weather we had left behind was about twenty degrees cooler. We were driven to the terminal to retrieve our suitcases and then onto our onward journey to the hotel.

I'm not sure what we were expecting. We knew we were on a budget and as long as the room we had was clean and there was a pool that was all that mattered. We were met with over twenty to thirty people standing outside the airport terminal holding sign boards above their heads with names on. Passengers were everywhere, scrambling to find their name on a board so they could get to their destination. Tripping over luggage, we made our way through the hordes of people to the board with our names on, children screaming and running round, mums trying to create some sense of order and the dads thinking how long it would be till they could have a beer.

Not once did Daniel let go of my hand, leading me through the crowds till we reached the coach. He moved both of our cases closer to the man who was loading all the luggage onto the coach before climbing aboard. We sat at the very front, side by side, eager to get to the hotel. One by one, the others joined us until the bus was full. The driver, already in his seat, was reading a book, patiently waiting for each person to get comfortable so he could depart. The last person to step on was a brunette lady, hair tightly pinned up and wearing clothes to resemble an air stewardess: a white shirt with a blue cravat, tightly fitted pencil skirt and high heels. She picked up the microphone attached to the dashboard as soon as the doors abruptly closed behind her. She cleared her throat then spoke.

'Ladies and gentlemen, welcome to Zante. My name is Estelle, and I will be your holiday representative. I hope you have all had a pleasant flight. We will now be on our way to your final destination. We have four drop off points along the way. I will give you warning before we stop so you can collect all your belongings and be ready to leave the coach. First stop is the Amari Hotel, we have the Browne, Murphy and the Sames families and should be there in approximately fifteen minutes. Please enjoy the views until then.' She cut off the microphone, sat on the other front seat on the other side of the aisle to us, crossed her legs and the coach began to move.

I couldn't believe how blue the sky was, not a cloud to be seen. I could feel the heat from the other side of the windows. We passed endless views of open land resembling desert-like scenery with occasional green patches and plants with pretty, pink flowers. The road wound around bends and hills until we reached a town laden with an abundance of stunning white buildings. The coach slowed down, reaching gates that had the metal words 'Amari Resort'. We had arrived. My baby was many miles away, but I was quite excited to see where we were staying. The gates opened, we drove inside and then it stopped again. Estelle stood up, tapped the microphone and began to speak again.

'Okay, we are here. If I could ask the Brownes, Murphys and Sames to please make their way off the coach, the driver will get your cases out for you and walk you to reception. I will be visiting your resort on Monday and Thursday this week but if you have any questions or issues during your stay and would like to get in touch, I am contactable on this number, or the hotel can call me for you.' She handed each family an envelope as they left.

Collecting our bags and making our way to reception, we couldn't wait to dump our bags in the room and jump in the pool. The heat and the journey had made us both hot, tired and uncomfortable.

In less than half an hour, we were checked in, led to our room and free to enjoy the week. Our room was basic, whitewashed walls containing a double bed, a basic cupboard and a dresser and that was it, but we weren't expecting much more. I wasted no time at all to jump on Daniel. There was something about the sunshine that made me more horny than normal and after being turned down on the plane, I took this chance to go for it.

'If I run the shower, do you want to join me before we jump in the pool? I'm desperate to get out of these hot clothes and into my bikini.' I gave Daniel the look I had given him before, hoping to entice him this time. Without getting a yes or no answer from him,

I made my way to the bathroom. It was lined from floor to ceiling with plain white tiles. There was a toilet, sink, a shower head above me and just a hole in the floor to collect the water. Plenty of room for two people to have a shower together.

Not long after I had turned on the shower and removed all my clothing, Daniel joined me, standing in the doorway. He didn't say anything, instead he just stood there looking at my naked body. He was appreciating me with his eyes. I moved over to stand under the water current, each droplet running down my body and dropping from my curves. With both of my hands, I brushed my hair back so the water made my hair wet and ran down my back. I closed my eyes imagining him to still be watching me and becoming increasingly aroused.

I never felt embarrassed or shy of being naked. Especially with Daniel. He had seen me at my best and most definitely seen me at my worst. I felt body confidence was important, if you couldn't be proud of what you have, how could you enjoy being intimate with someone and make the most of it?

I deliberately reached for the soap and lathered it between my hands. My eyes still closed. At first, I started round my neck, then to my shoulders, reaching my armpits, next circling my breasts at length. Taking time to go underneath, cupping the whole breast and then dropping them so they bounced when I let them go. I was even more aroused now, moving my hands to my belly button, my neat, tight stomach, moving down to between my legs, my fingers touching and cleaning every deep part of me. I was caught in the moment, almost carried away. I felt a cold hand join mine and touch my pussy.

I opened my eyes to find Daniel in the shower with me, his head resting on my shoulder and watching both of our hands touch me. I moaned deliciously as he rubbed my vulva. He knew exactly where to touch and how much pressure to apply as though he had years of experience. As if not already wet from the shower, I was soaking, wanting him to keep rubbing me. With my other hand, I reached back to find his already erect cock resting on my back. I took it in my hand and lathered his length till it was really soapy.

He kissed my neck gently, from my hair line to my shoulders until I couldn't take it anymore. I span around to face him. He pushed me against the wall, the water falling above both of our heads as we began kissing passionately; the room steamy from the heat of the shower. Our breathing in time with each other, I felt a tingling feeling all down the back of my head and down my spine. A feeling of pure ecstasy. His cock was pushing against my pussy. He lifted my leg up, wrapped it around his thigh as he pushed deep inside me. He was fucking me hard against the wall, my hands above my head and him cupping and massaging my breasts. We both had our eyes firmly closed. Every time he thrust, I clenched my inner walls, making it tighter and tighter up inside for him, bringing him to cum and me to climax. A whole-body sensation, my toes were sensitive, my cheeks clenching, a pressure building inside that I just couldn't control. I took a deep breath in, our tongues writhing with each other's and then it happened. We both came at the same time, our hearts racing, the release, the feeling of euphoria an orgasm so strong it took my breath away. My legs shook with sensation. Blocking out everything around me, I was completely and utterly caught in the moment. He let go of my other leg after gripping it so hard and had to steady himself with his hand on the wall. His mouth broke free from mine and he took a deep breath.

I couldn't get enough of the sexual tension that Daniel and I had. Each time he left me wanting more. It was like an addiction, a feeling of pure euphoria, a sensation that shook every part of my body each time. I lived for the moments of intimacy with him. No sooner had we had sex, I wanted to go again, orgasm after orgasm.

'You're incredible. Do you know that?' he whispered sensually to me. If anything, I thought he was the incredible one. How did I get so lucky? We were perfectly matched, not only in the bedroom but as a couple, a team. I couldn't think of anyone I would rather be with, even after everything we had been through. Losing him at any moment would be relative to losing a limb, a huge hole in my heart.

Leaving the shower running, he lifted me up and carried me out to the bedroom, throwing me on the bed. Both of us wet but we weren't cold. He began kissing me again, all along my neck like a ravenous animal, his hands wandering all over me. I grabbed his back with both hands, using my nails to dig in and create pain and tension. He kicked his head back as I loosened my grip and moved my hands down to his cock and balls. He was still erect and wanting more. I wrapped my legs back round his body, twisting and pushing him sideways so I could jump on top of him, straddling his waist.

I sat on his cock, impaled and in a sitting up position like riding a horse. The sensation of him deep inside me as I began moving forwards and backwards, clenching his girth up and down as I went. Slow and deep at first, then picking up pace till I could feel him bucking. Staring into his eyes the whole time, I pushed my breasts together, playing with them, pinching my nipples, teasing his view of me by pleasuring my entire body while he groaned in pleasure, his cock being pulled up and down inside me. He felt harder and harder as my insides felt waves of a pulse, a heartbeat in my pussy that exploded, sending a current through my entire body. I could feel him cumming at the same time, both of us soaking wet and dripping from out between us. I collapsed on top of him, us both rapidly breathing, my nipples squashed against his.

I rolled over, gripping the sheets. A huge smile on my face. *If only every day could be like this*, I thought. Our sex was amazing.

We lay next to each other for a moment, catching our breath.

Although we could have spent the whole day in the room, we decided to make the most of the hot rays of sunshine that were piercing through the hotel room windows and changed into our beach attire to lounge by the pool. It felt strange not having Jack around but in a nice way; it was good to enjoy some time together.

The hotel consisted of four blocks of apartments and a small reception area, arranged in a block formation around a central large swimming pool with rows of sun loungers. Next to the pool was an open-air bar that was open from 9 a.m. until 7 p.m. It seemed quite busy. There were more people at the bar than there were sunbathing, or swimming and it seemed mostly adults, where normally there would be children dive bombing into the water or running around screaming. It was basic, but it was all we needed really. We had definitely chosen the right hotel.

Daniel started to roll out his towel along the closest sun lounger but I was eager to head to the bar, being the outgoing person that I was and never turning down a drink.

'Do you fancy a cocktail or a beer?' I said, itching to head over to the bar.

'Yeah, go on then. Pick me anything you think I'll like.' He lay down, stretching out his well-kept body in the sunshine and perched his sunglasses perfectly on his eyes. Wrapping my sarong around my waist, I sauntered off to the bar to join the queue with everyone else.

'Hey, my lovely, how long are you both here for?' a stunning blonde lady asked me. She was one of the other families from the same coach as us, arriving at the same time. 'We're only here for a week, but it's enough to get a bit of sun and to relax. This is Tom and I'm Michelle.' She tapped the guy on the shoulder standing next to her, prompting him to turn around and introduce him to me.

'We're only here a week as well. We've left our little boy at home so a week was all I could stand being away from him. I'm Rose and Daniel is over by the pool. It seems a nice enough place. You look like you've had a cocktail already, what would you recommend?' They seemed a nice, chatty couple and a good distraction from missing home.

'Sex on the Beach, it's amazing.' Both Tom and Michelle laughed. My face made the expression of surprise. A bit more forward than I had been used to, but I liked it.

'The drink, lovely. The drink is called Sex on the Beach.' She laughed again but placed her hand on my shoulder as she did so.

'Oh, the drink. I'm sorry, I thought you…' My naivety caught the best of me and we laughed together. I looked at the bright red cocktail she was holding in her hand. It was in a curvy glass with crushed ice and a slice of pineapple resting on the side. It looked delicious. As I looked up, I caught her glimpsing at the top half of my bikini where my breasts were snuggly squeezed in and overflowing to show off my ample cleavage. She then moved her gaze up to meet my eyes. I wasn't sure what to say next, but I was fully aware that she was checking me out. I hadn't had that before; it sent a feeling down to my bikini briefs and into my pussy that I hadn't had before. We both smiled before I edged forward to try to get served.

'Two Sex on the Beaches please?' I hollered to the bartender. Standing back next to the couple, waiting for our drinks to get made, I tried making conversation again to avoid the awkwardness.

'So, where are you both from?' I said making idle chat.

'London. You?' she said taking a sip from her drink but looking at me the whole time.

'Berkshire. You're more than welcome to join us over by the loungers, if you fancy it?' I offered for them to join us, picking up the cocktails in my hand and began walking them back over to where Daniel was. They followed behind me. I noticed Daniel's face before I got close. He had the look of dread. He knew I was bringing people over to say hi and he was the shyest person I knew. Making small talk was not in his nature but he would warm up to them once they got talking.

'Hi Daniel. I'm Michelle and this is Tom. We're here for a week as well.' Michelle was so confident like me. Daniel got up, taking the

210

drink from my hand and stood next to Tom. They spoke between them while we chatted at length. Michelle was an events organiser for a big promotional company in the city and Tom was a builder. She had long blonde hair that she had piled high in a messy bun, alluring blue eyes and a cute, dimpled smile. She had a small chest, but it fit perfectly with her slim and petite frame. Tom, on the other hand, was a thick set, muscular man and looked like he spent a lot of time working out. Short, shaved dark hair and dark brown eyes. He was very attractive, very much my type, gorgeous eyes and a perfectly handsome smile that I would have fallen for had I not given my heart to Daniel. This was the first occasion where I had also been drawn to a woman and the way she kept looking at me seemed to give me the same opinion that she liked me too.

We spent over an hour talking about ourselves, sharing our backgrounds, laughing together and enjoying a few more cocktails. As the afternoon grew slightly cloudy, the conversations came to a natural close and we parted, agreeing to catch up again a little later. The drinks had gone to my head in the steaming heat, under the jealous watch of Daniel. I lay back on the bed and slowly closed my eyes, drifting off into my own little dream world.

After a long day of travelling and a few drinks by the pool, we were planning on having a relatively quiet evening. Finding a bar or a restaurant nearby for food and to see what the local town was like, we headed back to our room to find a piece of paper had been pushed under the door inviting us to a welcome dinner and drinks at the hotel's restaurant next door. Not having planned much else, we thought it would be a great idea to go to that and see what else was available for us to do during the rest of the week.

Wearing a short, strappy dress and wedges, I was ready to enjoy the night. Daniel looked his usual sexy self, chino shorts, a casual, short sleeved shirt and shoes. He always had the greatest fashion sense, his hair spiked in a wet-looking gel style and his freckles on display fuelled by the heat. Clutching hands, we made our way down to the lobby, unsure as to how many people we would be joined by.

Approaching the restaurant outside of the main entrance to the hotel, we were greeted by a couple of restaurant waiters. A few tables had been made up with tablecloths, glasses, lit candles and menus. The restaurant was on a pretty, meandering street full of bars, restaurants and small shops, lined with cobblestones. The view in front of us was beautiful, a dusky sky, free from clouds and meeting the sparkling sea, lit from the light of the moon in the distance. It was very romantic in an idyllic setting. It sounds funny but I could smell the salty sea air.

'Good evening to you both. Thank you for joining us.' A waiter served us a glass of house white wine each and welcomed us into the restaurant. *I could get used to this.* The weather, eating out in the evening, not having to cook and not working. I was sure going home would hit me with a really hard bump.

The restaurant was quite small but loud and crowded. Whitewashed wooden tables and chairs, all lit with candles and authentic-looking. Couples and families enjoying good food, drink and each other's company. That's how it should be, not caught up in the merry-go-round land that we all lived in back home. Eat, sleep, work and repeat. I was looking forward to spending a few hours with Daniel, talking as a couple and not having to discuss anomalies like bills, our bank balance or never ending to do lists to do with the house. We very rarely spent quality time at home together, just the two of us. The waiter pulled out our chairs in turn for us to take a seat, took the serviette from each placeholding and gently placed it on our laps.

'As a thank you from the hotel for joining us, there is a three-course choice on one side of menu, or if you feel like choosing something else, please take a look on the a la carte menu,' he explained to us in broken English.

The meal wasn't the best meal we had tasted but because it was just the two of us, the setting and the atmosphere, it was probably the most enjoyable meal we had experienced. We sat for hours talking about us, about our lovely little family and all the plans we were going to make. Taking us back to the first meal we had together for Valentine's Day when Jack was conceived. It was magical. We had the rest of our lives in front of us and we wanted to make the most of it. The adventures we were going to organise and the places we were going to visit in the future along with the lifestyle changes we wanted to make. Although we didn't have much money at that particular time, we hoped it would soon change and if we kept working the way we were, things would be easier later down the line. At least we were both on the same page and wanted the same thing from our lives.

We paid for the wine that had accompanied our free meal, leaving a tip on the small white china plate in the middle of the table and staggered back to our hotel; the pathway lit by the big bright moon, shining in a dark but clear sky. Both of us struggled to walk in a straight line but by leaning against each other, we weaved our way back and forth to our room.

That night, we slept like babies. After a day of travelling and settling into our new surroundings, we crashed into the room, stumbled into bed, trying to undress as we went.

The morning woke us abruptly; the bright sunshine bursting into our room through the curtains, at the crack of dawn. I tossed and turned, unable to settle, thinking of how Jack would normally be stirring in his cot, waiting for me to come in and be greeted with his cheeky, smiling face. He would be reaching his arms up, extended to me so that I could pick him up and give him the loveliest hug. Depending on the day of the week, we would either get him ready for going to his childminder or at weekends, it would be a lazy morning back in bed, cuddled up watching cartoons or Saturday morning television, all snuggled up in a duvet. I was so desperate to call home, just to check on him, just to say hi but I didn't want to wake Daniel up and disturb him. I closed my eyes again trying to think of something else. The light from the sunshine gently warmed my face through the glass.

'Can't sleep?' Daniel was awake too. I rolled over to face him, smiling.

'Morning. No, I can't. It's beautiful here but I was just thinking about Jack,' I whispered quietly to not wake any of the other guests in the hotel, in case they could hear me talking.

'He'll be fine. He'll be being spoilt rotten by your mum and dad. Relax and enjoy yourself.' I felt his warm hands slide their way up my thigh and stop just at the top, gently stroking my hips. I knew exactly what that meant. I ran my fingers through his hair and moved in to kiss his warm lips.

'Mmmm... I love you,' I said, continuing to feel his thick, dark hair as we kissed lovingly. I always liked to stare into his gorgeous, bright blue eyes but when our lips met, I couldn't help closing my eyes and enjoying the moment of pure passion. The most amazing feeling running down the back of my neck and into my whole body. I could feel goosebumps run down my arms and onto my breasts making my nipples hard and pointed. This wasn't because I was cold, this was all about the sensation.

Every time I was touched, it was like a drug running through my veins. It flowed, and I could feel the rush of adrenaline, like an energy that surged inside me. A tension that built up until climax when it was eventually released. Alcohol, drugs or anything else I had ever experienced before didn't bring me close to how I felt when I was making love. Never did I nor ever would I turn down sex or a fondle, even in the busiest of times. To me, it was a time to enjoy the moment, keep the excitement going. I believed at that time that a relationship without passion would become stale and stagnant.

I arched my back, twisting my body sideways so I could face away from Daniel. Pushing my bottom cheeks against his cock, he pulled me close into him and with both hands cupped my breasts, squeezing and teasing my nipples as he did so. I could feel he was rock hard and as he pushed between my legs, he felt how wet I was inside, gently easing the tip of his cock between my lips. It felt so tight, so sensual, as he pulled it in and out, slowly, deeply. He

215

seemed to be holding onto me like I was going to run away if he let go. His legs wrapped around mine so tight that I could barely move. I could sense the sweat from his efforts on his brow, his face next to mine and his deep breathing in my ear. I moved my hand down to reach between my legs, opening my lips and exposing my vulva to my fingers so I could touch myself while he was deep inside me. I knew he was close, so I had to smoothly circle my erogenous area to climax at the same time as him. The feeling was immense.

I squeezed every internal muscle I had to make him feel the tension, to bring him to cum and be out of control of his sensations. I could feel him gripping harder and harder, breathing deeper and deeper until I felt his explosion inside me. At the same time, the build-up of pure ecstasy had also made me cum. My whole pussy pulsed around his cock, my legs shaking, my heart racing. It took me a few deep breaths to bring myself back down again. He didn't say a word, just the noise of his soft breathing next to my ear as he unwrapped his legs from around me. His hands once again circling my breasts like a cool down routine after exercise. We both lay together for a while. I figured we were both deep in thought, each wondering what the other was thinking.

It was times like these that I thought sex couldn't get any better. I couldn't top a better feeling or with anyone else. I was completely satisfied, I had everything I desired. I wouldn't complain if it was more frequent but the actual sex itself was incredible...

It wasn't long before my mind started to wander and back to home and how much I was missing Jack.

216

'I think I might walk to the shop and grab some bottled water. We're completely out.' I reached for the edge of the covers and threw them back. My naked body stepped out and grabbed a pair of shorts and a bikini top from my suitcase that I still hadn't unpacked.

'You want me to come with you?' Daniel asked. I think he was just asking out of courtesy, but I didn't want him to go with me. I deliberately put more Greek coins in my pocket so that I could call home and speak to Jack without him knowing.

'Nah, it's okay, I won't be long.' I quickly stepped into my flip flops and walked to the door before he could say anything else. I felt like a fugitive. I ran down the corridor, and reaching the steps, I hurried down them as quickly as I could. The faster I was, the longer I could speak on the phone. The shop was almost opposite the hotel. Checking for traffic, I sprinted across the road and dived into the glass payphone. I picked it up and began to dial. The awful smell of smoked cigarettes on the handset filled my nostrils but I didn't care, all I wanted to do was speak to my baby. I dialled frantically the international code.

'Hello?' My dad had picked up; I knew his voice instantly.

'Hey Dad, it's me. It's Rose. How are you?' I missed his company. We used to be so close. I had always been a daddy's girl.

'Oh hi, is everything okay?' He sounded worried that I was in trouble.

'Oh, sorry. Yes, I'm fine, just missing you all. Is Jack okay?' I knew he was, but I wanted to ask.

'Hang on a minute, let me get him and your mum.' He disappeared for a brief second, but I could hear him calling out in the distance.

'Mum, mum, mum.' There it was my boy's beautiful voice. I wanted to cry happy tears. He was okay. Oh boy how I missed his cuddles. I felt my eyes welling up, wanting to just reach through the phone and hug him.

'Rose, are you all right?' my mum asked. 'Jack is fine. We went to the park this morning. He had a quick nap as he was playing on the swings and the slide. What's the time where you are? Two hours ahead, right?' She sounded like she was cramming as many questions in as possible as we would have limited time talking. I could see the money going down on the display, leaving me with not much time left.

'I'm fine, I'm fine. How are you all? We're having a great time. I just wanted to hear your voices and to make sure everything was great back home.' Of course they were fine, but I needed to speak to them to put my mind at rest. Just as I wanted to speak more, there were a couple of bleeps on the line warning me that my time was coming to an end.

'I can't stay long as my money is running out. Give Jack a big kiss for me. Love you both and will see you on Saturday.' I tried to hold back the tears.

'Love you too. See you Saturday.' There were a few more mumbles from Jack and the line cut off. I placed the receiver back on its holder and kept my hand on it for a while, staring past the glass booth and into the sunny distance. He was fine, that was all that mattered. I rubbed my face with both hands to wake me up and pulled myself together. I had to get back to Daniel before he had an inkling that I had called home.

I raced back to the room to find him still in bed, propped up with a pillow behind his back. As I opened the door, I tried not to look flustered. Looking down at my hands, I suddenly realised I had forgotten the water that I went to get.

'Shit,' I muttered under my breath.

'Hey, that was quick.' He looked a little surprised. 'Where's the water?'

'It erm… it was warm. They didn't have any chilled so I thought I would go back later. I didn't have enough change either.' I tried to shrug it off and walked to the bathroom to have a wee.

'You called home, didn't you?' he shouted to me. He didn't miss a thing. Always quiet, not saying much but watching and taking everything in. Did I admit it, or did I stick to my guns?

'Sure did.' Oops, there it was. I admitted I had been caught out.

'I knew you did anyway. The hotel filled up the fridge with water while you were out. I could see you were itching to speak to Jack. Is he okay?' Ah see, he wanted to know too. I walked out the bathroom with a big smile on my face.

'He was fine. I only had five minutes, but it was nice to hear him.' God, I missed his cuddles.

'Now stop it and enjoy yourself. I'll have a quick shower and we can head downstairs. Fancy a walk along the beach?' His young, defined body appeared from half under the covers and made his way across to the bathroom. I could hear him turn the shower on and climb in. I never tired of looking at his fit body. I still fancied him after all these years and the spark hadn't waned.

I opened the curtains and sat on the balcony in the warm, morning sunshine, watching the few scattered clouds slowly make their way across the stunning, bright blue sky. There were very few opportunities for me to ponder, to sit and just think. My life was normally a hectic chaos. Every minute was crammed full of work, activities, chores and more, and yet every night when I tried to sleep, everything I hadn't managed to do was whirling around my mind like a whirlwind.

Stuck in a daydream, I lifted my feet up and placed them on the chair opposite me. I leant back, soaking in the sun and closed my eyes. No more than five minutes later, I felt a warm hand on my shoulder, gently shaking me to wake up.

'Hey baby. I'm heading down to the pool. Are you coming or staying here? You looked so peaceful, I didn't want to wake you, but it's been nearly an hour and I'm hungry.' Daniel's face peered over mine. An hour? I must have been tired, either that or just the heat of the day had relaxed me so much that I dozed off. I rubbed my eyes, took a little stretch and got myself together. I probably could have slept for many more hours, but I packed our sun cream, towels and money into my beach bag, and we made our way down to the pool.

The pool area was busy. The air was filled by the loud noise of people having fun in the background, mixed with screams from the swimming pool and the music playing by the bar. The atmosphere here was great. The hotel staff made you feel welcome and want to be a part of the fun.

It was late morning but it would be rude not to have a cocktail or two already, I thought.

'I'll grab the drinks in. What are you having? A mojito? One? Two?' I sprawled out my towel as I asked Daniel.

'Don't go too mad, Rose. It isn't even midday yet.' Of course, I ignored what he said and headed straight for the bar.

'Two mojitos and two daquiris please,' I shouted to the bar man. I felt alive, the music pounding in my chest. After a quick sleep on the balcony, I felt refreshed and ready for the day ahead.

'Yes, beautiful,' he said in a Greek accent and winked at me. All the men over here had dark hair, olive skin and were woman charmers. I began balancing the cocktails onto a small, black tray so I could carry them back to the sun loungers without spilling them everywhere. I caught Daniel out of the corner of my eye shaking his head. He could see the drinks stacked up in my hands and realised I was ignoring everything he had told me. As I turned around, holding the drinks precariously, Tom and Michelle were standing right behind me, waiting for their turn at the bar.

'Good morning, my lovely.' Michelle smiled affectionately. I placed the tray back on the bar so that I could turn and talk to them without dropping the cocktails.

'We looked for you both last night but couldn't see you. Did you go anywhere nice?' She seemed to study my whole face, starting with my green eyes before moving to my lips each time I spoke. It was as if she was imagining a scenario in her own head and was fascinated with my every move. I had never felt such a connection with another woman before or maybe it was me that was studying her. Tom just stood in the background behind her, his glare was also on me. What was he thinking?

'Just to the restaurant next to the hotel. We were invited to a welcome dinner. Did you both not get the invite?' Just as I continued the conversation, Daniel began to walk over. I could see all the other women around the pool follow him with their longing eyes. I was a lucky girl; he was so handsome. His dark hair and blue eyes made him very attractive. He had a walk like James Bond that made him mysterious and desirable. Daniel was naturally quite hairy, so it only added to his sexiness, making him look older than he was.

'I thought I would come over before the ice in the drinks melted.' Daniel gave a cheeky laugh and shook hands with Tom. 'Morning, mate, did you have a good night?'

Tom and Daniel chatted between them whilst Michelle and I carried on our conversation.

'So, Tom and I were talking about you both last night and wondered if you wanted to join us tonight for dinner and drinks? We could go to one of the tavernas over the road and then perhaps take some drinks back to our room after the bar closes and carry on, if you haven't got any plans?' She placed a hand on my arm and began to stroke it up and down before placing it back on her hip. It sent a slight shiver down my back but I liked it. I could see Daniel was looking at us both and noting what she had just done. I wasn't a very affectionate person and wasn't sure if I was supposed to do the same back to her or whether I just carried on regardless. I stared back at her, keeping all my thoughts to myself.

'I'll check with Daniel but that sounds lovely. We would love to. What time are you thinking?' I asked.

Michelle turned to speak to Tom but in doing so, she placed the same hand on the back of Daniel's sweaty back just above his shorts waistband and slowly moved it down, so she was touching the top of his bottom. He jumped slightly but kept her hand where it was. I think he quite liked her touching him.

'Sorry to interrupt, gentlemen. I was just asking Rose if you both wanted to join us for dinner and drinks tonight. It would be great to enjoy the night together and then drinks back at ours. It's not as if we have work in the morning, is it?' She threw her head back, tossing her long hair and laughed out loud. It was flirtatious but friendly. I could sense Daniel was also quite nervous with her forwardness, but he just went with the flow. Tom seemed oblivious to what was going on and just agreed with everything Michelle was saying, occasionally looking over at me to check my reaction. 'I'm thinking 7 p.m. tonight?'

Daniel threw me a look, checking my facial expression first before replying. 'It's good with me if you're up for it?'

'Yes, fine with me,' I agreed, picking up the cocktails from the bar and handing them out to everyone. 'Cheers,' I said raising my glass in the air, gesturing for the rest of them to join me and toast to the night. I wasn't sure what I was expecting or maybe I had read into it completely wrong. Was she flirting with us or was she just being friendly? It didn't bother me in the slightest either way.

We stood by the pool bar for a little while longer, laughing and making general conversation but then we all returned to our opposite ends of the pool and our marked sun loungers. Both couples engulfed in our own books that we were reading and an occasional dip in the pool to cool down.

223

As soon as the steaming afternoon sun started to fade, creating shadows behind the building blocks of our surrounding hotel, it became noticeably chilly and a signal for us to take a shower and get ready for our evening out with Tom and Michelle. I had a slight sense of butterflies in my stomach, a new set of friends and a couple that we didn't know a huge amount about. I would have to curb my drinking before I got too out of control and embarrass both myself and Daniel. I had a strange feeling about the night ahead. I couldn't put my finger on it, but I felt like something was going to happen. Probably just my nerves. I continued to get ready and didn't say a word.

My curly hair was difficult to tame in the humidity of the night, but I did my best to style it into a neat bundle at the back of my head, held fast with a clip. My face rosy from a day of sun made my green eyes more prominent and my lovely long eyelashes blackened from a new coating of mascara. A short, black strappy dress, a pair of high summer wedges and I was ready to go. Daniel smelt so good, wearing a new seductive aftershave, his hair jet black and still damp from the shower that complemented his chino shorts and smart blue shirt. We both looked stunning, giving each other in turn a look up and down and an approving smile. If we weren't going out, I would have been happy to tear his shirt back open and spend the night in bed together.

He reached for my hand, pulling me to the door to follow him down the corridor as I grabbed my bag on the way out. We were quiet the whole way to reception. I was nervous and thought I needed a drink to settle my nerves. He, on the other hand, was quiet as usual. It suited Daniel not to make conversation for once.

As I had expected, Tom and Michelle were already there waiting for us. Her in a long, tight-fitting dress showing off her tall but slender figure, blonde hair flowing with bright red lipstick. Tom looked a little less formal, a linen shirt and matching shorts. This time we were greeted with a big, longer than average hug, one that was matched with one you would give to a loved one saying goodbye for the very last time. It felt good though, it was lovely and very endearing. Such affection and from two people who were really strangers to us. Tom's hug was strong; his builder arms right round me, he moved them up and down as if he had missed hugging someone. He smelt incredible too. The bristle from his stubble brushing past my neck and chin sent shivers down my body. A different man touching me other than Daniel was surreal.

'I've booked us a table. Let's go eat and have a good night,' Michelle said, turning to lead the way. The restaurant was almost opposite the hotel, so we didn't have far to walk. Two waiters outside the restaurant greeted us and took us to our table. Pulling out our chairs in turn, seating us and then draping our napkins over our laps, we were handed a menu each and then left to decide what we wanted to eat.

'Look at the two of you, such a beautiful couple.' Michelle didn't waste any time, she came straight at us with compliments. For once, I was shy. I wasn't used to this type of flattery, even from Daniel. Did I return the compliment or just acknowledge it?

'Aw, thank you.' I managed to find the words. 'You both look incredible too. I'm looking forward to tonight.' I felt a little nudge under the table but couldn't quite work out whether it was Daniel or one of the others. Michelle was looking straight at me, a naughty, luring type smile on her face. There it was again. Was she deliberately trying to give me signals or was I reading too much into it? I coughed and tried to look at the menu as if to break the ice.

'What is everyone drinking?' Diving straight into the drinks menu, I felt uncomfortable without a glass in my hand. A few sips down and I would feel more at ease and able to talk all night long. 'I'm thinking white wine, anyone want to share?' I spun Daniel a look who was sitting next to me.

'Yeah, okay.' I think he was feeling just as uncomfortable as I was and struggling to make conversation with the right words to say.

'We're into sharing and more than just wine.' There it was, that was the ice breaker. Tom bluntly batted that comment across the table to us and then sat there smiling waiting for our response. Not expecting it, I nervously laughed and just looked at Daniel who had gone bright red and didn't know what to say. Michelle nudged Tom like a naughty child at the dinner table but also sat there smiling like a Cheshire cat. It wasn't something we had discussed before, and I wasn't sure what I thought about it. Would I share Daniel with someone else? Probably but I knew he loved *me*. Would he share me with someone else? I didn't know. I shrugged off the comment, smiled back at both of them and scanned down the rest of the menu onto the food. I wasn't that hungry. It wasn't the choice of menu; it was more the feeling in my stomach as to how the night was going

226

to end. Anticipation, eating in front of strangers, a new scenario that neither of us had been in before.

'Right, that's me done and decided.' Daniel placed the menu down on the table and straightened his knife and fork so they were perfectly vertical. The waiter closest to us took this as a cue and walked over to us with his pen and paper in hand to take our orders. I wasn't a big eater, whatever I did have would be finished by Daniel, so I strategically ordered what I knew we both liked. Everything revolved around drink, food was secondary for me. The taste, the sensation, the thirst quencher, it was all an experience when you drank yet food was just something that stopped my stomach from growling in hunger.

Our orders were taken, and we resumed our small talk, where we worked, what we did, what we liked to do in our spare time, our family. They did more of the question asking and we fed into their inquisitiveness. As I lifted my glass of white wine, I took a sip and placed it back on the table, my hand still firmly around its base. Michelle moved her hand forward onto the table and with both her index and middle finger started to stroke my hand gently. Tom saw her do this and with almost military precision planning, our conversation took a sharp turn as he made another bold statement.

'So, Michelle and I like to experiment, what about you both? Are you into a bit of experimental fun?'

I didn't know what to say; my eyes watching her soft fingers caress mine. I hadn't even noticed if anyone else in the restaurant was watching what was happening.

'Maybe, depends what type of fun we're talking here.' Daniel had lowered the volume of his voice so only the four of us could hear. I think he was asserting the fact that he was in control of what was about to happen here. He was in charge, whatever he wanted to do I was game. If he didn't want any part in this then that was that. I trusted him implicitly and that was all that mattered. I had never been with a woman before and hadn't had a chance to learn what I was supposed to do. Had she done it before, would she show me? It was like being a virgin all over again. I knew what I liked but would it be the same for her? And what would the men be doing while we were together? Was she thinking that she slept with Daniel whilst I was with Tom? I had so many questions that I wanted to ask.

Instead, I kept quiet, taking Daniel's lead and almost becoming completely beholden to everyone else on the table. My wine was going down fast. Nervously I used my other hand to free the glass from the hand that Michelle had a hold of and gulped the remaining drops till it was empty.

'I'm sorry, we don't want you both to feel uncomfortable. Especially if it's not something you're into. That's not what we want at all, but if you are, we think you're an extremely attractive couple and would love for you to join us after dinner in our room if you know what I mean.'

Michelle withdrew her hand from mine and placed it back on her lap. She seemed to accept that this was a first for us and respected our decision whatever it was. This was like a red rag to a bull for me. Tell me not to do something and I would do it. Entice me into something and I was all in. The stroking of my hand, the quiet, discreet conversation in a busy restaurant setting and the talk of doing something naughty had me totally drawn in. If it was naughty, I was in. I felt horny just thinking about it.

Daniel looked at me, trying to read my mind. I looked back at him and shrugged giving him the okay signal that I was in. I felt a rush of adrenaline, a feeling of excitement, a level of nervousness but in a good way.

'Okay, we're in but if I say enough, then that's enough and we can stop at any time.' I loved it when Daniel was assertive and barked the orders. He meant every word he said; he had to be the alpha male in this situation. If he wasn't, he wouldn't have let it happen. Tom held out his hand to shake Daniel's. It was like a gentlemen's agreement, almost as if they were shaking on a bet or a sports game not sharing their wives with each other.

We continued the rest of the meal as if nothing had happened. We laughed, we joked, we got on really well and we both enjoyed each other's company but the pending event that we were anticipating was in everyone's mind. A looming event that was hanging over us all.

'Shall we make a move?' Michelle asked. 'Let's order another couple of bottles and take them to the room.' She called an end to our dinner and asked the waiter for the final bill so we could make a move. I think she was more eager than any of us to go. Like a big sister, she split the bill between us, paid the amounts, organised the bottles of wine and shoved them into her bag. Clutching at my hand, she guided us back up to their room. She had a way of making me feel completely at ease. I wasn't anxious or worried by this point. The only thing I wanted to be sure of was that Daniel was by my side and comfortable with everything.

All four of us, drunk from the amount of alcohol we had consumed during dinner and high from the feeling of what was yet to come, found ourselves waiting in the corridor outside of their room. Michelle, stumbling with the room card, finally opened the door and we all fell in. Tom grabbed a bottle from Michelle's bag. Twisting the screw top off the bottle, he took the bottle in his mouth and drank a couple of mouthfuls straight down. He handed it to Daniel to do the same and patted him on the back like he was handing over the baton in a relay race.

Michelle fondled around in her bag trying to retrieve the other bottle, before making her way to the bathroom. She handed it to me with a mischievous look on her face. I found her beautiful, attractive and sexy all at the same time. While she was in the bathroom freshening up, Daniel came over to me and pulled me to one side. In a drunken whisper, he asked me if I was okay and that I could stop at any time, prompting me to speak up but I was fine with everything. It was as though he was expecting me to say no, and I didn't want to go through with it.

As soon as Michelle made it back in the room, I took her place. Standing in their bathroom, I put both hands on the sink countertop, looking at myself in the large mirror. I had double vision, but I could make out a very drunk face, hair no longer neatly clipped back and makeup slightly smeared from the humidity. I pulled the clip from my hair letting its curls fall to my shoulders. My nipples were so erect and excited that I could see them pointing through my bra and my dress. Taking in a big deep breath, I adjusted my straps on my dress, freshened up and went to join them back in the main room.

I wasn't quite ready for what came next. As I opened the door, Daniel and Tom were stood together with Michelle in between them. Tom had one hand on her bottom and was kissing her neck while her and Daniel were kissing passionately. It wasn't that I didn't like it, I just wasn't prepared and was a little taken aback. She paused. Daniel saw my face and didn't know what to do next. Michelle walked slowly over to me, with no warning at all she got so close that her lips touched mine. Her hand smoothly followed my jaw to my ear and ended on the back of my head through my hair. I felt her other hand around my waist, down my hips and to my bottom. It felt different but amazing. She was the instigator in this whole scenario, she made the first steps with everyone, bringing us together as a group.

Her lips were softer, her tongue gentler than Daniel's. I was extremely turned on in a way that I could have never imagined. Caught in the moment and forgetting where I was, my eyes closed, my mouth and tongue completely entwined with hers. I wondered how gentle her tongue would feel licking me in other places. I moved my hand to reach round the back of her head, locking us in as we kissed, my other hand touching her small, pert breasts. I could feel her erect nipples through her bra and dress and wanted to peel both off exposing her naked body. It felt so right, it didn't feel wrong at all, but I hadn't known that until now.

She slowly lifted my shoulder straps and peeled them down my arms and off my body, unzipping the side of my dress. Letting it

231

fall to the floor, she left me naked except my knickers. I did the same, removing her dress so that the next time we kissed, our breasts touched. Each time our nipples pressed against each other, it sent goosebumps down my entire body. I could feel Daniel watching the both of us, Tom was starting to take his shirt off and remove his shoes, prompting Daniel to do the same.

Michelle told me to sit on the bed, pushing me backwards on the covers, tugging at the sides of my knickers to remove them. I was extremely wet, the thought of another woman touching me while two men looked on was such a turn on. With each movement, she was guiding me like a professional. This wasn't her first time. After removing my knickers and leaving me totally exposed, she ran her finger down from my belly button to the top of my vagina. She paused, looked at me and ushered both the men to join us on the bed. Tom on one side, Daniel on the other. Her fingers were soft and attentive, but she didn't touch me like Daniel did. She didn't know me like he did. She moved her head down to between my legs, pushing them apart. Daniel leant over to start kissing me while she began licking and sucking my clitoris in a way I had never experienced before. It was incredible. Tom was cupping and squeezing her breasts the whole time she was down on me but his eyes were on me, watching the pleasure she was giving me.

Tom stood behind Michelle, pushing his cock into her whilst she tasted the delights of my pussy. He didn't have his eyes closed; he was looking straight at me. It seemed like he was imagining fucking me instead of her. I writhed in pleasure, I pulled Daniel into my lips, kissing him while I enjoyed the sensations I received from Michelle.

Before I managed to reach an orgasm, Michelle lifted her head and saw Daniel's cock was being wasted. Pulling Tom's cock out from behind her, she made her way back up to my face and kissed me before moving over to Daniel and kissing him again. She climbed over to straddle his now fully naked body, her pussy hovering just above his cock, the whole time looking at my face to check I was okay with it. Daniel seemed to do the same, making sure I didn't want to stop.

I thought I would, I thought I wouldn't want to share him with anyone, but it excited me even more seeing him with someone else. As the two of them began to relax and enjoy the sensation of being with another person, I watched Daniel's cock enter her and a gasp of pleasure escaped from her mouth. Tom's attention turned to me; his rough hands started to fondle my breasts. It didn't turn me on as much as being with Daniel and even Michelle but I found him inquisitively attractive. It didn't feel like cheating even though Daniel was next to me fucking another woman, but I went with it. Instead of me getting on top and fucking him, he got up and rolled on top of me. His big body pressed against my large breasts. He was sensual, and he was attentive, but I didn't feel the power that I felt with Daniel. I closed my eyes and tried to imagine it was him touching me. He reached between my legs, feeling my moist lips from Michelle, his cock wet from being inserted into her before me. He was breathing heavily; I could tell he wanted to cum. He was quite rough, holding my arms above my head, restrained, with one hand and the other guiding his cock into my pussy.

I glanced over at Daniel. He seemed uncomfortable, but I could tell he was enjoying his cock being rode. With every thrust from Michelle, he lost a little more control and came closer to cumming. She became more and more erratic as she looked like she was just about to climax. I was more turned on watching the two of them writhe together than what was happening to me, almost pre-occupied. Michelle picked up the pace, back and forth on top of him until he closed his eyes and erupted. She had a smile on her face, she knew he was pulsing inside of her.

While Daniel and Michelle were calming down, I shifted my focus back to Tom. He may not be Daniel, but he was attractive in his own right. I was here and, in a way, I wanted him to enjoy his moment with someone other than his wife. I wanted him to look at me in desire and for me to be better than her in bed. As he let go of my arms, I began by cupping and pushing up my breasts, teasing him with the occasional view of my nipples through my pleasuring fingers. I had a dirty look in my eyes, staring into his the whole time. As his movement became more intense, I wrapped both arms around his side and started digging in my long nails into his back. He seemed to like the pain, so I applied more pressure with a big nasty grin on my face. He gave an awkward smile back but the sensation of him deep inside me made him close his eyes and concentrate on cumming. I had lost all sense of there being anyone else in the room. It was like we were alone together, and I was being a bad, bad girl. Before Tom had a chance to get much further, we both opened our eyes to Daniel struggling to push Michelle off him and there being a commotion.

'That's enough now. I think we're all done. Rose, get your stuff, we're leaving.'

Tom reluctantly stopped thrusting into me and pulled his cock out. We both looked at each other confused. Did something happen that I missed? I thought it was all consensual and everything was fine.

'What's wrong, Daniel?' The moment had completely disappeared, and he seemed to be freaking out.

'I think we've all had a bit too much to drink and things have got way out of control. Rose, get your bits, we're going.'

Michelle jumped off the bed with Daniel following. She tried grabbing his muscular arms to stop him, but he broke free. For a moment, both Tom and I weren't sure what was going on.

Daniel looked at me in a disapproving way. 'We're going.' He threw my knickers at me. Was it something I had said or done?

'Thank you for a great evening. Sorry, but we have to leave.' I pulled my knickers over my ankles and up over my hips. Tom was still sprawled on the bed with a look of confusion. I tried to find my dress which was crumpled in a ball on the floor along with my bag and bra. Before I had a chance to get completely dressed, Daniel latched hold of my hand and almost dragged me out of their hotel room, letting the door slam behind us and not looking back to see the reaction on their faces.

Outside in the corridor, Daniel pushed me against the cold, concrete white wall. 'I'm sorry but I had to get us out of there. Seeing you with him was killing me. I couldn't lie there and watch the way he was pleasing you like that. *I'm* your man, *I'm* the one who loves you. We have a connection that I don't want you to share with anyone else and that's that.'

He punched the wall next to my head in anger. It was so close that I heard the whack in my ear before I realised what he had done. He shouted as the impact of his fist against the wall split his knuckles and began bleeding. He lowered his eyes and head away from me, defeated and turned to walk down the empty and quiet corridor.

As I ran after him wearing nothing but my knickers and clutching my dress, bra and bag against my naked body, I tried to make sense of what he was talking about.

'But you said it was okay… you said…' I was worried what he would say or do next.

'I know what I said but I've changed my mind. It's not okay,' he said, continuing to our room.

I kept quiet, not wanting to aggravate him any further. We reached our room, he tussled with the room card, finally opening the door and crumbling onto the bed.

'Hey,' I said joining him. His face down on the covers, I leant over him and tried to move his head so he would look at me.

'I don't understand. You seemed to be enjoying it. You were fine with her and me and then what changed? Did I miss something? You know I love you. It didn't mean anything. You were right next to me.' I was trying to make sense of his rage.

'Rose, I thought I would be okay. I thought that it would be fine, but I can't stand seeing you with another guy. You're *mine!*' He was making out like I was his property, that he owned me and I had no right being with another man. Yet it was okay for him to be with another woman, *and* he was fine with her going down on me. It made no sense at all. None.

'I understand,' I said, completely contradicting what I was actually thinking. 'How are we going to face them tomorrow? It's going to be awkward.'

'Frankly, I don't care. We can go to the beach tomorrow instead.' He pulled back the covers of the bed, curling his legs under the sheets, laying his head on the pillow and closing his eyes as though he was hoping it would all go away. Not wanting to make the situation any worse, I cuddled up behind him, plumped the pillow up and did the same, closing my eyes, feeling the room spin as I tried to drift off. I lay there for hours trying to make sense of it all.

Chapter 21

Going Home

The following morning, I woke to an empty bed. I looked sleepily round the room, expecting him to be in the bathroom but he wasn't. Did I dream last night or was it for real? My head was pounding so I knew the part about drinking was true, but the rest of the night was a little hazy. The balcony door was slightly ajar, and the curtain was blowing in the wind. Yawning and with only my knickers on, I got up and made my way to the balcony. I could see Daniel sat there, his back against the wall, and he seemed to be staring into the distance.

I slid the door open slowly, just enough for me to squeeze through the opening. I didn't care I was half dressed, I couldn't care less if I was naked. Someone would have to be looking up at our balcony to see me so I continued and sat on the plastic chair next to him. Bringing my knees up and into my chest, I wrapped both arms around my legs and looked over at Daniel. He hadn't

239

taken his eyes off the horizon. I felt like a naughty child who was trying to apologise to their dad, yet they were ignoring me because they were disappointed in what I had done.

'Daniel, you okay?' I leant forward to ask. He seemed to snap out of his trance and turned to smile at me. What had we done? Was it a step too far and something that would either make or break us as a couple? Somehow, we always fell into situations and worried about them and the consequences afterwards. Live fast, die young was the motto that I wanted to enjoy my life by, but the more I was living fast, the more I was worried that I may die too young, and I now had a family to think about.

'I'm sorry, Rose. It just got a bit too much last night. Seeing you with him freaked me out and made me worry that I could lose you and I can't cope with that.' He edged sideways so he could sit closer to me.

'But we were together. It was lust, not love, there's a big difference. I don't *love* him, it was just a moment that we had together, and we were all wasted. I wouldn't risk what we have for anyone. What about her? You didn't seem to care that I was enjoying being with her, just him?' I wanted to understand how he felt.

'I don't care about you with women. I didn't realise you liked women as well until last night, but it isn't something I can compete with. With another man, it's different. I would compare myself to him and worry that you liked him more than me. I can't explain it, it's just how I feel. Is it something you want then? Do you want an open relationship? I don't know if I could deal with that.' He picked up my hand and held it, waiting for me to reply.

'So, what are you saying?' I still didn't understand what he was trying to say.

'I'm saying that I think you have needs and I don't know if I can fulfil them. You have a very dark side. What if I'm not enough for you? You like to experiment, to taste all the delights of the sexual world and whilst I love sex with you, maybe you need a dirtier world than I can give. I would do anything for you, you know that, but I will be constantly worrying about your desires.' This conversation was way over my head. I was sensual and seductive but I struggled talking about emotions and how I felt. 'I know that you want to experiment, that you are into all sorts in the bedroom. Last night made me wonder, what if I'm not enough for you and can't fulfil all your needs when it comes to sex?'

'Daniel, this is crazy. I love you, you love me, there is no question there at all. What happened last night, happened. It didn't mean anything to me. It was a drunken mess, and we need to forget about it and carry on. We'll look back at this in a couple of months' time and laugh about it. We have amazing sex, just the two of us. Let's go for coffee and breakfast and enjoy our last day here. If you want to, we can go to the beach, so we don't bump into the others. Then tomorrow we get to see our little boy. I can't wait.' I gave him a cuddle, reassuring him like a broken man and got up to get dressed.

Standing in the shower, letting the water run down my body, I could only think about what Daniel had said to me earlier. I knew I had a dark side; I couldn't beat the feeling of lust and love, but I could switch off my emotions like a tap. I had sex last night with a woman and another man, both practically strangers but I didn't feel any different. I could quite easily walk up to them at the bar and talk to them as if nothing had happened. Daniel, on the other hand, would feel socially awkward and uncomfortable. One thing was certain, I wouldn't risk losing him for anything so if it was an addiction that I had to curb then so be it. It did make me think about experience though. There was a whole world out there of other sexual practices that maybe we hadn't had yet.

We seemed to have sorted out our differences and it was a flashback to yesterday morning before everything had taken place last night. Daniel held my hand down the corridor to the hotel restaurant. He squeezed it occasionally as he always did but this morning, he looked a little more nervous than usual. We stood in the hotel restaurant queue to be seated, thinking we would miss Tom and Michelle as it was a little later than normal.

Out of nowhere, I felt an abrupt hand smack my bottom and then a familiar voice shout, 'Morning, mate.'

Turning around, Tom was standing next to us, reaching out to shake Daniel's hand. He was completely normal, behaving like he had complete memory loss.

Daniel returned the gesture of shaking his hand and replied, 'Sore head?'

'Not too bad, mate, but Michelle, on the other hand, feels rather delicate this morning and decided to stay in bed. I'm going to make the most of the peace and quiet without her and go for a walk along the beach before she gets up. Catch you both later.'

And off he walked. He almost had a spring in his step, and it completely cleared the air. I couldn't help but think there was way more to their story and relationship than they were letting on. At least we didn't have to worry about bumping into them for the rest of the day. Was she just too embarrassed like we were and had chosen to stay in her room? Or had they perhaps had the same argument we did? Even though I had told Daniel that it wasn't an issue, it was the only thing I could think of. It was like a built-up tension inside my body that was waiting to be fulfilled. I would have to suppress that urge for the rest of my life. If he was okay with me and other women, then maybe there was a way that I could keep a certain amount of kinkiness in our sex life.

We sat down to breakfast, a little more relaxed than we were earlier this morning.

'Hey Daniel, I've been thinking about last night and us as a family together. When we get home, why don't we get something that will bring us all together and have something to look forward to. It could be good for us.' I moved the food around my plate, not that hungry but it occupied me whilst he ate.

'You clearly have something in mind. What is this *something*?' He looked up at me, sipping his coffee and wiping the steam from his eyebrows.

'A dog. How about a dog?' Before he could answer me, I had to sell it and sell it quick. 'I mean, Jack would love it and we could go for lovely walks after work together. The house is so quiet when you get in that having a dog running towards you, eager to see you each day, would be so nice. Plus, I only work five minutes away from home so I could let it out each day. Imagine a cute little puppy. Jack loves watching 101 Dalmatians. Maybe we could get him one of those, they are beautiful. Please, it would be so lovely and...' I don't think he was listening to anything I was saying but hearing me go on and on was enough for anyone. It was sometimes easier for him to agree with me even if he didn't than to try giving me a counter argument.

'Let's talk about it when we're home.' He continued with his breakfast.

'So... it's not a no then?' I had hope but I was clutching at straws.

'Maybe.' He pulled his knife and fork together, finished the last of his coffee and sat back in his chair.

'Oh, it's going to be so exciting. A cute little puppy. Jack's face is going to be a picture. They'll be the best of friends.'

'Rose, I said maybe.'

I'll take that as a yes then. I had already got my hopes up and in my head, I was building a picture of going to look at dog litters, choosing one, his name and welcoming him to the family.

We finished breakfast and decided to go for a little walk along the main street outside the hotel and finish up along the beach. Daniel still seemed a bit quiet. I walked along next to him wondering what he was thinking. We found a nice quiet little spot on the sand dunes, tucked away from the swirling sea wind. The sun beat down onto the beautiful blue Mediterranean Sea, us both in deep thought. He placed his arm all the way round my shoulders and pulled me in close.

'You drive me insane, but I love you so much. We're going to grow old together, do you know that?' I wasn't sure if he was making a statement or asking me a question. 'You're like a whirlwind, but you are my whole world.'

I laughed. I knew it was true and he knew me so well.

He spoke the most loving words to me but I felt like he thought he was never good enough for me and I couldn't work out why. I think for some people they are never happy with what they have, and they never appreciate what they have till it is gone. For us, it wasn't the case, but we did try to live life to the fullest and to take every adventure we could. We could be gone tomorrow and there was no space for regrets. Having Jack at seventeen meant we had grown up well ahead of time and as a result wanted to cram in as much as possible before our time was up. It wasn't morbid, it was a fact and we both had the same opinion.

At that moment in time, I was torn between wanting to go home and see our beautiful boy, family and friends again, but I also didn't want this holiday to end. Daniel was right, it was a chance to rewind, refocus and take some well-earnt time out. I could sit on the beach cuddled tight up to Daniel forever, but we had to get back to reality at some point. My biggest wish would be to live in a world where money and materials didn't matter but this was just not the world we lived in.

'Love you too, baby,' I said. 'I'll remind you of that in twenty years' time when you've left me for someone half my age and are having a midlife crisis.' I jabbed him in the ribs before he could get all mushy again, flicked off my flip flops and ran to where the sea met the sand, dipping my toes in enough to see how cold or warm it was.

Daniel came running in behind me, picking me up in his arms and us both falling to the floor in the sea. It was slightly colder than bath water but not freezing. I let out a few screams but more from him tickling and splashing me. We wrestled, we played, and we laughed. We were so lucky to have found each other and more importantly, someone who was willing to tolerate me.

The day seemed to whizz past, the last day in the sunshine before collecting our bags from our rooms and dropping them in reception, ready for our coach to come and collect us, taking us back to the airport. We would have to get on the same coach as Tom and Michelle but it didn't bother me in the slightest. Daniel, on the other hand, was starting to get a little anxious again. I needed a drink to get me through the last hour of waiting so I ordered a double vodka and coke for me and a beer for Daniel. He sat there sipping, enjoying it like a Sunday afternoon tipple. I, on the other hand, drank the whole drink in less than five minutes.

'Oh, that was nice. I think I'll have another,' I said, hoping he would want another one too.

'Rose, seriously, we'll be on the coach soon.' He tried to reason with me but nope, too late.

'I had best be quick then.' Instead of ordering one, I ordered two doubles and sat back down. Was I in fear of missing out or the fact that I had been told to slow down by Daniel that I ordered two more, just to do the opposite? I wasn't sure which it was.

I drank one straight away and then the other before he had had a chance to finish his first pint. Consuming three drinks one after the other made me need to go to the toilet so I got up and walked to the other side of reception to the ladies. I sat on the toilet trying to go but I just sat there feeling disappointed in myself that after last night I couldn't stop when it came to alcohol. I felt a bit tipsy.

Concentrating on going, I pulled at the toilet roll but the whole roll came off in my hands and fell to the floor. Clutching at a few pieces, I wiped and then tried to coil the rest up and place it on the back of the cistern. Clumsily, I flushed and steadied myself with one hand on the door and with the other pulled my knickers up and unlocked the catch on the door.

I opened the cubicle door and was shocked to be greeted by the same familiar face from last night. Tom was standing in front of me. What was he doing in the ladies? He held one finger up against my lips, pushing me backwards into the cubicle and told me to shush.

'Look, I know I'm not supposed to be in here, but I just wanted to say something quickly in case I didn't get the chance to before we left,' he whispered. He didn't scare me at all. He was taking an opportunity and I understood that. I just blinked as if to give him the signal that it was okay to continue, and I kept quiet, intrigued as to what he wanted to say to me.

'I'm sorry for what happened last night. Well, I'm not sorry but I didn't want you getting into trouble. I heard him shouting at you outside. I heard the bang and wanted to make sure everything was okay. I felt like we pressurised you into coming back to our room, but I really connected with you until it was stopped abruptly. You see, Michelle can be a bit demanding at times and she *needed* it to happen, but you, you're different. You've got a way about you that I'm fascinated with. I think there's more to you than I met last night. A darker side, perhaps. I wished we had more time but—' His voice stopped instantly as there was the noise of someone walking into the ladies.

We both stood there in silence, hoping not to be caught out. How would I explain the two of us in a cubicle together? Especially after last night. He still had his finger on my lips, us staring at each other but quiet like frozen statues. The sound of a woman closing the door, going to the toilet and then just as she was about to flush, he whispered in my ear.

'I think you're amazing. I would love to see you again, just me and you and see where that takes us.' He pushed a folded-up piece of paper into my hand and at the same time as removing his finger, he gave me a long, slow, passionate kiss on the lips. I fell for it. I let him kiss me and it was good.

As the other lady washed her hands and the sound of her footsteps got quieter and quieter on the floor as she left, Tom let go of me, smiled and left the cubicle. I stood still for a moment, thinking about what that just was. I unfolded the piece of paper that he had handed me and looked at it to reveal a number signed off with just the letter T, presuming it was his mobile. I quickly rolled it back up and stuffed it into my bra. I couldn't afford for Daniel to find that and ask questions.

Adjusting my dress, washing my hands and drying them, I walked out of the toilets as if nothing had happened but as I looked over at where Daniel was sitting, I found Michelle and him in mid conversation. Without interrupting them, I stood by the side of the toilets, just behind the pillar that blocked his view from seeing me and watched them talking. What were they saying? He seemed just as confused as I was when Tom burst into the toilets. What did Tom mean by Michelle *needing* it to happen? I could see her hand on his waist, touching him like she kept touching me. I was jealous. I wanted to know what they were talking about. I went to walk over but just as I took my first step, she kissed him on the cheek in a friendly way and left.

As soon as I reached Daniel's chair, he was already sat back down, another pint in his hand and looked surprised to see me standing there.

'Oh, you took your time.' He took a sip of his beer and swallowed so loud I could hear it.

'Yes, sorry. I was just trying to freshen up.' He didn't mention Michelle coming over to him nor did I mention Tom in the toilets, but I was so eager to find out what she had said to him. 'Did I miss much while I was gone then?' I tried to make it sound out like I didn't know.

'Nope, nothing,' he said, picking up his bag. 'Just enjoying the view before we leave. We had better go. We're being ushered onto the coach.'

I picked up my bag, following him, holding my hand up to the side of my bra, praying that the little bit of paper I had put in there from Tom didn't escape.

Our suitcases went in the holding area, and we climbed aboard the busy coach. I scanned quickly to see where Tom and Michelle were so we could deliberately sit at the other end, but I couldn't see them anywhere. Maybe I missed them, and they were tucked away at the back. Maybe they had forgotten something and went back to retrieve it. I sat down, my mind in overdrive, thinking about what he had said and what she had said to Daniel. The driver began to count numbers, pointing at people as he did so and then sat in his chair and started the engine. How weird, where were they? I sat back in the seat, trying to change my thoughts. Leaning my head against Daniel's shoulder, I closed my eyes.

The flight was uneventful, from the moment we boarded I counted every minute until we landed. I got up, I sat down, I flicked through every screen on the panel in the headrest in front of me and I twisted and fidgeted throughout the entire journey. By the time we landed, Daniel had just about had enough of me. The only thing keeping me going was Jack standing there with open arms. Everything took so long: the queue for border control, our baggage collection and then finally customs.

We had reached the exit gates to be met with crowds of people all holding boards and shrieks of excitement as loved ones were returning home. I couldn't see my parents anywhere; Daniel towering above me was trying to sift through all the faces to find the ones belonging to my mum and dad. He raised an arm and pointed to a space in the middle of the crowd, and I followed his guidance. I could feel my palms getting sweaty, slightly worried how Jack would react to us being home and having left him for nearly a week.

The little baby we left behind seemed to have changed in such a short timeframe; his cute chubby face still the most adorable I had ever seen. He stood beside my dad in his little white Nike trainers that I bought him just before we went away, holding onto my dad's trouser leg and looking all shy. Daniel called out to him but his face hid. I wasn't sure if he was playing hide and seek, or if he was angry with us for going. I dropped my bags instantly and prodded him jokingly in the tummy. He cheekily looked at me, smiling and threw himself at me. It was the biggest hug I had ever had in my whole life. I squeezed him so tight and didn't want to let go, welling up inside. I was a whole person yet again.

'Oh boy, how I missed you, sweetheart.' I held the back of his head so tight against my chest and picked him up off the floor. Daniel wrapped his arms around the both of us and gave a squeeze. The family was back together again.

'Well, I hope you've managed to bring the sunshine back with you because the weather has been miserable here while you have been away.' My mum laughed and gave us both a hug. Jack was so heavy now and half the size of me, normally he would be walking around but as we had missed him so much, Daniel took him from me and began carrying him back to the car. I gave my mum and dad another hug in turn and walked back talking about the holiday, sensitively missing out the parts I didn't think I should mention.

'Oh, and we're getting a puppy,' I said laughing out loud so that Daniel could hear as well as my mum and dad.

'Here we go,' Daniel said to Jack. 'Mummy is back, another brilliant idea of hers...'

They giggled together.

Chapter 22

Some Friendly Help

That night after getting home, I was shattered. My mum and dad dropped us off at home and I emptied the suitcases, put washing on and spent hours sitting on the floor with Jack, playing with toys, watching cartoons and just spending quality time with him. Being away had given me the chance to take a reality check, what was important and what wasn't. I even debated in my head if I was a good parent or not. While I went to work, he was with a childminder and I missed the times that he had hurt himself and needed a cuddle, his first words, steps, so many firsts that I wasn't there for but if I didn't go to work, he would equally miss out on so much.

What was right, what was wrong? I hoped that one day when we weren't always strapped for cash that things would get better and as he grew up, he would be proud of how hard we had worked as parents to give him everything he needed in life.

Jack hadn't left my side. During bath time, he wanted to get out and be wrapped up in his hooded bathrobe. He had chosen his favourite book from the small bookshelf in his bedroom and climbed into our bed. Several attempts to get him back into his bed and in his room had failed and after missing out on days of cuddles, I was more than happy for him to sleep in our bed with us. Daniel jumped on the bed with us and listened as I read his book in an animated fashion to him. Before I had reached the end of it, Daniel was snoring, and Jack was chuckling at the noises he was making.

'Gain, gain.' He couldn't quite say the full word, but I knew what he meant as he began pushing the pages back to the beginning for me to read again from the start. His eyes were sleepy, and he was yawning, but how could I refuse his little requests? I had all the time in the world for him. I leant back on the bed, my head on the pillow, holding the book up above us as Jack nestled up into my armpit, the covers all snug around us. I barely managed to get past the second page as his eyelids were so heavy, I couldn't really see his stunning bluey green eyes. I continued through the pages to make sure he was sound asleep. As I lowered the book on the last page, I dropped it to my side and stroked his silky-smooth brown hair. *How did we create something so perfect and so beautiful?* I thought. I too closed my eyes and was gone.

The morning woke me abruptly with a foot kick to my face. Jack was lying horizontally across both Daniel and I. He was sucking his thumb and wiggling his toes at me.

'Good morning, cheeky,' I said grabbing hold of his toes and tickling his foot.

He laughed as he jumped on me, clearly wanting me to get up and make his breakfast. His favourite was Farley's Rusks, softened with milk and mashed up like a smooth porridge. Leaving Daniel in bed for a while longer, we got our robes and slippers on and headed downstairs together; Jack bumping on his bottom, one step of the stairs at a time. We counted out loud as we went.

I sat him in his highchair, him eagerly kicking the tray waiting for his breakfast. I opened the cupboard doors as quietly as I could to not wake Daniel up. I wanted him happy and not grumpy for our last Saturday together before returning to work. There was a clink of the letterbox and a raft of envelopes fell to the ground. I dreaded letters arriving as I knew that most of them were chasing something. You never received any good news through the post.

Tightening my dressing gown belt, I quickly scooted across the floor to pick them up. Four out of the five were addressed to me in brown envelopes. They looked official as I quickly scanned them, flicking through each one in my hands. I placed them on the kitchen side next to me while I returned to making Jack's breakfast.

He was at that age where he was able to feed himself but most of it went round his face rather than in his mouth. Quite independent, he would growl at me if I tried feeding him, now he had learnt to do it himself, so I just made sure he didn't make too much mess and wasn't wearing his best clothes. Getting more and more excited and clapping his hands, I gave Jack his plastic bowl and spoon drenched in his crushed-up rusks and milk. I hadn't even taken my hand away before he plunged into it and was eager to take his first mouthful. You would think he hadn't been fed for weeks at the way he was so hungry.

I stood back against the worktop, picked up my post reluctantly and opened them one by one. Debt, debt and more debt. We were struggling. The bills we had coming in were more than we earnt, and Daniel was completely unaware. We had a joint back account, but I made the payments every month. We couldn't set up direct debits because most months they would bounce and the bank charges they threw on top were colossal. One month I would pay the mortgage and bounce the other bills, the next I would then not pay the mortgage and pay the bills, so it was a constant challenge that we didn't lose everything. The washing machine had broken so that went on my credit card. Jack needed new clothes as he was outgrowing his current wardrobe so that also went on my credit card. The more interest that was applied, the more I couldn't meet the demand.

Instead of working things out, sitting down and talking to Daniel and admitting defeat, I did the opposite and buried my head in the sand. *It will work itself out*, I thought. I folded the letters back in half, returned them to their envelopes and, opening the cupboard where we kept all our cookery books, I got out the first biggest one I could find. I opened it right in the middle of the book and hid the envelopes in between the pages. He would never go in that cupboard or use those books. Sliding it back in the cupboard and closing the door, I carried on as normal. That would bide me a couple more weeks until I had to think about them again.

Jack was squeezing the leftover of his breakfast into the gaps in his fingers and smearing it all over the tray. I opened the fridge door and got out a Cadburys Twirl, taking a finger out at a time. I savoured the taste along with a strong cup of tea. I always kept a supply of chocolate in the fridge for when I needed it, and it had to be Cadburys.

'No, baby, don't do that. You've got it everywhere.' I couldn't help but smile at him as he whacked his hand up and down, spattering the kitchen cupboards and walls. There was a gooey mess everywhere, but I couldn't have cared less. I had more pressing things to worry about and a little bit of mess here and there didn't bother me in the slightest. He laughed back thinking it was a funny game. How could I be angry at that cute, chubby face?

'Right, let's get you in the bath, you little mess monster and hopefully Daddy will be awake by the time we're done.'

Lifting Jack from his highchair, we trundled back upstairs and into the bathroom. I plonked him into the bath, the smell of Johnson's baby bath and soap filled the air as he played with the bubbles around him. No sooner had I got him in and started to wash his hair, I could hear Daniel calling.

'You two better get a wriggle on as we've got to go and see a man about a dog,' Daniel shouted from the bedroom.

'You what?' I said half hearing what he said.

'I'm guessing you want to come and look at puppies with me so you and Jack better get dressed quick so we can go.'

Was he being serious? Bundling Jack up in his towel, I ran into our room with him on my hip.

'Are you being serious?' I said jumping on the bed with Jack.

'You said you wanted a puppy. I thought it would be good for us and spoke to a few people on our way back home. They aren't ready yet as they're only a few weeks old, but we can go and choose one, think of a name, get the house all ready. Unless you think it's a bad idea and have changed your mind, of course?' He raised an eyebrow at me, lifting Jack onto his lap and tickling him.

'Of course I haven't changed my mind. Who wouldn't want a puppy? Oh wow, I'm so excited. I'll be ready in twenty minutes if you can watch Jack.'

I ran off to the bathroom in a hurry, jumped into the shower and quickly got ready. I could see what he was doing. I think what happened in Greece had given him a bit of a shock, seeing us both with other people, me liking women. Him wanting to bring us back together as a family would bond us with a new addition. Giving in to everything I wanted. Maybe I should tell him about our finances, having a dog as well would put further strain on our cash flow but it would potentially rock the boat and I didn't want us to have any more upset. I wanted us to have something exciting to look forward to. I kept quiet and didn't say a word.

We drove for about an hour. Jack, as usual, had fallen asleep about five minutes after we left home. The silent rock of the car and him tucked cosily into his car seat always made him drift off. Daniel and I spoke about how we would look after the puppy during the first few weeks, getting a new bed, toys, dog food, bowls. It was like a brand-new chapter in our life, something else that needed to rely on us. By the time we got there, Jack was a sweaty ball of cuteness, sucking his thumb in his car seat. We pulled up to a large white house with a gated fence. It looked like an old farmhouse, large metal sheds towards the back and a neatly landscaped front garden. Our car slowly dragged along the shingled driveway and up to the big red front door. As soon as I opened the door, I could hear the faint sound of dogs barking and classical music playing inside.

Waking Jack from his deep sleep and slipping on his coat, we got out of the car and made our way up the cobbled path. There was a brass, circular knocker that was heavy to lift, but Daniel gave it a firm knock and waited for them to answer. He looked at me and smiled, a bit of a twinkle in his eye, the way he used to look at me when we first met.

A pretty, middle-aged, smartly dressed lady answered the door. She reminded me slightly of Mary Poppins, her dark hair pulled back into a neat style and secured with a pin, rosy red cheeks and a fitted dress.

'Ah, you must be Daniel and Rose. Do come in. Mind the dogs and the mess. We're in the middle of feeding time.' She left the door open for us to come in and follow her through the house. It was very elegant inside, stone flooring with the occasional patterned rug, old wooden furniture and lots of ornaments that looked very expensive. The house smelt a lot of dogs but that was to be expected. I shut the door carefully behind me and we followed her through to what seemed to be the utility room, next to the kitchen. There were at least three Dalmatians running around the house, but they were friendly, and Jack giggled as they brushed past him.

It was quite a dark room, a small lamp in the corner was lit. There was a small leather sofa that had scratches and rips all over it, hidden by a large throw that was draped across half of it.

'Take a seat please. Make yourself at home. I'll be two minutes. I just need to shut these ones out first.' She walked out of the room.

259

We heard a couple of other doors slam and then the sound of her feet returning to the room. There was a small bookshelf filled with what looked like old antique, collectors books. All the classics from Charlotte Bronte to Louisa May Alcott. I recognised them because of my love of literature. Beside the bookshelf was a square pen, another Dalmatian and the sound of several little puppies barely with their eyes open moved around. They were all white, the faint outline of dark spots were forming.

I just wanted to peer over the side and cuddle them, but I sat attentively waiting for her to introduce us to them. She sat down in front of us, flung one leg over the other, her hands weaved together and looked at us.

'And this must be...' She looked at Jack who was pulling at my coat to look in the pen also.

'This is Jack, our son,' I said, bringing him closer to me and lifting him onto my lap to keep him under control.

'Nice to meet you, Jack. What a little cutie. And have you ever had a dog before? Do you currently have any?' She made her way over to the pen and knelt on the cold floor.

'We don't have any dogs at the moment, but my parents have always had dogs. We had them from a very early age, so I'm well versed on how to look after them. We also want Jack to be around animals and brought up with them from an early age.' I had appeared to put on a posh tone to my voice. I didn't want her to look down on us or think we weren't capable of bringing a dog into the family, nor that we wouldn't have a loving, caring home for one of her puppies to go to.

'Come, come.' She put up her hand and motioned for us to join her without listening to what I had to say. We did the same, carefully sitting on the floor next to her. I put my finger up against my lips and told Jack he had to be a good boy and be quiet, so we didn't startle the puppies. He sat down, legs crossed and was patient, just like he did when I read him a story. The lady reached in and with both hands picked up one of the larger puppies, lifting it out and placing it on Jack's lap, keeping her hands on his so it was safe and secure.

'You must treat it like a baby and look after it very carefully. Stroke its back like this. Isn't it soft and velvet-like?' She was showing Jack how to hold it as it whimpered around; its eyes still closed.

'Can I ask, how old they are?' I took the opportunity to give it a little stroke as well.

'Yes, my dear, they're only two weeks old. Their eyes should start to open any day now. They'll be ready at eight weeks to leave and will be wormed and vaccinated before you can collect them. The pups are all kennel club registered and full pedigrees. We have three generations of winners so they will be beautiful. There are three boys and two girls, do you have a preference?' She looked straight at Daniel, rather than me.

'I'm thinking a boy please.' We spoke about it in the car. I didn't mind so I left it to him to make the decision.

'If you would like to pick up any of the others feel free to do so but just be gentle. Once you have a chosen pup, we will note it down. You're lucky as you are the first family to visit, so the full litter is available.' She smiled as she stood up, moving back to her chair to sit down whilst we were left to cuddle all the puppies in turn. It

261

was hard to decide. They were all cute but all so similar. Then there was one rather plump puppy, rolled up in the corner that caught my eye. An all-white one but with black spots on his nose and big front paws. He looked like the biggest one of them all, content and happy on his own in the corner.

'What about that one?' I turned to Daniel and Jack. 'He seems lovely.'

I leant forwards and picked him up. He was all warm; I had disturbed his cosy sleep. He stretched out, his eyes still closed and let out a little yawn.

'I hold,' Jack said holding out his hands.

I passed him over, being careful that Jack was gentle. He bent forwards and tried to kiss him. It was so lovely to see him being careful with something so small and petite, normally all his toys and cars were thrown, and he was so rough but, in this instance, he was very delicate and caring.

'If that's the one you want, then let's go for it. Can we leave a deposit so that you know we are serious?' Daniel asked the lady, hoping for confirmation.

'Yes, sure. I will just take down all your details. Let me get a pen and paper and we can go from there.' She got up to get them leaving us doting on the puppies, the big one in particular.

'Okay, Jack. Time to put him back into his bed. Let him go back to sleep so his mummy doesn't get too upset.' I helped Jack slowly place him back into the pen and sit on the chair with us, waiting for the lady to return. She was carrying a see-through plastic folder containing some papers.

'Now I am going to give you this. It's a cheat sheet for owning a puppy, the things you need to purchase, what food they have been fed on so far and some details of their pedigree. If you could just fill in this form for me which just has your contact information on so that we can transfer the pedigree into your name or names as the owner, and my contact information along with the date of when he can leave home. Do you have any questions?' She handed it over to us along with a pen.

Once we had given the lady all our details and a cash deposit, we said our goodbyes. Jack blew a kiss to the puppies but got a little upset. He thought we were taking them home with us today and couldn't quite understand that we had a few more weeks to wait. It was hard telling Jack to wait patiently until we could take our puppy home when I was over excited myself. I was like a child at Christmas with things like this, behaving more and more hyper until the day arrived. We got settled back into the car and promised Jack we would get some sweets on the way home if he was a good boy to distract him from the puppies. It worked and like clockwork, the rocking of the car moving sent him off to sleep.

Taking all the opportunity I could while Jack was asleep, I turned to Daniel and smiled naughtily at him. He took a double take at me as he noticed I was looking at him out of the corner of his eye.

'What?' He shot back at me.

'So, I was thinking, how about we get a takeaway tonight and go to bed early? I want to try something new and dirty,' I asked him, hoping his answer would be yes.

'Can do,' was all he could manage. 'I'm really tired, to be honest.'

263

I gave him a look that could kill.

'What?' he said again.

'Can do? If you don't want to then don't worry about it. I just thought...' I looked out of the car window and stared at the traffic passing us in the opposite direction on the other side of the road.

'I didn't mean it like that. Don't be mad.' He seemed to realise that what he had said annoyed me.

'I'll make it worth your while.' I spun my head back round to face him and smiled.

'Oh yeah, what have you got planned?' Daniel appeared a little more interested now.

'You'll have to wait and see when we get home.' Ever since the holiday, I had sex on my mind. I wanted to spice things up between us, to make things exciting and to make sure he was never tempted away by anyone other than me. I had to think of new things that we could do in the bedroom, something that he would never do with other people. I was open and game to try anything and everything.

We stopped off at the local shops on the way home to get some essentials, a bottle of wine and I picked up a candle. I wanted it to be romantic just as much as it would be seductive. And a bar of Cadburys chocolate. That was on my essentials list, chocolate was part of my five a day. The cheapest takeaway was fish and chips and whilst it wasn't something I really fancied, I was conscious that we had little to no money despite Daniel putting down a deposit on the puppy earlier that day. We would have to tighten our belts even more than we already were.

I carried the warm bag of fish and chips in my arms, enjoying the heat it was giving off and the smell of salt and vinegar filled the air with an aroma that was making us both extremely hungry. We had managed to keep Jack asleep the whole time I was at the shops. Almost as if he knew, turning the last corner before home, Jack began to stir, waking up with a sleepy smile and bright red cheeks.

I asked Daniel if he wouldn't mind getting Jack quickly changed and into his baby grow, ready for bed so that he could have his dinner and last bottle of milk before bed. While he was upstairs, I set up the table with three mats, one for each of us with Daniel and I sat opposite each other and Jack in the middle. I couldn't find a candlestick holder, so I got a bottle of Rolling Rock from the fridge, emptied the contents into a glass and then stuck the tall white candle into the top of the bottle. As I lit it, the wax ran down the side and onto the bottle, and I placed it in the middle of the table. Knives and forks out along with condiments. Candlelit fish and chips, what could be more romantic?

Both my boys walked into the kitchen, Daniel tickling Jack and him chuckling like they always did. We may have had him young, but Daniel was such a good dad to him, and he was his world. He would have done anything for that little boy. Daniel laughed as he saw the table and how I had improvised with the candle.

'I love it,' he said, kissing my forehead. We sat down to dinner, music playing in the background rather than the television as it forced us into conversation and not locked onto whatever was on the screen. We had a hi-fi stacking tower music system that included a record player at the top, two cassette decks in the middle and a CD player at the bottom. There were two large speakers either side that I had tuned into the radio, playing a variety of songs for us to listen to. It was a gift for my sixteenth birthday from my parents and I had it on all the time.

I had a glass of fizz; Daniel had his bottle of beer to which Jack would hold up his beaker and say cheers to us every time we took a sip. We laughed and spoke about so many things from the puppy and what we were going to call him to what needed to be done next to the house when we could afford it. Again, I avoided the topic of money and I felt like it was going to be forever before we could afford anything at all. My mind was wandering to what I wanted to do to Daniel in the bedroom as Jack kept rubbing his heavy eyes. That was the signal I needed to take Jack up to his cot and I could then get ready for Daniel.

'Say goodnight to Daddy.' I picked up Jack from his highchair and walked him round so he could give Daniel a kiss before bedtime. He gave the cutest kiss, puckering up his lips and pinning it on Daniel. Jack scrunched his hand up and waved back to his dad as I walked him off to bed.

'Give me fifteen minutes, Daniel, and then come up,' I shouted to him as I made my way upstairs.

Jack loved his sleep. Every night I would place him in his wooden cot, fold over his baby duvet so that it was tucked under his armpits, and I would stroke his soft golden-brown hair as I read him a story. Very rarely did I make it past the fifth page before he was fast asleep.

Slowing the strokes to his head, I stood up, inserted his book back between all the others on his bookshelf and tip toed out of his room leaving only a glowing night light to guide my way. I went to the bathroom to quickly freshen up but then realised I had left something downstairs. With nothing but my dressing gown on, I went into the kitchen; Daniel still at the table finishing his beer and tapping his feet to the music. I opened the cupboard door and took out a small glass tumbler. Removing an ice cube tray from the freezer, I popped out some of the ice cubes into the tumbler and headed back upstairs.

'Are you coming up?' I called for Daniel to join me. I ran round the side of the bed to his chest of drawers and took out a tie, the only one he owned, and placed it on the side. I could see the flicker of light getting brighter and brighter as it reached our room and Daniel was standing in the doorway holding the bottle of Rolling Rock in his hand, the candle in it melting away.

'Should I be scared?' he asked as he laughed quietly, trying not to wake Jack.

'Absolutely. I want you to sit on the bed and do everything I tell you to do.'

I had removed my dressing gown and had on a sexy black lace underwear set. I didn't have many sets of underwear; Jack's clothes came first and then whatever money was left, if any, I spent on my own clothes and underwear. Most of them had holes in or were fraying but I had a few nice ones for special occasions like this.

Daniel set the candle on the side next to the tie and sat on the bed. I moved to stand between his legs and kissed him. With both my hands around the side of his face, I pushed my breasts against his chest and my thighs right up close to his cock hoping to feel him get

267

hard. I started to unbutton the top two buttons of his polo shirt and pulled it off over his arms and upper body. Moving back in to kiss him again, my hands ran down his neck to his chest and to his belt. He reached up to touch my breasts as I undid his zip and asked him to stand up so I could remove his trousers and boxer shorts leaving him completely naked and vulnerable. I liked being in charge and telling him what to do. It was the only time I was in charge of our relationship, of his actions and the only time he did what I was telling him to do.

'Now lie back on the bed with your arms above your head.' He looked at me confused and I think a little worried, but he did it anyway. 'Close your eyes.'

I straddled him on the bed. As he closed his eyes, I kissed him again, even more passionately than I did before, our tongues writhing together as if they were one. I took the tie from the side with one hand and with the other moved his arms so his hands were touching each other. I wrapped the tie around his wrists a couple of times and then started to feed it through the metal headboard attached to the bed.

Daniel opened his eyes. 'Rose, what are you doing?' He looked worried.

'Shush… close your eyes and go with it. Enjoy it. I'm not going to hurt you.'

As soon as the tie was wrapped around his wrists and tied to the headboard, his hands were tied together, a knot in the end to keep them tight. So now he was where I wanted him. He couldn't touch me and I could do whatever I wanted with him. I kissed his lips, his eyes still firmly closed.

I whispered in his ear. 'How much do you want me to suck your cock?'

He didn't open them, he just whispered back. 'So much, take it all the way down. As far down your neck as you can.'

I started by kissing his neck, his chest and next his stomach. Long, slow, wet kisses, my hands following me all the way down, touching his body as I moved. I reached his cock but before I took it in my mouth, I pulled his legs up so I could fit between them and ran my tongue from his balls down to the space just before his arsehole. The skin there was so soft. I took his balls and sucked them into my mouth, paying attention to what he enjoyed. I felt for the tumbler glass on the side with the ice cubes in and popped one in my mouth. It started to melt instantly, making my tongue and the inside of my mouth tingle from the ice. My teeth were sensitive from the cold. I swirled the ice cube around and around so that the whole of my mouth was frozen.

As I looked down, Daniel was rock hard from the suspense of what was going to happen next. His legs dropped back down leaving his cock standing on end, ready for action. I cupped his cold, wet testicles with one hand and with the other held his girth like a strong handle. The tip was pulsing like it was ready to explode. I placed my lips on the tip. Like a purse, I gently opened one side of my mouth to let a trickle of ice-cold water run down his shaft. He let out a gasp as the cold hit him, running down to the bottom. I did the same on the other side letting more water run down his length, so it was completely covered.

My hand that was holding his testicles was drenched. I used this to massage into the area between his perineum and his cock, his trimmed pubic hair wet and glistening. I gently stroked, rubbed and massaged him, his face showing pleasure as I went for it. Like a suction cup, I wrapped my mouth around him, taking his cock in my mouth, careful not to let any more of the water out. I sank down to his base, the tip reaching the back of my throat till I couldn't take it anymore without gagging. His member was completely submerged in a cold cave of ice-cold water. I pumped up and down, occasionally swallowing a small amount, so I had room for his stiffening cock. He began moaning but they were dampened by having to keep the noise down. His hands and arms were taut as he could feel the pressure and wanted to hold my head as I increased the pace.

Harder and harder, faster and faster, up and down I pumped. All the ice had melted but I was left with a small amount of water in my mouth, keeping his cock moist, massaging his testicles as my lips pursed tighter together to make him cum. I was so turned on seeing him in pleasure, I had full control of his bodily functions. There was nothing he could do to stop me and I got off on pleasing him. His body buckled, his cock bulging ready to explode. I swallowed and felt him shoot his load down my throat. I swallowed again to taste his thick, salty cum, his legs and toes shuddering. I didn't stop there. Once my mouth was empty and I had taken down every last drop, I used my tongue to circle his red tip. He was tingling with pleasure. Opening his eyes, I could tell he couldn't take any more and was trying to force his way out of the tie. I kept going, his hands broke free and he had to grab my hair to stop him from shouting.

'Stop, stop, I can't take any more,' he tried to say as he regained control. He took in a deep breath as he held my head, his face flushed and his wrists red from being strapped so tight. He took in more deep breaths as if he had run a marathon and closed his eyes, concentrating on bringing himself back down again.

'Come here,' he said pulling me up to him. 'That was amazing. It felt so good. Give me five minutes to get myself back together.'

It didn't bother me that I hadn't cum. I was extremely turned on but that was from seeing what I had done to him and how I had made him feel. I pulled up the corners of the duvet to cover us. I tucked myself in under his armpit, my head resting on his shoulder. His eyes still closed, he looked relaxed but as though all his energy had been sucked out of him. I closed my eyes too.

Monday morning and the routine started as normal. I opened my eyes and had the feeling of, 'oh no I don't want to go back to work'. I was enjoying being off with Daniel and Jack, not having to rush around and cram as much as I could into twenty-four hours. There was the potential of calling in sick, but my mum had always taught me that unless you were dying, you went to school, or you went to work, and I stuck with that theory.

Lying next to Daniel, who was fast asleep and snoring, it was nice and cosy, wrapped in a thick duvet. My legs were frozen on the bed, not wanting to venture out into the cold. I was psyching myself up to move. I could hear Jack playing in his cot with his toys and talking to himself. He must be patiently waiting for me to come and get him. *I must get up. I'm going to be late if I don't get ready.* But the energy and excitement for the day just wasn't there. I dangled one foot out of the corner of the bed, then the other but then tucked them back in again. Daniel rolled over, fidgeting, before opening one eye, looking at me as if I had been caught out.

'What time is it?' he said yawning.

'6:30. I need to get up, but I don't want to,' I said.

"Uuuggghhhhh…' He closed his eyes again and screwed up his face before returning to sleep. He didn't have to get Jack up and ready, feed him his breakfast or have long hair that needed washing, drying and styling. He had it easy and could afford to go back to sleep for another half an hour.

I plucked up the courage to get up, picking my dressing gown off the floor from a pile next to my bed and tied it as tight as I could. Walking into Jack's bedroom, I was greeted by his warm smile and messy hair. He stood up, clutching at the bars and peering over the top. He could quite easily climb out, but I don't think he had quite figured out how to yet. Reaching over the top, I picked him up. He was so warm and cuddly, and he was also getting heavier and heavier, but his cuddles were so lovely that I carried him around everywhere with me.

'Good morning, gorgeous.' I hugged him as he wrapped both arms around my neck and hung on. 'Hungry? Let's get you some breakfast whilst Mummy has a cup of tea and some chocolate.'

We made our way downstairs, me careful not to fall down the stairs as I couldn't quite see where I was going. It was still quite dark in the mornings, but I didn't want to turn on every light in the house. The only light downstairs was the streetlights glowing into the kitchen from outside and the light of the moon. I reached underneath the cooker hood and flicked on the small, square light so I was able to find my way around the kitchen. I hated early mornings, they made me feel nauseous. Even though I was polite, I told people not to talk to me until at least 10 a.m. After that point, you would get the better side of me. I placed Jack in his highchair, filled up the kettle and began making his breakfast.

Bang, bang, bang. There was a knock at the door. What on earth? Who would that be at this hour in the morning? I felt sick, something was not right. I stood still, not wanting to answer it as I had a bad feeling.

Bang, bang, bang. There it was again. I had to answer it. Giving Jack his bowl and spoon so he could start eating, I went to answer the door. I unlocked it quietly and as it creaked open, I found a huge man standing there. He must have been taller than six feet, stocky and very serious looking. Who was this and why was he knocking on my door when the rest of the neighbourhood were fast asleep in their beds?

'Erm, hello? Can I help you?' I looked at him puzzled. I could hear Daniel shouting from bed asking who was at the door.

'Are you Rosemary and have you seen letters from Ashworth?' he said in rather a deep, stern voice. My heart pounded; I knew who he was.

Ashworth were the company that had been chasing me for payments on my credit cards, the ones that I had folded back up and put in the cupboard without telling Daniel. I knew this was serious and I was in trouble.

'I am and I have.' I admitted it straight away. I could lie, but where would that get me? After all, it was 6:45 a.m., I was in my dressing gown, and I had a scary-looking giant at my door. Now was not the right time to act dumb.

'Okay, so I have come to collect the sum of £800. We have written to you and called numerous times without a response. I must leave today with the money or remove goods to that amount.' He wasn't joking.

'I… erm… I don't have that sort of money,' I said panicking. How did I get out of this one? Daniel called to me from upstairs. It was all happening at once.

'Can a family member or friend lend you the money?' he asked.

'Not at this time in the morning, no.' I didn't know what else to say. I had to think fast. 'Can I have some time to pay and make an arrangement?' I thought maybe he would be nice and give me a chance.

'We have given you time to pay. You have ignored us and so this is the last resort. It went to court. You didn't attend the hearing and so now it is with me as a debt collector to either get the money or remove goods to that amount. Your cards also have been blocked.' He stood there motionlessly. He didn't care one little bit. It was his job not to care.

'Goods? What do you mean by goods?' I was thinking any minute Daniel was going to come steaming down the stairs and I would be in trouble.

'Stereos, jewellery, televisions, basically anything of value that we can sell to cover your debt, madam.' He had an envelope in one hand, a mobile phone in the other. He wore an identification badge around his neck with his picture on it. I could tell he was getting impatient.

'All I have is £100 in my purse. *Please,* is there any way you could give me forty-eight hours to get the money together?' I was half expecting him to say no but he looked at me. He could hear Jack in the background talking. He must have finished his breakfast and now wanted a drink.

'Okay, seeing as you look like a nice lady, I'm going to hand you this envelope. Inside is my number. I will take the £100 now *but* I need you to give me a call within forty-eight hours and make payment by card or I will be back the following day to take things. Do you understand? This is *serious.* If you don't answer the door, we have the right to phone the police and gain access. Understand?' He passed me the envelope.

I nodded as I went to retrieve my purse from the bottom step of the stairs. With shaking hands, I took out five twenty-pound notes and handed them to him. I should have asked him for a receipt or confirmation of our agreement, but I just wasn't thinking. I wanted to get rid of him as quickly as possible.

'Thanks.' He almost snatched the notes out of my hand. 'Have a good day,' he said as he stuffed the notes into his pocket, turned and walked off.

I shut the door behind him and stood with my back to the cold plastic, closing my eyes to pause and think. *That's all I need to start my day.* Jack in the background was getting louder and louder from the kitchen.

'Rose, who was that?' Daniel called down again to me but still not getting up.

'Just the electricity company come to read the meters and see if we wanted to change our tariff,' I shouted back up to him.

'At this time in the morning?'

'Yeah, how rude. All done now though.' I went back into the kitchen to settle Jack, finding his beaker from the cupboard and filling it with milk from the fridge with my shaking hands. I needed to think of a way of fixing this and quickly before Daniel found out. That wasn't the only bill either. If I paid this one, it still left me with another five or six debts still to pay. Short of robbing a bank, I had no way out and for every pound I earnt, I had two that I owed. I put my masked face on, acted completely normal and got ready for work. Daniel was none the wiser.

That morning at work, I wasn't myself. The mundane job that it was left me working on auto pilot mode whilst I occasionally stared at the screen wondering how I was going to get myself out of the hole that I was in. Daniel would understand why we were in debt, but I also knew he would go into panic mode and lock down every penny. He would be angry that I had let the situation get out of control and would ration things, stop us going out and he would be in a bad mood all the time. I didn't want him to resent us moving out, or us settling down so I just wanted to keep everything as it was. Living in a bubble where everything was okay. *There'll be less arguments and we'll be happy this way*, I thought.

At work, Teresa and George had both made several attempts to come over and talk to me during the day but I just wasn't in the mood. George's inappropriate comments were starting to annoy me and Teresa's daily dramas made me realise just how petty they were. *Try living in my world where the ends don't meet.*

'Hey, what's up, Rose?' Teresa sat on the edge of my desk on all my papers so I couldn't process them.

'I'm struggling right now. No money, bills coming out of my ears, and I can't meet the demands.' I finally opened up, pushing the papers across the desk and pulling them out from under her bottom.

'I can help. What do you need? Fifty quid, a hundred?' She kindly offered to help me but she had no idea.

'More like a thousand. I had a debt collector turn up this morning before work. Daniel doesn't know and I've got forty-eight hours to pay the remaining seven hundred. Where am I going to find that sort of money? I can't ask my parents as they'll tell me to move back home if I can't afford things.' I felt sick inside that I had let it get this far and out of control.

'Oh, I see,' she said, clearly thinking how she could help. 'I could maybe stretch to £500, but I have a lot to sort out on my car this month, otherwise I would lend you the whole amount and then just pay me as and when you can. I know you'll pay it back. Besides I know where you work and where you live.' She laughed out loud. I couldn't believe she was trying to help me. 'I can go to the bank at lunch, you can pay it in yours and give the guy a ring.' She made it sound so easy and it was a relief but at the same time, I was borrowing more money to pay a bill that I still had to pay back.

'Really?' I said looking at her. 'I owe you and I promise to pay it back as quickly as I can.' I stood up giving her a hug and letting out a huge sigh.

'You're welcome but I must insist that you come out with me for a drink one night this week or next as a thank you. I need a drinking buddy and you have just said yes.' She leapt up from the desk and wandered back to her workstation.

Thirty minutes later, George came over to my desk, hovering around.

'Did you want something, George?' I peered up at him from my screen, expecting him to make a sarcastic comment. He was acting all sheepish, like he had a question to ask but didn't know how to approach it. Very unlike him.

'Rose,' he said, now leaning against the corner of my desk. I carried on working whilst thinking he was wasting my time.

'Yes?' I replied.

'Don't be mad but Teresa said you're a bit strapped for cash and I thought maybe I could help?' He paused, waiting to catch my attention. I instantly looked up, mad that Teresa had said something.

'What? She said what?' I didn't know what to say.

'She's only trying to help. You know that, right? I want to help you too. That's what friends are for. I've had a chunk of commission this month so I can give you some if it would help you out of a situation?' He smiled at me and I felt guilty for thinking he was wasting my time. 'I can get it this afternoon for you.' His beautiful brown eyes had a slight twinkle in them as he smiled at me. I couldn't quite believe that they would both help me. I also felt guilty that this was all a secret from Daniel, and he had no idea.

I still had to find a way of making extra money. I couldn't work any more hours than I was already doing as I didn't see Jack enough as it was. I had been in this job for nearly a year, if I could get to a salesperson's role rather than admin, I could make more than double what I was currently making but how did I get to the next level up? I needed experience and how did you get experience when you haven't done it before? I decided to speak to my manager to see what career progression meant and how I could climb the ladder. I knew I was more than capable. It was whether someone would give me the chance and believe in me.

My manager was very rarely in the office. She spent her time on the first floor of the office, surrounded by the account managers and only came downstairs with her team when something went wrong or to check on us. She had very poor people skills and I found it difficult to talk to her but what did I have to lose? I started to type out an email to her.

'Good afternoon, Anne,' I wrote. 'I know you are extremely busy, but I wondered if you could spare me thirty minutes of your time to discuss career progression. As both my manager and a highly respected peer within the company, I would really appreciate the ability to ask your advice on a few matters.' I signed off: 'Kindest regards, Rose.'

I read it about twenty times in my head before finally clicking send. She may not reply to me but if I didn't do something, I could risk losing the house and my debts spiralling out of control, more than they already were.

Less than five minutes later, my computer made a dinging sound, and I got a notification that meant she had replied.

'Yep. Can do 2 p.m.' That was all she wrote but I guess at least she had replied to me.

I had less than an hour to prepare and think of what I wanted to say to her, what I wanted to get out of the meeting and how I would justify me wanting to step up. I got out my notebook from my drawer and my half chewed, black biro pen and started scribbling down all my positive attributions. Why would I be perfect for a sales role? Why should she consider promoting me to all the sales managers in the business? My day couldn't get any worse, could it?

Anne came stomping through the office, her coffee cup in hand and her phone in the other. No smile on her face as usual. She walked up to my desk. 'Come with me. We can use the back office for a chat.'

As I stood up, I noticed everyone in the office watching. Normally if Anne wanted a chat, you were either fired or in trouble, so I could only imagine what they were all thinking. I smiled reassuringly at everyone, so they knew I wasn't concerned. Nervously, I followed her to the back office.

She sat down at the head of the table, taking a sip of her coffee and told me to sit next to her, interlinking her hands and fingers on the desk in front of her. I did as I was told, crossing my legs and placing my notebook and pen on the table.

'So, what did you want to discuss?' She cut straight to the chase. No chit chat, no small talk. Just straight to the point. I had to act confident. I knew what I wanted, and I needed her help.

'Thank you for taking the time to sit down with me. I… erm… wanted a little advice from you.' I was staring straight at her, serious and assertive.

'Go on,' she said.

'Basically, I want to move into sales. I've worked very hard here since I've been in this role, and I want to know what I need to do to progress.' I stopped talking, waiting for her reaction and hoping to take a steer from her.

Anne didn't move a muscle. I could see her thinking, before her expression changed to a smile and then a laugh. She flicked her dark hair backwards and laughed at me in a taunting manner, instantly making me feel stupid that I had even thought she would help me. *Where do I go from this?* I thought.

'So, you want to be a salesperson? And what makes you think you're ready? You're just an administrator at the moment. It takes skills, confidence and experience to move into sales.' She picked up her coffee again and took a bigger, longer sip, sitting back in her chair and folding her arms. Normally I would just sit there and bite my lip, but I wanted this and had to prove my point.

'I am confident, and I do think I have the skills to be very good in sales. I may not have the experience, but I am a quick learner. I've shown you that from learning my current role quickly. I process way more orders than the others, I finish first every day. I just need the opportunity to—'

281

She stopped me in my tracks before I could continue justifying myself. 'I'm going to stop you there. I have a very busy day ahead of me today, I appreciate you reaching out but maybe we will have this chat in another year or so. Okay?'

I nodded without choice. She stood up taking her coffee and phone with her, leaving the door to slam behind her. I took a few moments just to sit there and reflect on what had just happened. I stared out the tall, floor to ceiling windows, fitted with slatted blinds and into the car park beyond. My small car at the end of the row surrounded by flashy sports cars. *Well, that didn't go according to plan.* I heard a tap on the door, thinking that she had come back to apologise for her abrupt departure but as I turned around, George was standing in the doorway.

'Hey, you okay? What was that all about, she didn't fire you, did she?' He looked concerned. 'I came over to give you your money but saw you both walk off to the meeting. As soon as she walked out, I thought I would make sure you were okay.' Why was he being so nice to me? Why did he care whether I had been fired or not?

'No, quite the opposite. I asked her for a meeting. Thank you so much for the money. You've literally just saved my life.' I stood up to give him a big hug as he handed me a white envelope full of cash. Money had never felt so good or been so appreciated.

'Anytime,' he said mid hug. As we let each other go, he looked down at me and said, 'So, are you going to tell me what the meeting was about?'

'I stupidly asked her how I could move into sales, but she practically laughed in my face. I don't get it. How do I get in if

I'm not already in it and no one will give me a chance without experience? There are no formal qualifications so what do I need to do?' I flooded him with questions.

'Right, sit down. Let's have a little chat.' He put his hand on my shoulder as he sat in the same chair as Anne had sat in. 'You don't learn sales, you either have it or you don't. A good salesperson is a people person, if you know what I mean. It takes confidence and no self-doubt. If you believe in the product you're selling, then people will want to buy it. Don't be pushy. You have two ears and one mouth which means you need to listen to the customer twice as much as you talk. Understand what they want, why they would need something, how it would benefit them. Make them then feel like they don't *want* your product, they *need* it. Get it?'

Somehow, he had managed to speak the wisest words I had ever heard and was so motivational, yet he was the one person that I always thought spoke complete rubbish. He was so right.

'But how do I get into it? How do I talk someone into giving me a chance if everyone just laughs at me and doesn't take me seriously?'

'Not everyone will laugh at you. Anne laughed at you because she's arrogant, and she's threatened by you. A younger, prettier, talented woman in her team that wants to progress could overtake her and more importantly, she doesn't want you to leave her team because right now you're killing it. Top performer, intelligent, it takes a lot to find a good employee like you. Don't let her dampen your enthusiasm or you wanting to succeed. Ignore her, be bolder and more determined than ever before and you will be successful.' His words were imprinted in my mind. He was so encouraging; I couldn't believe it and here he was handing me money to get out of my situation.

'Why are you being so nice to me?' I asked. 'You've given me money and now this advice. I wish I had asked for your input and not hers from the beginning.' I threw him another appreciative smile.

'I'm not giving you money. I'm loaning it to you, and I hate to see someone with such enthusiasm be shot down like you just have. I'll introduce you to my sales manager and I'll also help you prepare for it. Stand up in the room and tell him why he needs to hire you, why you would be good for the team. If his goal is to hit a target, how can you help him hit it? Put yourself in his shoes and try to think of what he would want to see from a salesperson. That's how you'll convince him, okay?'

Wow, he was like a fountain of knowledge, and he had just told me everything I needed to know. I was looking at him in a whole new light. He was successful and now I knew why.

'Okay, you got this?' he said looking me straight in the eyes.

'Yes, I've got this. I can't ever thank you enough. You don't know how much this means to me.' I was blushing.

'I think I do, and I'll think of how you can repay me.' George winked one of his stunning brown eyes and chuckled a naughty chuckle. I didn't know whether he was joking or serious and whether I should hug him again or just fist bump him. It became slightly awkward, but I laughed it off instead and punched him jovially in the shoulder. 'We better get back to work or someone will think we're up to something in here, if you know what I mean. Now, go pay your debts and go home tonight thinking positive.' He got up, patted me on the back and walked out of the room.

I sat in the chair and thought for a few moments more. I couldn't believe my luck and that I had managed to find the best of friends here at work. I took a big sigh of relief, straightened my blouse, collected my things and left the room. This time when I sat at my desk, I was calm knowing I had the money to pay the debt collector and I had the potential of a possible route into sales. My day was definitely going to end better than it had started.

I worked through my lunch break so I could finish slightly earlier and pay the money George had given me into my bank account. Finishing my final order and having it entered onto the system, I switched off my screen, pushed my seat under the desk and said good day to everyone. I practically ran to the car, drove as fast as I could to the high street, sweating and trying to catch my breath. I approached the counter, handing the lady the envelope of cash from George and my bank card. I tapped my nails impatiently on the screen between her and me. She glared at me prompting me to stop. She printed off the receipt and I said thank you. As soon as I was outside, I took out the piece of paper that the debt collector had given me earlier that morning and began to dial his number.

'Hello?' he answered straight away.

'Hi, my name is Rosemary. You called at my house earlier this morning to collect some money. I'm calling to pay the rest. My reference number is 543—' I didn't finish giving him the number before he interrupted.

'Yes, I know who you are. Okay, do you have your long card number and I will take the eight hundred pounds.'

'What? Wait a second. I gave you a hundred pounds this morning so it leaves seven to pay.' I was confused.

'I'm sorry, madam. I don't remember taking any money from you this morning. Did you get a receipt?'

Was he joking? I definitely got the money out of my purse and handed it to him. I wasn't dreaming that.

'Well, no I didn't get a receipt. I just presumed that—'

He cut me off again and was quite rude. 'In that case, you didn't give me any money.'

He had stolen my money this morning but what could I do? I had no proof; he had completely taken advantage of me and my predicament. I couldn't tell Daniel and I couldn't prove that I had given it to him.

'Hey, that's not fair. You know I gave you that money this morning. Please don't. I couldn't even afford the eight hundred let alone another hundred. I've had to borrow this and will have to pay it back.' I began to cry, just when I thought things were looking up.

'I'm really sorry, madam, but I don't know what money you're talking about. You really should be more careful in the future and look after it.'

How could he do this to me? I had no way other than to accept it. Slowly, and trying to hold back the tears, I began to read out my card number and details. The tears were more from anger than upset. I was angry that I was so stupid. What a lesson learnt.

'Okay, that's gone through. Here is your reference number.' He gave me a string of letters and numbers which I noted and without saying thanks or bye, I hung up. I was annoyed at myself. That was a hundred pounds that I didn't have. Wiping the tears, I made my way back to the car so I could go and pick up Jack from the childminder and get home.

I was beginning to realise that in this world there are some genuine, honest and loyal people but there are also those who were untrustworthy and deceitful and the only way I was going to get anywhere was to be smarter and not play by the book. I already had a problem with trusting people, and this only strengthened my opinion.

All I wanted to do was go home, be with my baby and my man. Being angry made me frustrated and there was only one way I could alleviate that frustration and it was drink or sex or, even better, both. If I had been taught one lesson today, it was to take control of my life and to take control in the bedroom. That was the one place that I ruled, and I took charge. Boy was Daniel going to get it tonight.

Daniel was his usual quiet self when he got in. He gave me a big kiss and Jack a big cuddle. 'How was your day, beautiful?' he asked me.

'Yeah, not bad, thanks. Yours?' I shrugged off the day's events, not mentioning anything that had happened.

'Same shit, different day,' he said. He seemed down.

'Well, once dinner is done, you and me are going to have an early night.' I turned around and smiled cheekily at him.

'Oh, I like the sound of that. Does it involve ice cubes again?' Daniel laughed under his breath as he spun Jack around the kitchen. He was giggling from the way his dad was holding him like a plane and swooshing him back and forth. I laughed back. While I was chopping the vegetables, I was thinking of ways I could top the ice cube episode and make him think about it all day tomorrow.

We ate dinner and spent some time playing with Jack in the bath. I always filled the tub with so much baby bath that the bubbles piled high around him. Jack had so many toys, from foam letters and numbers to submarines and fish that he would fill with water and pour back out again. Daniel and I would both arrange the letters to spell a rude word every morning in the shower for the other to see, at Jack's age he didn't realise what they spelt but it made us both laugh.

Drying him down and dusting Jack in talcum powder, I wrapped him up in his pyjamas and got him into bed, reading him his favourite book before he fell asleep. I walked back into the bathroom to clear the bath of bubbles, wipe down the tiles and take out all of his toys. I had stripped down to my underwear because Jack had got my clothes so wet from all the splashing. As I was bent right over the side of the bath with the shower hose in my hand, Daniel appeared.

'Need a hand with that?' I knew he wasn't asking if I wanted a hand. He was asking if I wanted a *hand*. I liked the sound of that. Turning off the shower and wrapping the metal cord round the bath taps, I left them running to fill the tub back up as I turned around to face him.

'Well, I am quite wet.'

He looked at my half naked body and with one hand and his middle finger, he ran it round the top of my knickers, pulling them out towards him, letting them go so they flicked against my skin. That tease only made me feel naughtier than I was already feeling.

I tip toed up to kiss him, unbuttoning his trouser zip at the same time. I could feel he was already hard; I only had to touch him or talk about sex for him to get horny. I was the same, a touch from him left me wet and excited. Opening his trousers to expose his Calvin Klein boxer shorts, I pulled them down over his bottom letting them drop to the floor. His socks came off one by one. His T-shirt was next, up and over his shoulders and off to join his trousers on the floor. Daniel reached behind me and unfastened my bra. My breasts fell out, my nipples instantly turning hard from the cold of the room.

'Pinch them,' I said. 'I want you to pinch my nipples like this.' I grabbed his and pinched his really hard.

'Argh, Rose!'

I had given him the okay to be hard with me. Flicking my long hair over my shoulder, I turned around grabbing hold of the sink basin and bent over showing him my round and voluptuous bottom cheeks. Looking over my shoulder at him and biting my bottom lip, he moved over standing right behind me. He didn't take my knickers off, instead he pulled at the thong between my cheeks and pulled it to one side, slipping his fingers down to reach my soaking wet pussy. He eased a finger in so he could feel it disappear as it sunk deep inside. I groaned as it felt so good. His other hand worked its way round from my hips to my front, cupping both my breasts in turn, pinching and squeezing my nipples till they hurt. The harder he did it, the more I liked it and the louder I got.

'Fuck me,' I whispered loud enough for him to hear. 'And fuck me hard.'

He looked surprised. I moved his hand from my breasts to my neck. I wanted him to hold my throat while he was fucking me hard. With my foot, I pushed the door closed and could see us both in the mirror on the wall behind the door. As I watched his reflection, I saw him pull his cock from out of his boxer shorts and slip it between my cheeks. It began to slide further in before completely disappearing. I could feel his full girth inside me, rock hard, filling me up and stretching me over the basin. I felt trapped, totally dominated. My throat tight, my breathing restricted but I was enjoying it. The rougher he got, the more my senses were heightened. He began thrusting; the cold porcelain against my hips hurting with each bang. Daniel also seemed to be getting off on hurting me but I had asked him to. He wasn't doing anything I didn't want him to. He loosened his grip on my throat but moved it to my hair, wrapping it around his hand. He gripped and pulled my hair while he was fucking me. It was pure lust, pure animal sex with passion and it was great.

My face was pushed against the bathroom cabinet; my hands gripping on the side of the basin as he fucked me the hardest he had ever done before. My knuckles white from such a tight grip. I could feel the tension in his cock as he was close to cumming inside me.

He leant forwards and whispered in my ear. 'You dirty fucking bitch, how much do you like it?'

Just the way he spoke to me like a piece of dirt made me more aroused than I already was, and he was clearly enjoying it. He clenched his bottom as I tightened every internal muscle to make it as tight as possible for him. He stopped still, holding me tightly, I could feel him pulsing and filling me. He groaned, his heart rapidly pumping against my back and his sweat pouring from his forehead from the heat of the bath filling the air.

He pulled his cock out, spun me around and told me to get in the bath. Ready for what he had in store for me next, I did as I was told, tearing my underwear off and throwing it on the floor with the rest of the clothes. I lifted my legs up, dipping my toes into the boiling hot water. It was up to my knees. My skin instantly turned red; the heat added to the sexual tension. Daniel watched me climb in. He stepped over to join me and got in but before I sat in the water, he asked me to sit on the back edge of the bath. He knelt down; the water now close to the brim. Pouring some tea tree and mint shower gel into his hands, he lathered them together. He placed both hands on my knees pulling my legs apart. He worked the lather round and round, moving up my inner thighs. The sensation was incredible; it tingled and turned my skin cold, goosebumps appearing all over my legs. The anticipation of where he was making his way to was unbelievable, every hair on my body standing on end.

Finally, he reached my pussy, a small landing strip of pubic hair covered the area above my opening, the rest was shaved daily with oil leaving it smooth and silky to the touch. He ran his fingers down both sides, parting my lips to see the perfectly pink inside of my vagina. With the tip of his finger, he gently pressed it in, watching my face fill with pleasure. It didn't go in all the way, he was teasing me, my body arching with tension. Leaning forward, he bowed his

291

head between my legs, his tongue making full contact with me. I held the back of his head with one hand and pushed him into me. His gentle kisses and licks made my body quiver in ecstasy. My hips moved in time with his every stroke, he could taste my juices flowing. Every stroke of his tongue was like a drug flowing through my lower body, my veins filling with a sensation of adrenaline ready to explode. My toes curled, my hand pressed against the tiles. I let go of everything I had, an orgasm clenching my body and taking over. I was a shuddering mess of euphoria. I had to pull his head away from between my legs as I couldn't take anymore. He looked up at me, wiping his face clean as I sank into the hot bath water, my body limp as if I had run a marathon and he had done all the work. Daniel kissed me so I could taste my own scent. I couldn't love or find anyone more attractive than him.

'So, you like it rough now, do you?' he asked, sinking back into the bath too. It was a tight squeeze with both of us in it, but I neatly tucked in between his legs and lay back against his hot, wet body, both calming down and enjoying the relaxation of the warm water. Every so often, he would pick up the bath sponge from the water and ring it out on me so I didn't get cold. I lay there thinking, *could sex get any better than that?* It was nice to have slow, affectionate sex but I also liked the way he had taken full control and been as rough as he could. You needed trust in someone to take it to that level without going too far. Some women may not like it like that, but I found it seductive having a strong man take advantage of me.

Before our fingers and toes became too wrinkled, I got out and ran to the airing cupboard to grab us both fresh towels. We got ourselves dried and cuddled up in bed together, watching random television programmes until we fell asleep.

Chapter 23

Moving On Up

Tue to his word, George had had a chat with his sales manager and managed to get me a meeting with him. The next step was to prepare for his valuable time. I was nervous but I knew I needed to do this to get my foot in the door and I wanted it to go so well. I turned up to work and George was already sat at my desk, scribbling on my notepad and swinging on my chair.

'You're welcome,' he said, pleased with himself.

I laughed as I threw my bag under my desk and tried pushing him out of my chair. 'Thank you, George. How did you manage that?' I switched on my screen and took my notepad away from him, so he stopped drawing on it and gave me his attention.

'How did I manage what? I spoke to him, said you would be great in sales and that he should give you a chance and he agreed. That was that. The next thing you need to do now is wow him. I'll give you a few pointers and the rest is up to you.' He made it sound so easy. 'Just be yourself and you'll be fine.'

I knew he was right; it was just easier said than done.

'Then when you get offered the job, we can go out for drinks and celebrate. Deal?' He shook my hand and got up to leave.

'Deal, you're on.' I watched him walk away as I sat down to get on with work. Anne had given us our daily telling off for being louder yesterday than we should have been. Claire looked like she wanted to cry, and the warehouse manager rushed back and forth pulling his hair out as the previous days' worth of orders hadn't been shipped. He was now under pressure to get them out the door. The busier it was at work, the more I enjoyed it. It made the day go quicker.

The sales manager, Dave, had given me a time slot for the following day to sit down with him. I kept it quiet. I didn't want Anne to think I had gone around or above her, and it wasn't guaranteed that he would offer me a role in his team.

The last day of the month felt like minutes rather than hours and I was already checking out for the day. I had so much that I needed to do. I wanted to get my suit out of the wardrobe. The same suit that I wore to the interview for my current role. A fresh night's sleep and my hair and makeup done in the morning. I wanted to look to impress. I had managed to work myself up so much that I felt sick, my stomach was upside down and my patience ran out quicker than normal.

Back at home, Daniel and I were clearing away the dishes in the kitchen.

'Rose, chill. You'll be fine. He will love you, who wouldn't?' Daniel flung his arms around me and kissed me on the head. He was always so supportive of me, but he didn't know how much I wanted this job. I didn't just want it, I *needed* it. *We* needed it for the family, for the money.

'You say that, but what if he doesn't? It will knock my confidence.' There wasn't much that he could say back to that.

'Then he's an idiot and doesn't deserve you in his team.' If only Daniel was the one interviewing me, but he wasn't. 'Pretend I'm him and you are you. Rosemary, why do you want to be in sales?' He wanted me to do role play with him but not in the role play sense that I liked.

'I'm not doing role play with you but thank you, honey. I think I'm going to go to bed early before I stress myself out anymore. Are you coming up?' I asked him, putting away the last plate and wiping down the sides.

That night, I barely slept. I tossed and turned all night long. I was hot, then I was cold. I could hear every sound that the house made. The heating turned off, then on again in the morning. The radiators creaked. I could hear cars outside and even Jack kicking in his bed as he dreamt. It wasn't the beauty sleep I was hoping for, but I had to clear my mind and get ready for the day ahead.

As I left, Daniel smacked me on the bottom and said, 'Good luck today. I know you don't need it, but I'll say it anyway. Give me a ring when you can speak.'

I got to work early. I prepped in my head what I was going to say. I had typed out some bullet points and printed them out to take in

297

with me. My meeting was at 10 a.m. so I didn't have to wait too long. I had never spoken with Dave before, but I had met him briefly in the office before, so I knew what he looked like. The first floor very rarely mixed with us admin staff downstairs. George was the only one, but this was because he spent the whole day anywhere in the office other than at his own desk.

At 9:50 a.m., I took the stairs upstairs. It was like stepping into a new school on the first day of term. As soon as I opened the door onto the main office floor, everyone turned round to look at me. I had to walk through the middle of everyone's desks to the other end of the building. Dave was sat in his office. The door was shut but I could see him at his desk, his eyes glued to his screen. Eagerly, I knocked on the door and then waited for him to invite me in. I suddenly felt like a naughty student being sent to the headmaster's office and my nerves got the better of me. As I took a few deep breaths in, I heard him call out.

'Come in.'

I reached for the silver handle, twisting it downwards to release the lock, and stepped forwards.

'Good morning. Is now a good time?' I asked politely.

'Why, of course. Come in, come in and take a seat.' He pointed at the chair across the desk from him and stopped what he was doing. I shut the door behind me, clicking it back into its frame. His office was lovely. I could smell the aroma of his wooden desk, scattered with picture frames facing him of what I presumed were his family. A large green potted plant stood in the corner, and he was rested, leaning back in a black leather chair, his hands making an arrow shape as he studied me up and down. I sat, crossing my legs, my papers and hands resting on my lap, so it forced me not to fidget.

'Thank you for taking the time to see me, Mr Ashcroft.' I started the conversation. Silence made me feel awkward.

'Dave, please call me Dave,' he said. He had dark hair that was greying, thick lines embedded in his forehead and a thick set frown. I couldn't quite read yet whether he was personable or not. He had hazel-coloured eyes and a dark complexion. When he finally smiled, his teeth looked like he was either a smoker or a lover of red wine, or perhaps both.

'So, George tells me you want to make the break into sales, why is that?' He pushed his hands together and then back into an arrow shape again. He was calm and collected, clearly a very respected man within the business. I had to be careful how I answered each question from him.

'Yes, George is correct. I feel that my personality would be well suited to sales. I take the time to understand and listen to a customer before recommending the right product or solution to fit their needs. I am intelligent, hardworking and I want to progress. I know that sales can be very stressful, but I enjoy the challenge and I think I would hit and exceed any targets I am given. I'm quite competitive and I have excelled downstairs in administration. I'm just asking for the opportunity to prove to you that I can do it.' I didn't want to beg for the job but at the same time I wanted him to know that I was serious and really wanted to be given a chance.

'I understand that you have a little boy. That must have been hard work raising a small child, continuing with your education and working. I like your tenacity and drive. I did a little background check on you and I do think you would be good in sales. What is your appetite? To earn money?' I wasn't sure if he was asking me a trick question or not.

'You're right, it has been tough, but I want to work hard and earn money for my family. I want to earn lots of money. Every day I look at the cars in the car park and I want one too.' Was that a step too far? Would he think that I just wanted the job for the money?

'That is the right answer. Money motivates every salesperson, that's why they have tough targets. If money doesn't drive you, then you aren't motivated by commission. I like your attitude. I need a junior account manager that will support the account directors. You can watch and learn from them with a gradual target. How does that sound?' He sounded like he was offering me a job. What would I say to Anne after she had basically laughed in my face?

'That would be fantastic. It sounds like the perfect role. I won't let you down and I'll work so hard.' I didn't want to sound too desperate, but I was over the moon and struggled to contain my emotions.

'I'll speak to Anne in a second and let her know that you'll work out the week in her team and move over to mine after that. What salary are you currently on?' He leant forward and started tapping on his keyboard.

'Thank you, really appreciated. I'm currently on seventeen thousand per annum.' I pursed my lips together, hoping he would give me a pay rise.

300

'Subject to human resources agreement, of course, but I would recommend a base salary of twenty-two thousand with commission of five percent on top of everything that you work on and close with the account directors. After a successful probation of six months, I'll look at a small car allowance for you. Is that okay with you?'

I could hardly believe what he was saying, I almost had to pinch myself to make sure I wasn't dreaming this. 'Erm yes, that sounds great. Thank you very much.' I remained cool on the outside but inside I wanted to scream, and fist pump the air.

'Okay, well done. Don't let me down. Is there anything else you would like to ask me before we wrap up?' He finished typing again and glanced in my direction. He was so quick and to the point. No time for dilly-dallying around.

'No, I think you've covered everything and thank you again for this opportunity.' I picked up my papers that I hadn't even shown to him and went to walk out the door.

'Report to my office next Monday morning at 9 a.m. and I will walk the floor with you, introducing you to your new team. Understood?' he said before looking back at his screen.

'Understood. Have a good week. See you Monday.' I held out my hand to shake his out of courtesy. He shook it back and smiled at me. His stern face weakened and turned to one of warmth. I was sure he would be a better boss than Anne was and would learn a lot. 'And Mr Ashcroft... I mean Dave... thank you again for giving me the opportunity.' I stopped there, smiled at him and went to leave the room.

Trying not to skip out and slam the door, I walked back out of the first floor to the stairs and did a little dance of happiness in the corridor. All I wanted to do was call Daniel and tell him. This was huge for us, the increase in salary would make such a difference. All I needed now was to not fuck this up.

I went outside to my car and sat in the driver's seat. I wanted to speak to Daniel, but I didn't want all my colleagues listening in to our conversation, especially before Dave had had a chance to speak to Anne.

Picking up my phone, I dialled Daniel's work number. It only rang a few times before I heard my favourite voice. 'Good morning. DPDE, Daniel speaking, how can I help?' He went silent waiting for a response.

'Good morning, sexy Daniel,' I replied.

'Hey Rose, you all right?' He was always worried when I called him in case there was a problem with Jack.

'So… I had my interview with the sales manager, Mr Ashcroft… well, Dave, and he offered me a junior sales role. I can't believe it.' I couldn't contain the excitement in my voice. 'And he's given me a pay rise, an extra four hundred pounds a month plus commission.'

'No way, that's great news. See, I told you that you would smash it. Now don't go running off with any rich salesmen, you hear me?' He worried so much about money and that I would find someone else, making my life easier. It wasn't about the money, but it would definitely help us with all our outgoings.

'It's great, isn't it? I think we're going out for a few drinks after work to celebrate. Would you mind picking up Jack and I'll be home a little later?' I asked.

'Oh okay. Maybe we can celebrate tomorrow?' He seemed disappointed.

'Of course we can. I should really have a few drinks with them. I wouldn't have got the job in the first place if it wasn't for the team helping me.' I was trying to justify why I should go. I didn't mention that it was mainly George who had helped me. He would only get jealous and ask questions as to why he was so helpful.

'Rose, you did this. Yes, they set up the interview, but you got it because you are you. You're clever and confident. The most amazing woman I have ever met, and I love you.' I couldn't ask for a more supportive boyfriend.

'Thank you. Love you too. I better head back in as they'll wonder where I've gone. See you later, yeah?'

'Yes, see you later. I'll get Jack. Have a good night.' The phone clicked off; he had gone. I put my mobile back in my pocket and made my way back into the office. Teresa was perched on the end of my desk, a big grin on her face.

'So, how did it go? Tell me, tell me, tell me.' I think she was more excited than I was.

'I got offered the role of junior salesperson. Looks like I'm moving up to the first floor next week.' I burst with pride.

'No way!' she said, jumping off the desk.

'Yes way!' I said. 'I can't quite believe it. I owe George big time.'

'You do, but you also owe yourself a big pat on the back. If Dave didn't like you and hadn't seen how hard you have worked since you've been here, he wouldn't have offered it to you. You're a credit to yourself. Have you told Daniel yet?' She gave me a hug and jumped up and down. 'We're going out for drinks tonight to celebrate, aren't we?' I knew she would suggest drinks, hence me warning Daniel beforehand and making sure he was okay to pick up Jack for me.

'We sure are. Yes, I spoke to Daniel and he's going to pick up Jack, so that means we're out, out.'

'Amazing. I'm so excited for you. This is the start of greater things.' Just as she said that, George came waltzing over.

'I hear you got the job. Well done you.' He held out his arms to hug me as well. I had never had so much affection. It was like winning the lottery.

'All thanks to you, George,' I said, accepting his hug.

'Welcome to the first floor.' It sounded like a members' club that I had just been accepted into. Claire and the others were wondering what was going on. What was all the commotion? Just as we were mid conversation, I could see Anne appear from the end of the office and she was making her way towards me. Her face was as miserable as it always was, coffee in hand, strutting between the desks to where we were all standing. She looked angry. Was it me she was angry with?

'Rosemary Murrell, back office now please?' She didn't even look at me. Teresa and George looked sheepish and wandered back to their own desks, leaving me to follow Anne like a naughty schoolgirl. She even called me by my full name.

'Shut the door behind you,' she ordered. I didn't even have a chance to sit down before she started yelling at me. 'How dare you go behind my back and speak to the sales manager. Especially after our conversation. I've come into the office to hear that you're moving teams and I wasn't even consulted. Do you know how stupid that makes me feel?'

My face flushed. I didn't want to shout back, I had to remain calm and collected. I wanted to be the better person here. There was no doubt that the rest of the office could hear everything she was shouting.

'I'm really sorry, Anne. It was never my intention to make you feel stupid. I had the opportunity to meet with Dave and he was very accommodating.' I was trying to diffuse the situation.

'Mr Ashcroft to you. He has only given you the role because you put him on the spot. There are so many other people in this company that would be better suited to the position than you but that's his decision and not mine. You need to make sure you have everything completed, all orders on the system and a hand over with Claire before the end of the week.' She slammed down her coffee cup on the table. It spilled all over the sides. She glared at me and then walked to the door, slamming it again on the way out.

I was left standing there, not knowing what to do. Thank goodness I was leaving her team. I picked up her cup and took it to the kitchen, placing it into the dishwasher. I collected a couple of paper towels and went back in to clear up the mess she had left.

Claire walked over to me. 'Are you okay?' she asked. 'I heard her shouting from my desk.'

'I'm okay. She's not happy that I've been offered a job in Dave's team on the first floor without telling her,' I explained.

'She'll get over it. She's always like that. I think it's jealousy if I'm honest.' Claire smiled sympathetically at me. 'Just ignore her and go for it. I think you'll be fab and well done.' Claire spoke very rarely but when she did it was only nice. Her words of encouragement meant a lot to me.

'Thanks, Claire. I'll miss working with you and the team, but I couldn't be happier to move away from her as a manager.' We both laughed.

The afternoon dragged, after the excitement of the morning and upsetting Anne, I put my head down and flew through all the orders on my desk. Conscious that I had already raised a drama in the office, I didn't want to cause any more arguments.

As soon as 5 p.m. hit, both George and Teresa were standing beside me, hurrying me along.

'Come on,' said Teresa, 'We have a pub to get to and drinks to drink. Do the rest tomorrow.' She almost switched off my screen for me and carried me out the door.

'Okay, okay, I'm coming.' With my bag over my shoulder, I joined them like the three musketeers. I had no idea where we were going or how long we would be but the both of us clambered into George's gorgeous sports car and off he drove. I clung on in the back as he drove so fast, his car sounding like a Formula One racing engine. We arrived at a small local pub called The Berkshire Arms in less than five minutes. I opened the door feeling quite sick.

As we approached the bar, they already knew who George was. He must have been a regular.

'Evening, George. Same as usual?' the bartender asked.

'Yes please. Ladies, what are you drinking?' George turned to both of us to ask.

'White wine please for me, large.' Teresa didn't waste any time.

'Erm… same for me please.' It was easier for me to go with what everyone else was having. I hadn't been in this pub before, but it was lovely and quaint, a traditional British public house. The original beams hung low in the ceiling above us, I felt like even I had to duck to walk through. Everyone seemed to know everyone else, laughing and talking in small groups. There were pockets of cosy seating areas with blankets and cushions and the sound of coin machines being played. It was only a Tuesday night, so I wasn't expecting it to be this busy. Hung across every wall were framed photographs of the village in bygone times. Scenes of horse and carriages, post houses and bakeries could be seen along with ladies and gentlemen in clothing from what I thought was around the early 1900s. They could have been even earlier. The pub's impressive crown glass windows looked like they hadn't been cleaned in many years but the last of the sunshine was still attempting to beam through.

'Let's go grab a seat,' George said, picking up his pint and handing us both our large glasses of wine. We followed him through, ducking as we went. He found a quiet part of the pub where nobody else was and as he sat down, raised his beer. 'Cheers to Rose joining the team. Here's to many more drinks together.'

Our three glasses chinked, all of us taking a sip and enjoying the wind-down from a crazy day in the office.

'So, I hear Anne wasn't very happy,' Teresa said, laughing. 'She needs to get off her high horse and stop being so rude to everyone.'

'She needs a good man in her life and sex. That'll make her lighten up a little,' George piped in. I just sat there laughing. I didn't care now that I knew I had the week to finish and then I wouldn't have to work for her again.

'Trust you to say that.' Teresa nudged George with her elbow and fell about laughing too.

'What did your man say about your promotion?' George asked. 'Is he quite supportive of you at work or is he a jealous type of guy?'

'Why would he be jealous of my work?' I thought it was a strange question for him to ask me.

'Well, you know, a successful woman, working with a group of men with lots of money. It's only time before you see how great life can really be and off you go... in the arms of another man. Only a matter of time before he loses you to someone else, if you know what I mean.'

'George!' Teresa nudged him again. 'They're childhood sweethearts. It'll take more than money to separate them. Money isn't everything.' She looked at me and smiled. She always had my back; Teresa was almost like an older sister that watched out for me.

'It helps.' He laughed, taking another sip of his pint. 'She looks naughty as well. I could teach you a thing or two. I'm older, more experienced.' I wasn't sure whether he was being serious or winding me up, so I went for the latter and just laughed it off.

'I'm fine, thank you. I don't want someone just for their money. Daniel and I are happy and besides, we have Jack together, I would never jeopardise that. Right, who's up for another drink?' As per usual, I had drunk my wine like a fruit juice and was already finishing the last mouthful. They, on the other hand, were still more than half full. I stood up to go back to the bar, taking their orders with me.

Just a few drinks, I said over and over in my mind, but I couldn't resist the temptation of ordering more when I got to the bar. 'Two white wines, a pint and three shots please?'

The bartender nodded but before making the drinks, he just stood there staring at me. I felt awkward as if I had asked for something unusual.

'Oh, you are eager. It's only 5:30, must have been one hell of a day today. Maybe you need a good wind-down. Here on your own with work colleagues? No boyfriend, I see?' He smiled and began pouring the drinks. What type of question was that? It may have been innocent, but he made me feel slightly uneasy. I just smiled and waited for the drinks to be ready.

Walking back to the table, Teresa and George must have had a bit of a talk as they were both quiet when I returned.

'Here you go,' I said, presenting a black tray with all the drinks on.

'Shots? Wow, it's a Tuesday night.' Teresa laughed but lifted them off the tray and onto the table. 'Tomorrow is going to be a heavy day in the office.'

The drinks kept flowing. One after the other we sank them, and it wasn't long before I had double vision. We spent a couple of hours putting the world to right, talking about all the people in the office and them giving me advice on who to trust and who not to. George got closer and closer, and Teresa was struggling to keep up.

'I'm sorry. I'm going to have to love you and leave you. I have a taxi coming in ten minutes. Will you both be okay getting home?' Teresa leant forward and kissed me lovingly on the cheek. 'I love you, gorgeous, don't ever change.' I had no idea what that meant but I put it down to drunk talk.

'Don't worry. I'll make sure Rose gets home okay.' He gave me a wink and laughed.

'I'm going to have to make a move soon as well. I've left Daniel to pick up Jack and put him to bed so I can't be too late home.' I got up to go to the toilet one last time as Teresa left before heading home. Just as I approached the ladies, I felt someone following me. I turned round quickly to find that George was behind me. *Oh, it's okay, he's heading to the gents,* I thought. But he wasn't. I paused before pushing the door open as he walked up to me.

'Rose, I need to speak to you before you go.' He was drunk and trying so hard to stand still without swaying back and forth. He steadied himself by placing his hand on the wall next to me. He wasn't making much sense. Somehow, he had gone from slightly drunk to completely wasted.

'Okay, what's up?' I too was drunk but I could just about comprehend everything he was saying to me.

'Now that you're working on the first floor, it means we're going to be working closer together.' He seemed to be studying my face, looking at my eyes, my nose and then stopping at my lips.

'It does,' I replied.

'Well, it means that we need to get along with each other.' I wasn't sure where this was going.

'We do, don't we?' I said, half acknowledging his words.

'I mean, *really* well with each other.' His words stumbled out of his mouth.

'George, what are you talking about?' He wasn't making any sense.

'You know how much I like you. I mean, *really* like you and I just think you could do so much better.' He placed his other hand on my shoulder as if he was talking sense into me.

'We aren't on about money again, are we? I've told you before, I—'

He cut me off before I could continue. He pushed me back into the door so that it flung open from behind me and I fell back onto the cold, tiled floor, him falling on top of me. I whacked my head with a thud and felt a cold sensation down my neck. It didn't hurt because the alcohol had dampened the pain, but the room was spinning. I moved my arm up to my head where I had hit it, but George didn't seem to notice, he just carried on with his slurry sentences.

'I'm trying to tell you that I find you really attractive and I want to be more than just friends.'

I wasn't listening to what he was saying. My head was throbbing, my fingers felt wet and as I brought them back down to my face, I noticed they were covered in blood. I had cut my head. George was still persistent in telling me how he felt and was trying to move my hand away from my face and kiss me, still on the floor, still on top of me. I was struggling to push him off.

'George, stop. I've hurt my head.' The blood was everywhere, on him, on my shirt and the more I tried to wrestle him, the more he was fighting back. He had hold of both my wrists, holding me tight, trying to calm me down and edging closer to my face, to my lips, to kiss me. I didn't know what had gotten into him.

'Hey, you two. What on earth is going on?' The bartender had heard the noise and was coming over. 'Are you okay? George, what the fuck?'

George dropped his head on my chest like a lead balloon, almost as if he had passed out comatose. The bartender pulled at his upper arms to try to get him to his feet. A couple of the other drinkers in the pub also rushed over to lift him up and get him to a chair. They then helped me up from under him and saw what I had done to my head.

It was beginning to really bang, the blood still running down my face, neck and shoulders. The toilet looked like a crime scene.

'Lady, your head. Hang on.' One of the men ran in, grabbed toilet paper and held it to my head to stop the bleed. 'I think we need to get you to hospital. That's a lot of blood.'

Although it was banging, I couldn't see exactly what I had done, only the shock and expressions of everyone that came to our aid. George had his head down on the table, cradled in his arms. He was out for the count and completely unaware of the situation. It was pure chaos, people running back and forth, someone on their phone.

'Is there anyone we can call? Anyone that will come and pick you up or shall we ring for an ambulance?' the bartender asked.

'I'm okay, I'm okay. It's just a small cut,' I reassured them, walking to the car park, leaving the toilet in utter chaos.

Daniel is going to be mad at me, I thought. Here I was again, creating a scene of destruction, like a whirlwind in flight. Calling him on a Tuesday night, intoxicated and with a knock to my head was not what he would be expecting. I chose the alternative option and decided to call my dad.

He never lost his temper with me, despite the times when he really should have. It would have probably knocked some sense into me. I dialled his number, praying he would pick up. It rang a few times then he answered.

'Hello?' He sounded like he was asleep. Surely, I hadn't woken him. It wasn't that late.

'Dad, it's me, Rose.' You could tell I was drunk.

'Had a few drinks, have we?' He knew instantly.

'I may have had one or two…' That was an understatement.

'Do you need picking up?' He could read my mind. I missed out the part about my head but by the time he picked me up, I was hoping it would have stopped.

'Dad, you're a legend. That would be amazing if you could. Would you mind?' I was over friendly and soppy due to the copious amounts of alcohol I had consumed.

'Of course, I don't mind. Where are you?' I could hear my mum in the background asking if I was okay.

'The Berkshire Arms.' The tissue I had pressed against my head was soaking through with blood and I needed to change it quickly before he came to get me.

'Okay, I'll be fifteen minutes.' The phone went dead.

I ran back to the toilet but as my head pounded, I felt dizzy. I bent over, one hand on my knee, the other on my matted hair, giving me five minutes to get my senses back. I felt strange and unusual. Sure, I had been drunk before but I felt different. My head wouldn't stop bleeding. No sooner had I replaced the tissue on my head, it was soaked through again and again. Feeling more sick than normal and lightheaded, the floor started to move beneath me. I could feel myself falling again to the floor but no matter how hard I tried to grab hold of someone or something around me, it was too late. It went dark. I lost all control of my body. I crashed to the floor, my body limp.

I felt a bright light shining in my eyes, a torch or bright rays of sunshine flooded my pupils. I jolted up but then the pain in my head forced me back down again. I looked around. Where was I? My feet were beneath a hospital bed sheet, railings on the end. I glanced across the room. My mum sat on a chair looking upset and my dad stood next to her with a steaming plastic cup. She looked up, suddenly aware that I had woken.

'Oh, you're awake. Thank goodness for that.' She rushed over to my bedside.

'What? Where am I?' I was confused, one minute I was in the pub, the next here.

'You're in hospital. Looks like you banged your head and lost a lot of blood. The alcohol didn't help.' She looked angry.

'Jack… where's Jack and Daniel? I should have been home hours ago.' Now I was really in trouble.

'It's okay. We called Daniel. He's worried about you, but he and Jack are at home. He told me to call him the minute you woke to

314

make sure you're all right. What were you thinking? It's a Tuesday night.' There she was, always concerned for my welfare and worrying that I was safe.

'It was only supposed to be a couple of drinks and I was going to come home. I banged my head, and I don't remember much after that. I have one hell of a headache.' I groaned as I tried to touch the back of my head again, feeling for what I had done.

'I wouldn't touch it. You have ten stitches and a big old bump.' She held my hand. 'You really are a nightmare. You worry me sick when you drink. Can't you calm it down a little?'

'Mum, I…' The nurse walked in before I could finish.

'We have your scan results back. No head trauma, just an almighty bump to the head. The stitches should stop the bleeding. How are you feeling?' She placed the clipboard on the bed beside me and was checking on the monitor screen that I was connected to.

'I feel fine, just a bit of a headache.' The alcohol was beginning to wear off, so I was feeling the full effects of what I had done.

'Would you mind excusing us for a minute or two please?' She turned to my parents, asking them if they could leave the room. *That sounds serious,* I thought. 'The paracetamol should kick in shortly. As long as you don't feel nauseous or lightheaded, you're free to go. However, I wanted to bring something to your attention.' She stopped momentarily and I wondered what she was about to say. 'Do you have any recollection of who you were out with last night? Friends, family, any strangers?'

I was confused why she was asking me about my night out.

'Just some friends from work, I think… I remember being with them at the table and then everything is just a blur after the last drink, I…' I touched my head again, trying to recall but it just wasn't there.

'It's just that your tests showed a chemical in your bloodstream, similar to that used as a date rape drug. Did you take any drugs or substances from anyone? Anything you can think of?'

I sat up, startled as to what she was trying to say.

'It could be why you passed out or why you can't remember anything. That along with the copious amounts of alcohol you seemed to have consumed. There doesn't appear to be any foul play. You were lucky, but it could have ended up so much worse than it did.'

'Are you saying my drink was spiked?' There was that creepy guy at the bar who didn't stop looking at me and the only other person that got me drinks from the bar was George, but he wouldn't have done something like that. George was someone I could trust, wasn't he? I found myself internally arguing with myself about who I could and couldn't trust. Surely George wouldn't, he was my friend. It must have been the bartender.

'Just mind how you get up and no driving, not for the next twelve hours or so. Understood? I'll ask your parents to come back in, as long as you're okay. There are lots of people you can talk to if you ever think you are in danger.' She seemed genuinely concerned about my welfare as she started disconnecting me from all the leads so that I was free to go.

The clock on the wall showed the time to be just after 2 in the morning. My poor parents had been waiting with me for well over five hours. A supposedly grown woman with a child of her own, in the accident and emergency ward because she was too drunk and incapable to look after herself. I felt ashamed. Why did this always happen when I drank? I said after the last time that I needed to slow down. Maybe I needed to give up completely, but it felt so good, I couldn't resist.

With my name tag still wrapped around my wrist, my parents walked me back to their car in the cold, pitch black early hours of the morning. They drove back in silence. I stared out the window trying to remember the episodes that made up last night, but I couldn't, it was a blur. I remember getting up to go to the toilet so I could make my way home and then nothing. A blank block of memory in my brain till I woke up in a hospital bed.

'You sure you're okay?' My mum turned to me in the car before my dad got out and opened the door for me.

'Yes, I'm fine. Thank you for picking me up and staying with me. I'll try to behave myself from now on.' With my bruised pride and guilt, I gave my dad a cuddle, thanking him for getting me. I got out of the car and walked solemnly to my front door. I knocked and waited for Daniel to answer. It took a while, but he eventually opened the door, standing there, shaking his head at me.

'Look at the state of you. What were you thinking? It was a Tuesday night.' My second lecture of the morning and we were only a couple of hours in. I deserved it though, I couldn't agree with him more.

'I know, I'm sorry. One turned into two and then I don't remember. My head hurts so much.' I started to feel sorry for myself, a blood-stained face and my hair all over the place.

'Get in out of the cold,' he said, pulling me inside. 'I'm glad you're okay, but it could have been so much worse. Think of Jack, he needs his mum. He doesn't need to see you like this.' His words made me feel even worse. I had responsibilities that were way more important than drink. I had to sort myself out.

'I know, I know. I won't do it again. I'll stop drinking.' It was a promise that I wasn't sure I could keep but I made every intention of doing so.

Daniel had a cup of tea already made and handed it to me. 'I love you though and was worried about you. If you don't get into bed and go to sleep, it will be time to get up again and I need to leave early.' He walked upstairs and I followed, taking a sip of tea. I climbed in the other side of the bed, where we met in the middle. I was in bed at home, where I should have been hours ago. I felt so bad and had let everyone down, that alone was a sobering thought.

I tossed and turned all night. My wound was damp and weeping and despite me taking painkillers, my head throbbed. I had no sympathy from Daniel, nor would I if I woke him up so I lay there on my side staring into a black abyss for hours, waiting for the early sunrise to wake up Jack and be able to get up and get ready for work.

The birds began chirping outside, daylight creeping in. I had a matter of minutes before the early alarm sounded. My whole body was aching, resembling being in a boxing ring with a professional. Not that I had ever been in that situation, but it was how I imagined being in a boxing ring would feel like. I didn't really want to go into work either, but they all knew we were out for drinks and after me getting my promotion, it would look like I was just hungover. I had to go in, I simply had to.

Jack's babbling got louder and louder as he became more impatient.

'I'm coming, sweetheart,' I murmured quietly as I got up to get him.

His cuddle, his sweet, sweet smile made everything suddenly all right. Jack made me get up every day and work for what I wanted in life; he gave me a purpose. My family, Daniel and everything I had was everything I needed. They brought out the best in me. It was nights away from them and the evil, evil drug they call alcohol that lured me away and showed my alter ego for the world to see. Did I have two sides to my personality? The family orientated, dedicated mother and soul mate to my boyfriend and then there was the party goer come addiction fuelled nightmare that couldn't say no to anything: alcohol, drugs and sex. Which one would eventually win?

That morning at work, I turned up as normal, still with the raging headache from the episode the night before but minus the memory of what had happened. *If only I had a rewind button.* I parked the car, nervous and apprehensive, wishing the day to end yet it was only 8:45 a.m. and the day was only just beginning. Snatching my bag from the passenger seat, my car filled with empty wrappers and rubbish, I slammed the door behind me and walked across the car park into work. Teresa was sat at my desk, as per usual, waiting for me to get in. Her high heels and long legs wrapped in tights were outstretched, crossed and resting on a box beside the chair.

'There she is,' she said as I walked over to her. 'What the hell happened last night after I left? George was texting me all night long. He said he couldn't remember much but that you hit your head and an ambulance turned up. After that, I couldn't get hold of him or you. I wasn't sure whether to text or call you this morning to check you were okay.' Teresa got up and came to look at my head where there was a visible patch of dressing covering my wound. 'Ouch, that looks nasty. Are you all right? You shouldn't really be in today.'

'I don't remember. I… all I recollect is getting up from the table when you left. After getting the drinks and downing mine, the rest is a blur. The nurse said I had banged my head and needed ten stitches but other than that nothing at all. What did George say? Is he… is he in yet?' I needed to find out answers from him. He must know what happened. I wasn't going to say anything about my drink being spiked, not to Daniel, Teresa or even George. I would soon know by the way he acted if it was him or not. If Daniel found out, he would never let me out again.

George then came slowly over to where we both were. He had shades on to dampen the bright lights of the office. He looked just like I felt and feeling very sorry for himself.

'Rose, mate, I'm so sorry. I should have been there for you last night. I was fucked. What happened? We were all at the table together, I downed my pint when Teresa said she was leaving and then I don't remember a thing. I saw the ambulance and you being carried over to it, but they wouldn't let me ride in it with you.' He gave me a hug, but not just any hug, one where he seemed just as broken as I was, and it lasted way longer than usual.

'You tell me. I don't remember anything after those last drinks, it's like a complete blackout.' Our hug ended as he raised his glasses to show two bloodshot and solemn dark eyes. 'All I know is I banged my head and I have one hell of a throbbing headache, even now.'

Teresa told me to sit down in the chair and ran to get me a cup of tea.

'Rose, look, while Teresa is in the kitchen, I wanted to apologise.' George seemed sorry-looking, his eyes watery and a distained look on his face. 'One, I should have looked after you and secondly, the bartender was arrested last night just after you left. We were sat at the table with a couple of the other regulars. Apparently, he had been caught slipping things into people's drinks and it wasn't the first time.' He continued to talk as I was watching his lips talking, lip reading them rather than listening to what he had to say.

'Go on,' I said, attentively.

'He got caught with Rohypnol. It appears that a few women had complained in the weeks before and they were watching him. I feel so guilty. I'm sorry.' He hung his head in shame, not wanting to look at me. 'I was so worried that he had slipped something in your drink.'

'Why do you feel guilty? It wasn't you.' Now I was beginning to feel bad that I was self-questioning him this morning when the nurse spoke to me. Of course, it wasn't him. He had done nothing but try to help me the past couple of weeks. How could I think it was actually him?

'It wasn't me but I took you to the pub. If we hadn't gone there, none of this would have ever happened.' He was clearly feeling sorry for himself.

321

'Hey look, we all went there. I drank stupid amounts of drink, as I normally do, and it could have been so much worse, right?' I stood up and placed my hand on his shoulder. I wanted to shake him to snap him out of his solemness, but he looked up at me with those brown eyes.

'I said I liked you last night and I meant it. I'm sorry, I'm really sorry and I will make it up to you.'

I didn't reply, instead I was re-playing his words back. He said he liked me but I don't remember him telling me that at all. George liked me in *that* way? I had absolutely no idea.

'Well, this looks a bit emotional,' Teresa said at the top of her voice for everyone to hear. She laughed bringing us back to reality again. 'I feel a group hug coming on.' She darted in between the two of us, flinging her arms wide and pulling the pair of us in together. 'Aw, besties.'

She laughed again, removing any atmosphere or emotional connection between George and I. She always had a way of clearing the air, changing the conversation when situations were awkward and generally reading people when things were a little frosty. It was as if she knew or had heard our whole discussion and was smoothing things over between us and for that I was ever appreciative.

Chapter 24

One Thing After Another

J ack hadn't forgotten the trip to choose our puppy. Every time we
walked past a dog, he would point and say 'Harry'. I would have
to correct him and explain that we would be getting one soon. As
the sleeps got closer and closer to picking him up, I got more excited
than Jack did. We had decided to call him Harry because Jack had
chosen it and he sounded cute when he said it. It sounded more like
'Hawee' so it had stuck.

We had the bed, bowls and toys all ready for him. I had borrowed
a cage for him from my parents. At night, we could keep him
contained, so he wouldn't chew half the downstairs furniture and
the floor wouldn't be ruined if he messed himself. We were ready for
yet another responsibility in our lives. Or so we thought.

We drove back to the lady's house that we visited before but
instead of tiny little puppies with their eyes barely opened, we found
seven larger than life puppies running around in the garden causing

bedlam. All of them were now completely covered in the cutest of black spots. The peace and quiet and classic music that we visited before had been replaced with lots of yapping and sharp pin-like teeth. Despite all that, it was the cutest image I had seen. Other than Jack, of course.

Our chunky little quiet puppy called Harry was now a big pawed, clumsy black and white spotted Dalmatian. He came running up to us as soon as we got there. Daniel grabbed him with one hand, lifting him free of the floor and cuddled him into his chest. His big brown eyes beamed in the sunshine, licking Daniel all over his hands and face. Daniel giggled like a child holding a new toy.

I couldn't wait to bundle our puppy into the car and take him home for the rest of the family to see. Daniel paid the rest of the money to the lady, and she handed over the pedigree certificate and other forms in a plastic folder along with a small blanket that had been in the same pen as all the others. Apparently, it was to comfort him during his first couple of nights away from the pack. There was no cup of tea, no long conversations and a sit down. I think the lady wanted to resort to some form of normality and had a lot of puppies to hand over to their new owners.

I walked with Jack, hand in hand back to the car, strapped him into his car seat and climbed into the back of the car next to him. As soon as I was settled in, and my seatbelt secured, Daniel passed me the blanket and sat Harry on my lap.

'You all good?' he asked before shutting the car door on me. Harry wriggled, whined a little but then seemed to get himself settled into the softness of the blanket and the warmth of my lap. He nestled his nose into the inside of my elbow and curled up. I stroked him just like I did every night to Jack, gently coaxing him into falling asleep. Jack had his hand stretched out from his seat trying every opportunity to stretch and stroke Harry, but he couldn't quite reach. Giving in, the motion of the car made Jack's eyelids heavy and before long, he fell asleep as well as Harry. *How hard could it be bringing up a dog and a small child?* I thought.

Harry was so quiet and content the whole journey home back to the house, it was as though he had been riding in cars his whole puppy life. Reaching home, I sat tight, waiting for Daniel to open the door and collect him from my lap whilst I then got out and collected Jack from his seat.

Following behind Daniel, he opened the front door, waiting for me to get inside and shut it behind me. He set Harry down on the floor letting him sniff and get used to his new surroundings. He looked so small and timid on his own, his tail between his legs and ears down. He sprinted to the dining room, ran underneath the table and chairs and sat down, watching us with his big brown eyes. Daniel turned the kettle on while Jack and I joined Harry. I sat down on the cold, laminate floor, my legs crossed. Jack copied me doing the same but to the side of me. I puckered up my lips and made a kissing sound for Harry to come out. Patiently, I sat there waiting for him to creep back out. His tail back up and wagging, his ears up and pleased to see me, he plucked up the courage to let us stroke him. Jack made several attempts to grab his tail and yank it, but he soon learnt that it was naughty and not to do it.

Harry playfully rolled around on the floor, biting our hands gently every time we tried to rub his tummy. I paid careful attention to make sure Harry was gentle with Jack, not biting him too hard to put him off dogs and that Jack wasn't hitting him or pulling his tail. It wasn't long before they became the best of friends. Wherever Jack went, Harry followed and vice versa. Jack even tried curling up in his bed, wanting to sleep with him. We fed him, he ate it, we let him out, he went to the toilet in the garden, we called him, he came. It was one of the best decisions we made, and the house instantly felt more homely.

That night, we lined his crate with newspaper in case he didn't make it through the night, his bed tucked in at the back and a small bowl of water in the corner. Using treats, I coerced him into his cage. Blowing him a kiss, we left him for the night. I felt nervous but just like a child, he had to get used to his new surroundings and we had to teach him from day one that night was night and day was day. I got into bed and all I could hear was his cries, his yapping turned to louder barking until it finally reached a howl.

'Oh, bless him. Do I get up and sit with him?' I rolled over to Daniel, wanting to put plugs in my ears to deafen the sound.

'Absolutely not, Rose. He needs to learn, otherwise he will keep barking every night till we take him out.' He made sense but every part of me wanted to go downstairs, let him out and cuddle up with him till he went to sleep. 'He will give up and go to sleep in a minute, you'll see.'

'You're right, I'll leave him. He's fine.'

Ten minutes later, he was still barking. Twenty minutes passed and still going. He was going to wake Jack if I didn't get him to stop.

326

I got to thirty minutes and couldn't stand it. Daniel could see me getting more and more impatient.

'Let me just reassure him and I'll be back up.' I pulled back the covers, put on my dressing gown and tip toed downstairs before Jack awoke. Harry was going crazy in the cage, wagging his tail, the newspaper shredded, the bowl of water upside down and standing on his bed.

'Hello, gorgeous,' I whispered. I couldn't be angry at him; he was so pleased to see me. I was so weak when it came to babies or animals. I bent down, opening the door as he jumped up at me. Trying to calm him down, I climbed half in the cage, straightened his bed and removed all the wet newspaper and his bowl. The cage was now all tidy, so I lifted him up, put him back in and closed the door. Straight away he began to cry. This wasn't going to work. Admitting defeat, I opened the door but instead of letting him out, I stroked him in his bed so that he settled.

'There you go. It's not so bad in there.' I was talking to the dog just like I would a human. I stroked his velvety fur as he lay down and was calm. His eyelids closed and he drifted off to sleep.

I edged backwards, him still asleep, and re-bolted the cage. Just a little attention was what he needed. Quietly I stood back up and went to walk out of the room but as the floor creaked, he opened his eyes and immediately got back up, barking at me like a burglar entering a home. I had been rumbled.

'Shhh... shhh... It's okay,' I whispered to him, this time he seemed to acknowledge me and stopped barking. I took the opportunity to keep walking and climbed back upstairs and into bed. I lay down, closed my eyes and there he was again. I could hear him whimpering quietly but as long as he wasn't too loud, I chose to ignore him.

Every couple of hours throughout the night, I awoke to hear his little cries, but I drifted in and out of sleep. I had work the following morning and couldn't afford to be awake all night long. It was like having Jack all over again and being sleep deprived. I needed to be hard on him. Harry had to know who was boss but if Daniel wasn't by my side telling me to ignore him, I would have cuddled up on the sofa with him or brought him up to our bed and let him sleep on the end of the covers.

It was 5:30 a.m. and I didn't need an alarm clock. Harry was barking, Jack was babbling away in his cot, it was time to get up. Daniel groaned, rolled over and pulled the pillow over his head so he couldn't hear. There was no getting away from it. I had to get up. I walked into Jack's room first, smiling as always. I took him downstairs to greet Harry.

'Hawee, Hawee,' he kept saying.

I let him open the cage door, releasing Harry for his early morning wee in the garden. Quietly, I opened the patio doors and in the dark sky of the morning, Harry zoomed round the grass before returning indoors. I stood there patiently, half asleep and shattered from the lack of sleep. My daily routine would now consist of feeding Harry, getting myself and Jack ready, dropping him off at the childminder, coming back home at lunchtime to check on Harry, and either Daniel or I rushing home after work to make sure he was okay. It worked out quite well as the days where Daniel was on a later shift than me, he was only left for a couple of hours at a time. I looked forward to coming home when Jack and Harry were both as equally excited to see me after a long day at work.

Before long, Harry had settled in. We soon learnt not to leave anything lying around the house as he loved to chew my heels, the skirting board, the legs of the table and chairs and practically anything he knew he shouldn't. He ignored us telling him off, he didn't do a single thing we told him to, but he soon learnt how to sit and hold up his paw. Harry also quickly learnt that if he sat by the side of Jack's highchair he would be fed small bits of food that Jack didn't like. They became thick as thieves.

By week twelve, he was allowed outdoors. He was a strong dog and as much as we tried to train him, he wouldn't walk to heel. Harry was one of the naughtiest dogs I had ever known. If I let him off the lead, he didn't come back. He ran up to people, stole food from the side as soon as he could reach and generally did as he pleased but I loved that dog so much. From the moment we brought Harry home, it was chaos. Never a dull moment. He would bark, whine and his claws on the floor trip-trapped all the time. He never sat down or slept except at night. Even an hour-long walk didn't tire him out, but I wouldn't have changed him for the world.

I remember the day so clearly, like a momentous day in my ever-changing life, I was out walking Harry when my phone rang. As per usual, he was pulling on the lead. I had to walk at such a fast pace that I was almost running whilst pushing Jack in his pushchair. He would giggle and try to hold onto the lead with his chubby hands. Occasionally, I would yank him back to give me the opportunity to catch my breath. The sun was shining but I could still see the mist lingering between the trees in the woods across the field, the grass frosty and if I looked close enough I could make out the patterns of spider webs between each blade. The birds were chirping away from high up watching the limited number of people out walking at such an early hour. It was a Saturday morning and Daniel was at work, so I had taken the opportunity to wear out Harry and then spend the day at home tidying up and carrying out all the much-needed housework from the week.

I didn't recognise the number on my mobile phone, so I was reluctant to answer but I felt a deep-down need to.

'Hello?' I was half expecting it to be a sales call.

'Rose, is that you?' A man's deep dulcet tone asked if it was me. Who was it? He knew my name. 'Rose, it's Tom.'

I froze, instantly slamming the brakes on the pushchair and stopping Harry in his tracks. He was panting heavily but stopped and sat down.

'Rose, can you hear me? It's Tom, we met in Greece.' He spoke again, his deep voice bellowing through me right down to a place that hadn't been reached in a long time. There was no doubt in my mind who it was. How could I forget him? 'Rose, don't hang up.' He sounded desperate. What on earth could he want? Why was he calling me and how did he get my number?

'Yes, I'm here.' That's all I could manage. I wanted to hear what he had to say.

'Rose, I need to speak to you. I need to see you. There's something I must tell you.' I could sense panic in his voice, but I was confused.

'Tom, how did you get my number?' I asked him outright. I never expected to see or hear from him again after the toilet incident on holiday. What was it about me with men and toilets? *I think I will have to avoid them in the future.*

'I got it from Michelle's phone. Remember? She took it on the first night so we could stay in touch. Daniel and Michelle have been in contact so I waited for her to go to sleep the other night so I could get it and speak to you.'

I froze for the second time. Daniel had been in contact with Michelle? Why would he be speaking to her? I never did ask him about them speaking before we left as I watched them both in conversation. Was there more going on that I had even realised?

'They have been in contact with each other, why?' I quizzed him to see if I could get more information. I suddenly went from a warm sensation, hearing his voice, to feeling sick from the pit of my stomach. I felt cheated and began creating a scenario in my head where Daniel and Michelle were having a full-on affair behind my back. Why else would he be calling me? I was hurt. Surely Daniel wouldn't do this to me.

'I can't tell you over the phone, but I need to see you and explain everything.' Once again, he sounded desperate. Was it just a plea to see me or was there actually more going on that I didn't know about?

'You can't leave me hanging like this. I need to know what's going on and why you desperately need to see me.' By this point, I was sounding just as desperate as he was.

'Meet me in an hour in Reading. Can you get there? I've told Michelle that I have an errand to run and need to pick up something for work. Give me half an hour of your time and I will tell you everything.' He stopped silent.

'Where do you want to meet and what if someone sees us together? How do I explain that?' I had to think quick, maybe my mum could have Jack for me and I could meet him. I knew this was dangerous, seeing him again and all the emotion of what happened while we were in Greece, followed by the conversation in the toilet before we both left for home. The ringing alarm bells in me meant I had to go. I had to find out what was going on.

'No one will see us. Meet me at the Reading services. I'm driving a black BMW. I'll park, if I can, in the furthest most corner of the car park. I'll wait by the car till you arrive.' He waited tentatively for me to reply.

'Okay, I'll see what I can do. I need to drop Jack off and I will meet you there.' I hung up.

A million questions were racing around in my mind. Why hadn't Daniel said anything? What was he up to? What had they spoken about? Why didn't I know? How could he do this to me? What other secrets did he have? What else wasn't he telling me? What did Tom want to tell me? I felt betrayed.

I turned in the opposite direction, heading back home. I wanted to run so I got there quicker but Harry was already rushing me along like a horse and carriage, pulling us with all his might. I called my mum and asked her to have Jack for a couple of hours. I told her I needed to help a friend move some furniture into her new apartment and I couldn't watch Jack properly while doing so. Of course, she said yes. She loved having her grandson at every opportunity she could

332

but I felt bad that I was lying. I knew full well it was a lie on top of another one.

I raced to get changed. I raced to drop off Jack, guilty that what time I had with him at weekends was precious and that Tom's reason for meeting better be a good one. I had to find out the truth and hopefully move on from whatever was troubling him.

The traffic wasn't too bad; my little car was under pressure as my foot was flat to the floor on the accelerator, breaking every speed limit there was. I still had that sick, stomach-turning feeling and my heart was racing. I couldn't work out if it was through dread or through anger from what I was about to find out. Maybe it was both.

I spun the car round the corner of the junction leaving the motorway, screeching to avoid cars like I was trying to be first in a race, impatiently beeping at other cars in my way until I reached the entrance to the car park. I hadn't seen him since Greece, and I had no idea what to say. Would it be awkward? I was so nervous, but it was the unforgettable events on holiday that had brought us back together.

I could see Tom right at the back of the car park. He was propped up against the side of his car smoking and looking on edge. Glancing round the area, there weren't that many people out and it wasn't too busy, so I pulled up next to him in my beaten-up Renault Clio. I didn't want to get out of the car, I even questioned whether I should. Did we both stand there and chat? Did we walk and talk? What was the protocol? Meeting strangers in car parks wasn't something I had done before, although he wasn't that much of a stranger. I had seen him naked after all.

As I got out, he walked over and proceeded to kiss me on both cheeks like a true gentleman. I didn't speak, for once I couldn't think of the words to say.

'You're looking as beautiful as ever.' He smiled and turned to walk back to his car door, unlocking it. 'Get in the back and I'll tell you what's going on.'

Without thinking, I walked round the other side of the car and pulled at the handle to open it. I didn't even question getting in the back of his car. For all I knew, he could kidnap me and drive off. Never once did I feel unsafe in his company. For some reason, he had always made me feel completely at ease, just as Michelle had done.

I sat on the plush, leather back seats of the car, and he joined me. He sat there for a few moments just looking at me like an excited schoolboy with a new toy.

'It's lovely to see you,' he said.

'You too,' I agreed and it was.

'I'm sorry. I realised that I probably left you on the other end of the phone earlier wondering what the fuck was going on.' He wasn't wrong.

'I don't understand. Why are they talking to each other?' I felt vulnerable.

'It's a long story, so I'll start from the beginning.' I was listening to everything he had to say. 'The thing is, Michelle and I have been trying for a baby for the last five years. It's all she's ever wanted but I couldn't give it to her. She started to resent me. Having sex with each other turned into a chore, and we began bickering. It just wasn't fun after a while and our relationship has been on the rocks for a long, long time. Our holiday was supposed to make or break us. To be honest, Rose, being in bed with you was the last time that I had feelings and another woman had touched me in such a sensual way that it made me feel alive again. You gave me that spark again. I was so disappointed that it ended the way it did.' I could see raw emotion in his eyes. He was pouring his heart out to me. I felt genuinely sorry that he felt that way but I couldn't understand where this was going.

'I'm sorry to hear that but what has this got to do with Daniel and Michelle?' I asked.

'Let me finish and you will see.' He reached out for my hand on my lap and squeezed it, his large hands warm and rough as they engulfed mine. 'As I said, all Michelle wanted was a baby. It felt like she was just using me. We had test after test, neither of us had any real reason as to why but we just couldn't conceive. I thought the holiday would be the end of us. I want a woman that wants to be with me in the bedroom, to connect with *me*, not just for my sperm.' He paused, swallowing heavily. 'Then you both came along, and Michelle seemed to lighten up. All she could do was talk about how getting into bed with you as another couple would breathe life into our sexual relationship. That it would bring us back together. I didn't realise until it was too late why.'

'I still don't understand. I—'

He stopped me from asking questions and interrupted me. 'She's pregnant, Rose. She got what she wanted.' He looked relieved by blurting it out.

'That's great news. I'm really happy for you. So, she got what she wanted.' I squeezed his hand back.

'You don't get it. It's not mine. It's Daniel's.' His eyes glared at me waiting for my expression to reveal all.

'You what?' There it was again, that pained feeling of sick from the bottom of my stomach. I was speechless.

'She didn't want *me* or *you*. She wanted *him*. She wanted a baby so bad that the only reason what happened in Greece happened, was because *she* planned it. That was her intention the whole way along, I was just too stupid to realise. I was so caught up in the moment, from the first time I placed my eyes on you, I wasn't interested in her. I just wish it was the two of us and not the four of us.' He brushed his head, taking some time to breathe and realise the truth of what he had just told me.

I sat back, staring up and out through the sunroof. 'So, does he know? Is that why they have been in contact?' I had to know the truth, even if it hurt me.

'No, no, no. I've read the messages and the missed calls.' He pulled my head towards him so he could look in my eyes as he explained more. 'She tried making contact not long after we found out she was pregnant. Messages from her to him say how much she liked him and that she wanted to meet up, saying how much she enjoyed their one night of passion together, but Daniel was clear from the beginning that he didn't want anything to do with her. He said there was no way on earth of them having anything other than what he called "a mistake" and telling her not to contact him again. He also said that he loved you and wasn't interested.'

'He said that?' I wanted to be sure.

'Yep, he even told her that if she kept calling and texting him that he would block her. I think he has because there has been no response from him for weeks. I have searched through her phone but can't see anything from him at all.'

'Really?' I needed reassurance.

'Yes. To be fair to him, he really loves you.' He seemed jealous.

'So, how does that leave you both?' It was none of my business but what did I do with the information he just gave me?

'We're still friends. I said I would help her with the baby, and I would make sure she didn't go without or struggle, but I can't help but think that I'm not part of her plans. The passion between us is gone. I don't think we will ever get that back, it was lost a long time ago. I want someone to lust after me, to make me feel like a real man the way you did that night. Even though we didn't finish, there is something in you that I crave. You have something so unique that most women don't have, like a drug, that drives men crazy. I can't explain it.'

I knew exactly what Tom was describing. There was a sensation so mind and body numbing, I only experienced it when I was in the bedroom at the point of ecstasy, something that filled my veins with desire. I couldn't control it and I didn't want to.

We both sat there, caught in the moment but not doing anything about it. What was he thinking?

'So, Daniel still doesn't know anything about the baby?' I finally asked.

'No, and it looks like he's blocked her. I just thought you ought to know. Do with it what you want to.'

Was he expecting me to tell him? How would that change us? What if he felt an allegiance to her and wanted something to do with the baby? It wouldn't be the three of us anymore. I didn't want to risk anything jeopardising our little family. How were we in this situation? It was all just a bad nightmare, haunting us time and time again.

'I've got to go.' I reached for the door handle to let myself free. 'I need time to think about what I do with this.'

'Rose, don't go. I want to get to know you better,' he pleaded with me.

'What in half an hour?' I threw back a sarcastic comment. I didn't mean to, I was just frustrated with the situation. It was always one thing after another, thrown at me to see how I handle different situations. 'I'm sorry. I didn't mean that.'

'Do you think there is even the slightest possibility that there could be something between us?' He tried lighting the tiniest glimmer of hope.

'I'm really sorry, Tom. You seem like the loveliest, sweetest guy but I love Daniel and I love what we have. We brought Jack into the world as the result of an incredible relationship. In all honesty, Michelle's baby will be the result of a one-night stand and I can't help that. It was her choice, as unfair as that sounds, and I would hate for any unborn child to be born into a world without a father but that's not my responsibility or Daniel's to some degree. It would ruin what we currently have.' I sounded horrible saying that, but it was how I felt, and he needed to hear it.

'I get it.' He looked disappointed. 'In that case, Michelle's secret is safe with me and you won't hear from me again.'

Maybe if Tom and I had met in different circumstances. He was, after all, a really nice guy and he was extremely attractive, but he just wasn't Daniel. He lifted my hand gently to his lips, his eyes firmly locked on mine and kissed it.

'If you ever change your mind or go through a rough patch, you have my number. I would never ever turn you down.'

I smiled in an appreciative way. He was tempting, he was desirable, but I had to say no.

'Thank you. I'll keep your number.' I smiled in a seductive but restricted manner. Our hands released from each other, it felt similar to a breakup. I felt bad but for all the right reasons, tugging at the door handle again as it clicked open. Without looking back at him, I stepped out of the car and into the cold of the semi-empty car park, my keys jingling in my hand.

A mixed bag of emotions, anger, sadness and hurt, filled my eyes as they began to water. A small trickle of a tear rolled down my cheek. I couldn't contain them. Wiping the tears from my face, I closed the door behind me leaving Tom in the back of his car. The blacked-out windows restricted my view of him as I walked round the car, back to mine.

I pressed the unlock button on my key fob, my car making a blipping sound to open. Sitting in the driver's seat, I gripped the wheel and cried but my tears meant nothing, nor did they solve anything. I didn't care who could see me, Tom even more so. I had been told one of the biggest secrets of both mine and Daniel's lives. He had a right to know, but what I pondered next was whether to keep it a secret or to tell him and risk our perfect little family.

UPCOMING TITLES FROM KATHRYN LOUISE

COMING SOON...

20 YEARS YOUNG

Rose and Daniel continue along their epic journey called life, but do they go their separate ways? A dark secret spills into their relationship causing shockwaves of emotion. A grand arrival means more decisions are to be made. A darker, more enticing story of erotic episodes and passion.

25 YEARS YOUNG

Rose's need for excitement and adventure causes problems. How naughty can she really be without losing everything that means something to her? Split personalities and dangerous situations create endless pain. Can she really supress her inner demons and make a change?

30 YEARS YOUNG

Times are changing. Dirty thirties have arrived. Years have passed but history has a habit of repeating itself. The skeletons in the closet keep presenting themselves. Experience has its advantages. You can forgive but you can't forget. What happens when a relationship has more downs than ups?

40 YEARS YOUNG

Naughty forties sound exciting. Interesting events take a turn for the worst. Rose thought she opted for the quiet life but what happens when the shoe is finally on the other foot? Emotional blackmail creates a stir. A new character causes a big

wave. The grass isn't always greener, but it was fun while it lasted…

Lightning Source UK Ltd.
Milton Keynes UK
UKHW012218040722
405365UK00005B/148/J